THE
ASSAILANT

Also by JAMES PATRICK HUNT

Goodbye Sister Disco
The Betrayers
Before They Make You Run
Maitland Under Siege
Maitland

THE
ASSAILANT

JAMES PATRICK HUNT

 MINOTAUR BOOKS ✿ NEW YORK

THE ASSAILANT. Copyright © 2009 by James Patrick Hunt. All rights reserved. Printed in the United States of America. For information, address St. Martin's Press, 175 Fifth Avenue, New York, N.Y. 10010.

Library of Congress Cataloging-in-Publication Data

Hunt, James Patrick, 1964–
    The assailant / James Patrick Hunt.—1st ed.
        p. cm.
    ISBN-13: 978-0-312-54578-9
    ISBN-10: 0-312-54578-9
    1. Police—Missouri—Saint Louis—Fiction. 2. Prostitutes—Crimes against—Fiction.
    3. Saint Louis (Mo).—Fiction. I. Title.
    PS3608.U577A9   2009
    813'.6—dc22

                                                                    2008045675

First Edition: June 2009

10 9 8 7 6 5 4 3 2 1

For my parents

ACKNOWLEDGMENTS

The author wishes to extend his gratitude to his editor, Matt Martz. Also to Lieutenant Darrell Hatfield, Oklahoma City Police Department (Ret.); Lieutenant Mike Denton, Owasso Police Department; and Special Agent John Jones, Oklahoma State Bureau of Investigation.

Niceness is a decision. It is a strategy of social interaction; it is not a character trait.

—GAVIN DE BECKER

THE
ASSAILANT

They brought a kid in tonight with a gunshot wound. He was black. Young and thin, probably around sixteen. He'd been hit in the head. He didn't want us to operate on him. He denied that he'd been shot, even when we pointed to the bullet that was right there beneath his skin, raising it as if a small stone were tucked under there. There were policemen waiting for him, apparently, and he didn't want them to know that he had been in a gunfight. I guess he'd shot and killed someone else and the bullet that was lodged in his skull proved that he had been there. I thought the incident was amusing. But Ogilvy, the new resident, said the boy was "chilling . . . the kid's eyes were vacant, and without feeling." Silly man, Ogilvy. He was being dramatic, wanting to comment on what he believed was the "human condition." Ogilvy does not understand people. He wants to believe that the little gangster feels remorse and pain beneath the tough exterior. Ogilvy wants to be . . . assured in some way. Ogilvy is an adolescent. A dull, single-minded mediocrity. I could have asked him if he was familiar with Nietzsche and he would have said, "Who?" He does not understand that strong men maintain the pure conscience of a beast. That they can return from a succession of murder and rape with contentment and joy in their hearts. It's not in men like Ogilvy to understand such things.

. . . I've started to walk at night. I come home from the hospital and even after working an eighteen-hour shift, it's hard for me to sleep. I should be physically exhausted, but my mind is still working. The walking helps me think. But I'm still restless. Not anxious or worried, but restless. I need to stop putting it off.

ONE

"Ashley?"

The young woman of twenty-two slowed her walk. She heard the name called again and then she turned to look at the caller.

"Ashley," he said. "It is you. Hey," he said. Smiling now.

Ashley waited to see if she recognized the man. Well dressed and professional. A soft, almost feminine way about him. He had not called to schedule an appointment tonight. But she thought she might have remembered him from before. A convention . . . ? She gave him her working smile anyway. The all-American college girl smile.

"Hey," she said, her voice bright without being warm.

The man said, "What are you doing here?"

"Just, you know, chilling."

Some of them liked it when you used kids' words. Chilling, hanging, balling. Middle-aged men with money, wanting to feel young. She could help them with that sort of thing. Anything to move things along.

The man smiled at her. And some part of her recoiled at that. His toothy smile beneath his spectacles. Discomforting, even from a customer.

They were standing on Market Street in downtown St. Louis. A November evening, the threat of cold rain in the air. The Cardinals had won the Series a few weeks earlier and the city was relatively quiet.

The girl's name was Reesa Woods, but when she was on duty she was called Ashley. She had left a hotel room at the Adam's Mark only a few minutes earlier. The client had been an old man, older than this guy in front of her. Sixty at least. He had made a lot of money in something called options and he was from England or Australia or someplace like that. He had dressed well and he had been a gentleman. She had been with him before. Tonight, he had done it to her only once, but then asked her if she would stay with him for a second hour and told her he would pay for it. Pay for her company. Another $450. Ashley had agreed to do so.

For the second hour, the old man was back in his clothes and had actually started to lecture her about her career options. Her future. He told her that she was a courtesan, not a prostitute, and there was a difference between the two. He told her that she had been born in the wrong country and probably the wrong century. He told her that she would have made a good Frenchwoman and that he meant that in a good way.

Reesa "Ashley" Woods had heard this sort of thing before. An old, lonely man with money, perhaps he wanted to believe she was something more than she was. A French courtesan as opposed to a girl from Springfield, Missouri, who had simply gotten bored with small-town life and a creepy, abusive boyfriend and had left it all behind as soon as she finished high school.

She had enrolled in classes at the University of Missouri, St. Louis (UMSL), starting with twelve hours for the semester and soon scaling it back to six because it was harder than she'd thought it would be. She believed she was smart enough to handle the load, but she felt there was no hurry.

When she was twenty, she took a job as a dancer at a strip club near the airport. It paid well with tips, and after a few months of that she was asked to have a drink with an older woman who looked a little like Jacqueline Bissett. Older, but sexy and mysterious. The woman's name was Bobbie Cafaza and she was the madam of what she said was the most exclusive escort service in the St. Louis area. One of the first questions she put to Reesa Woods was, "Are you using drugs? Don't lie to me, because if you do, I'll know it."

Reesa said she was not.

Bobbie said, "That's good. Because I can't have that in my house. I won't have it. At least half the girls who work at these strip clubs are addicted to coke or heroin. But I don't see the signs with you."

Reesa said she wouldn't touch it.

Bobbie Cafaza, at that time, was the madam of four escort services. But the one she had in mind for Reesa Woods was Executive Escorts, which was a part of Tia's Flower Shop. She told Reesa that their clients were not street-corner bums but high-class: doctors, lawyers, CEOs, and politicians. She told Reesa that she had that college, fresh-girl look that the clients were after.

Bobbie said, "There are escorts and there are whores. I run a professional outfit. When you're working, you wear a dress or a skirt. No shorts or pants. If you're standing on a street corner and you look like a whore, you're not doing it right. You need to look like you could be working for these men. Or with them. Like you're about to go to one of their meetings. That's what they're paying for. The illusion. Do you have a tattoo?"

"No," Reesa said.

"Good. Get one and you're fired. When can you start?"

Reesa quit the strip club and started a week later. Now she had been with the Flower Shop about a year. In that time, she had netted about ninety thousand dollars, all of it tax free. She owned a secondhand Mercedes convertible and had an attractive apartment in the Central West End. She believed that her working, "Ashley" identity was separate from that of Reesa Woods.

Walking away from the hotel, downtown on an evening that was turning cold, was she Ashley or was she Reesa Woods wanting to get home and take a shower?

The man on the street was sort of hovering around her now. "You keeping busy?"

She knew what he meant by that. Asking if she was working. "Yeah. How about you?"

"Oh, I was down here for a meeting. Bunch of pointy heads talking about administrative procedure. You know how that can be."

"Yeah," she said, though she had no idea what he was talking about. She was used to going along.

He said, "Are you busy now?" He was smiling at her again.

"Well," Reesa said, "you're supposed to go through the agency, you know."

"Oh, is that how it works?" he said, and Reesa picked up a bit of scorn in his voice. Like he needed to tell her he wasn't stupid. Creep. He said, "Can't you do things on your own?"

Reesa sighed. "Look, I can, but . . ."

Jesus, he was starting to pull his hand out of his pocket. A roll of bills.

"Christ," Reesa said. "Don't pull out money here."

"Oh. Sorry." He put it back in his pocket.

"Jesus," Reesa said.

"Well," he said, "if you're in such a hurry."

Shit, Reesa thought. Bobbie fired any girl caught freelancing. Bobbie's view was that she took good care of her girls, and if any of them thought about not reporting jobs to her, thought about skimming for themselves, they could go stand on the street corner with the rest of the whores because she'd fire their little asses pronto. Reesa believed she would too. But hell . . .

Reesa said, "I can give you an hour. Okay? That's it."

"Sounds great," the man said.

He walked her to his car. He opened the door and shut it after she got into the front seat.

It was when she got into the car that she started to worry. Because the car didn't really fit the man. It was a secondhand Ford Crown Victoria. Stripped, utilitarian, and plain. She expected him to have a Jaguar or a BMW. A secondhand car, but the man was wearing a nice suit and a Burberry raincoat. They didn't go together. A small alarm went off then. She could hear Bobbie's counsel from the earliest days: *You sense danger, you get out of there. . . .*

Reesa said, "Where did we meet before?"

The man kept his eyes ahead, on the road. They were south of the I-64 overpass now, heading toward the loading docks beyond Laclede's Landing.

The man said, "The pharmaceutical wine-and-cheese party. It was a couple of weeks ago."

"Oh," she said. And now she was looking at him again. "So you're a doctor?"

He nodded, smiling again. Pleased with himself.

And Reesa said, "Is this your car?"

"It's a loaner," the doctor said.

Soon they were stopped. And she could sense the Mississippi River not far off. Dark and cold and abandoned buildings were on both sides of them. And he had shut off the ignition to the car, and Reesa was not liking this at all. She was not the sort to work in cars. Hotel rooms, homes, apartments, that was her thing. She thought about her purse and the small mace dispenser inside, hoping she was wrong.

"Hey," she said, putting some harshness in her words because often that tone could put guys like this in their place. Particularly the professional ones who worried about exposure and scandal.

"Hey," she said, "I don't like this."

That's when she noticed him pulling on the black gloves. Not looking at her as he pulled them on, and then when they were pulled tight, he turned and punched her in the face.

The force of the blow did not knock her unconscious. In her last few seconds, she started to wish that it had.

TWO

Dr. Raymond Sheffield arrived at the emergency room at St. Mary's Hospital ten minutes before the beginning of his shift. It was a twelve-hour one, midnight to noon. He went to the locker room and changed into medical scrubs. On some days, he wore his business attire with a doctor's smock over, the tie showing. Today he chose not to.

In the locker room were Dr. Ogilvy and Dr. Tassett. They were interns in their late twenties. Dr. Sheffield was thirty-three. He was not an intern. He was a regular working emergency-room physician. His contracted annual salary was a little under four hundred thousand dollars.

Dr. Sheffield regarded the younger physicians. Robert Ogilvy, graduate of the University of Missouri medical school. Chubby, loud. A mediocrity. Slightly more intelligent than the typical shaved bears one saw out of state schools, but not much. Liked to repeat jokes he heard on cable television, get the laughs as if he deserved the credit. A fool.

Harry Tassett. Another mediocrity. Only he didn't know it. Graduate of the University of Texas medical school, but had gone to Penn undergrad. Ivy League, but the school you went to if you couldn't get into the others. It was no Dartmouth. Harry came from Dallas and he seemed not to be ashamed of it. Harry was not loud like Robert was, but too self-assured.

When they first began working together, they had shown some deference to Raymond. They did this even though he was not the director of the ER and didn't hold a teaching position. He was merely older by a few years and had concluded his internship. In Boston. In a real hospital. They had tried to be friendly to him at first, but he hadn't responded to their jokes. He found them tiresome and immature. It took them a while to figure out that Raymond Sheffield was not shy but perhaps superior. Above things. This suited Raymond.

Yet, as much as they may not have liked it, they did think he was a better doctor. And when they needed help, when they genuinely thought they might be lost, it was Raymond whom they consulted. Raymond could tell that they didn't like doing this and it pleased him all the more.

·

St. Mary's Hospital was located in North St. Louis, a high-crime area of the city and county. Near interstates, construction sites, industrial workplaces, and not a few crackhouses. St. Mary's emergency room rarely suffered for lack of business. The ER was supposed to be used to treat medical and surgical emergencies. But patients and doctors alike treated it like a clinic.

The "working" physicians and interns generally logged twelve-hour shifts, while the nurses worked eight-hour shifts.

An hour into his shift, Raymond Sheffield was suturing a laceration to a teenaged boy's calf. He was being assisted by one of the staff nurses. Sheffield kept the sutures tense but not too tight. He wanted to avoid scarring or edema.

"Dr. Sheffield?"

Raymond tilted his head.

"Dr. Sheffield?"

It was Helen Krans, an intern. She stood far enough away to prevent infection to the patient.

Raymond said, "Yes, Helen."

"I have a patient, a woman in her early thirties, came in saying she fell down the stairs and thinks she may have cracked a few ribs."

"And?"

"Well, the X-rays don't show any rib fracture. But she's complaining of considerable upper-abdominal tenderness."

"Muscle guarding?"

"I think so."

"Get a flat plate of her lower abdomen. Stat."

"Yes, sir."

Raymond Sheffield smiled. "Don't call me sir. We work together." He turned to the nurse assisting him and said, "Give him a tetanus booster plus intramuscular penicillin. Okay?"

"Yes, Doctor."

He cleaned and met with Dr. Krans later. Together they looked at the flat plate. Raymond Sheffield said, "That's what I was afraid of. A ruptured spleen."

It was bleeding under the capsule but had not yet come apart. Once it did, the patient would either bleed to death or die of peritonitis. She could also suffer paralysis of the intestines.

Helen Krans said, "Is she going to have to have a splenectomy?"

"Yes," Dr. Sheffield said. "Or she'll die. The capsule's on the verge of exploding now."

Dr. Krans said, "I'll call the attending surgeon to assist."

"Who is it?"

"Dr. Lipkin."

"Okay," Dr. Sheffield said. "Why don't you assist me as well?"

"I'd like that," she said. "How did you—"

"We need her authorization, don't we?"

"Yes, Doctor."

Dr. Sheffield said, "I'll speak to her."

The patient's name was Tilda Mercer. She was heavyset and unattractive, and she looked like she wanted to go home.

The physician said, "Mrs. Mercer, my name is Dr. Sheffield. We've been looking at your X-rays and we believe we need to remove your spleen."

The woman's lower lip quivered. She said, "Why do you need to do that?"

"Because it's been ruptured, and if we don't do it soon, there's a good chance you're going to die."

"But it's just . . . all I did was fall."

"Fall where?"

"On the floor."

"I thought you said you fell down the stairs?"

"Yeah. The stairs."

She was looking away from him.

Dr. Sheffield said, "Mrs. Mercer, where is your husband now?"

"He's at home."

"You drove yourself to the hospital?"

"Yeah. I mean, he's busy."

"Mrs. Mercer, pardon me for being blunt, but I don't think you've given us an honest history. Did you really fall down the stairs?"

"Yes. Yes."

"Or did you and your husband have an argument?"

"Well..."

"Mrs. Mercer, we can't help you unless you give us an adequate history. Did your husband hit you?"

The patient sighed. She said, "He didn't... *mean* to. He'd been drinking and I called him something and he pushed me down."

"Was that it?"

"And then he kicked me."

"In the stomach?"

"... Yeah."

After a moment, Dr. Sheffield said, "Okay, then. We'll need

you to sign some forms, and then we're going to conduct the surgery. I don't foresee any problems."

·

The surgery went well. After it was finished, Dr. Sheffield instructed the ER chief nurse to notify the police and report Mrs. Mercer's husband for assault and battery. He further instructed her to notify him when the police arrived so that he could give them a statement for their report.

Dr. Helen Krans caught up with him in the hospital cafeteria. He was sitting at a table by himself with a cup of coffee and reading the *New England Journal of Medicine*. He looked up at her and gave her a gentle smile and said hello.

"Hi," Helen said. "I just wanted to tell you that you were terrific. I didn't know—I didn't think about the spleen being ruptured. What I'm saying is, you saved that woman's life."

Dr. Sheffield said, "She's a patient."

"I know," Helen said. "But you followed it up and called the police and—well, it was very impressive. May I sit?"

"Of course."

Helen said, "How did you know?"

"How did I know that the spleen was ruptured?"

"Well, yes, that. But what I meant was, how did you know that she's been abused?"

Dr. Sheffield said, "That was simple. Obviously the trauma had to come from somewhere. She could have fallen, but that didn't really comport with her injury. I presumed she'd either been punched or kicked. She was kicked."

"Yet she tried to protect him."

"Tried to protect her husband, you mean?"

"Yes."

"Yes. Well, that's very typical."

"Of women in general?"

"Yes. Of victims, I suppose." Raymond Sheffield smiled. "I don't mean to sound callous about it."

"You don't . . ."

"I suppose I do. I'm in my early thirties, by no means old. Not even middle-aged. But it wasn't that long ago that I did my internship. In Boston. And I came out of there a much different person than when I went in."

"I understand."

Raymond frowned, paused. He wanted to convey that he was a sensitive, thoughtful person. He held the pose for just long enough. Then he said, "You learn to form a shell. Not just to sickness and trauma, but perhaps to human trauma as well. Spousal abuse, child abuse. When I first started, I wondered if Boston was the most violent, hateful place in the world. But then I found out that it was no worse there than it was anywhere else. St. Louis or Bedford Falls, Pennsylvania. It's not the place, it's the species."

Helen said, "Don't you worry?"

"About the patients?"

She smiled, seeming to believe in that moment that he was selfless. She said, "No. I mean, about yourself. That you're getting too hard."

"Yes. There's always that concern. That you can become inured to it. But if you give in to those feelings, you won't be much good as a physician. What you have to do is find that line. That midpoint. Find it, become comfortable with it, and somehow straddle it. It helps to have faith."

"Religious faith?"

"Yes. And faith in humanity as well. And your work. We did something good, didn't we?"

"*You* did," Helen said. "Do you go to church?"

"Not as much as I used to," Raymond said. "Not the Catholic Church. But I feel myself searching for something. I believe I'm a spiritual person, if not an orthodox one." He smiled. "I suppose that makes me sort of an anachronism."

"No," Helen said. "I think it's nice, actually."

Raymond gave her a brief look. His expression became shy, perhaps even embarrassed. He said, "We should probably get back to work."

THREE

Carol McGuire opened her eyes and closed them. Opened them again to see the numbers on the alarm clock take form. A little after eight o'clock. Her alarm was set to go off at six thirty, but she had not set the alarm last night. It was Saturday. Saturday morning.

Saturday morning. Hadn't . . . George stayed with her last night? He had. They had made love after they got back from a party. The party had been hosted by a schoolteacher who was married to a public defender, and they had both invited friends from their respective workplaces. The teachers and the lawyers had not mixed well. The teachers being decent, upright sorts who laughed at clean jokes and the lawyers being morbid and cynical. George had found one or two people he thought were tolerable if not interesting and then stayed in conversation with them to make the evening pass more quickly. Carol knew that George was not much of a socializer. His stomach was too sensitive for wine, and he had never been much of a drinker. Plus he was quiet in the way that some cops are quiet. While the loud ones were like cowboys, the quiet ones always seemed to be watching. George was a quiet one, his eyes not resting even when they seemed to be.

Carol would say, "You're always judging, aren't you?"

"I don't judge," he'd say. "Sometimes I watch, but that's not the same thing as judging."

Carol did not consider him restless. She would not have wanted to spend much time with someone like that. But the more she got to know him, the more she came to believe that he was the sort who could relax only on his terms. He would go to a party with her and not complain about being bored or put off by people, but she could see that he was doing it for her. Not enjoying himself, but being dutiful. She knew that policemen were tribal and, in their own way, quite snobbish. She had known that going in.

One of the differences between them was that he was incapable of sleeping in.

This morning, she knew that he was still in her apartment. Indeed, she could hear him moving around the kitchen now. Probably he had already made a pot of coffee and was sitting at her kitchen table reading the newspaper. He could be in bed with her, but she was asleep, as far as he knew. On a weekend, she could sleep to eleven or even noon. He seemed incapable of that.

She heard movement. Out of the kitchen now . . .

He was standing in the doorway of the bedroom. Wearing pajama bottoms and a white undershirt. She almost laughed at him. She knew that he had forced himself not to get fully dressed. At least he had given her that much consideration. He was holding a cup of coffee.

Carol said, "What are you doing in here?"

George Hastings said, "Just came to say good morning."

"You've probably finished reading the paper, haven't you?"

"Yep."

"And you could've been here."

"Doing what? Sleeping?"

"Holding your girlfriend. Keeping her warm. Making sweet jungle love to her."

"While she's asleep?"

"You just can't sleep in, can you?"

"I would if I could." He walked over to the bed and set his coffee cup on the nightstand. He sat on the bed and leaned down to kiss her.

"Wow," she said. "Brushed your teeth and everything." She pulled him down on top of her. They were pulling each other's clothing off when the cell phone rang. Once, twice, and then a third time.

Hastings said, "Shit. It's mine. Hold on." He walked over to the chair where his pants were hanging and got the cell phone out of the pocket.

"Yeah?"

"Lieutenant? This is Sergeant Wister. We got a body down here by the river. Sorry if I called at a bad time, but you're the one listed on call."

"That's all right. Tell me where you are." He shook his head at Carol to tell her he was sorry.

•

Hastings's police unit was a brown 1987 Jaguar XJ6 with a powerful, rumbly Corvette engine. It had belonged to a drug dealer who was a car buff until it was seized by the police pursuant to the RICO act and given to the homicide squad.

Hastings loved the car. A few months ago, he had smashed it into another car to prevent an assailant from shooting him. The assailant had died of internal injuries. The Jaguar had been considered a total loss by the department's insurance company. They'd asserted that even with the Corvette engine, the car was not worth salvaging. But Hastings had taken it to the city's maintenance division and persuaded them to rebuild the front end. It would not have been easy to replace a car like this one.

Carol's apartment was in Clayton. Hastings picked up a coffee to go at the Starbucks on Wydown Boulevard, leaving the Jaguar running in front, its Police tag prominently displayed in the windshield. There was a time and a place to exploit the little benefits he had, and he didn't mind doing it. He set the coffee cup in its holder, picked up Interstate 64 at Hadley, and took it downtown.

It was a cold morning, gray and overcast. St. Louis weather in the fall.

Hastings had grown up in Nebraska. They hadn't discussed such things when he was a kid, but as a man he realized that his roots had been what people called lower middle-class, if that. Luck and athletic ability had gotten him a baseball scholarship to Saint Louis University. His hopes of a baseball career had more or less petered out by the time he was twenty. But he had finished college and gotten a degree in something called communications. Within a year of graduating, he had enrolled in the police academy with the goal of becoming a detective. In that he succeeded, and he felt fortunate to have done so. He had been in St. Louis longer than Nebraska now. St. Louis was his home.

He pulled the Jaguar off the exit ramp near Busch Stadium and descended into the city. South of the Poplar Street Bridge and drawing toward abandoned buildings looming by the river. He slowed the car and the scene came into view. Emergency vehicles and police cars, their bright authoritative colors set off against the brown and gray background. Hastings parked the Jag and walked toward the yellow tape cordoning off the primary crime scene.

He signed the crime-scene sheet, indicating his time of arrival. Then he found the patrol sergeant in charge, whose name was Paul Wister.

Sergeant Wister said, "This way."

They walked toward the river.

The Mississippi, as big as they say when you get up close to it. Big enough that you can hear it and smell it. It can intimidate you when you're next to it. Hastings remembered the flood of 1993, when the water got high enough to dislodge entire houses from the ground and send them downstream like bathtub toys. The river commanded respect.

They were in the shadow of the Poplar Street Bridge and the coal-black railroad bridge that was south of the interstate. They got close to the shore and Hastings saw the medical examiner bent over the body of a girl.

Hastings walked closer, and Henry Donchin, the M.E., looked up and acknowledged him.

"Hey, Henry. What have you got?"

"It looks like a strangulation. There's a contusion to the face that may have knocked her unconscious before she was strangled."

Hastings said to the sergeant, "Identification?"

"Yes. Her name is Reesa Woods. She has a driver's license and a student identification. University of Missouri, St. Louis."

Hastings looked up at the bridges. Traffic rumbled over the interstate bridge, probably thousands of vehicles in the past few hours. Who would look down and see a dead girl? Who would be able to?

In the middle of the river, a set of massive barges was being pushed downstream.

Hastings said, "Who reported this?"

"A river-patrol boat. They saw her near the shore about a half hour after the sun came up. They figured she'd jumped off the Eads Bridge and washed up. They didn't know."

The crime-scene photographer walked up. He exchanged greetings with the other officers and asked if he could start taking his pictures. Hastings said he could and stepped back. He looked around again. Empty, abandoned buildings, bridges passing over, maybe a mile south of the Arch. The killer had hidden the girl in plain sight. If she had screamed, had anyone heard?

Hastings said to the sergeant, "Have your patrol officers found any witnesses?"

"No, Lieutenant. There was a car here. We can see that."

"Where?"

The sergeant pointed. "Probably there, we think."

Hastings walked away from the body. He used his hands when he spoke, playing it out with the sergeant.

Hastings said, "Parked here, killed her in the car, if not already, and then threw her out. Or ..."—and now Hastings was looking at the river—"or, he tried to take her to the river and throw her in. But got close and realized that would be harder than he thought."

Because when you got close to the edge, the banks of the river sloped down. You could see that when you got close. You could slip on that slope and end up in the river yourself. Slide in and good luck getting back out when the current got hold of you.

But, Hastings thought, you're surmising. Maybe the killer had just pushed her out the door and taken off.

Hastings said, "Her identification was on her?"

"Yes."

"Anything taken from her? Jewelry, money?"

"No."

The crime-scene van was pulling up now. The technicians climbing out and walking over to the sign-in sheet. Middle-aged guys with stomachs and pasty faces who looked like they worked for county government, which they did. The crime-scene-unit guys always complained about not getting enough funding for their work, and they had a point. Their van was a Chevy panel truck painted black and white like any other police vehicle; they weren't getting a shiny new Humvee anytime soon.

Hastings returned to the M.E. and said, "Are there any indications of rape?"

Henry Donchin said, "It's only been cursory, George. But . . . so far, no. Just death by strangulation."

Hastings was looking at the girl again. Pretty, young . . . dressed professionally. Classy, yet not really looking like a student.

Hastings said to the patrol sergeant, "Is this girl a prostitute?"

The sergeant said, "We checked her wallet for ID. But her purse is, well, we haven't looked through that yet."

"Where is it?"

"Over here."

Hastings pulled a pair of latex gloves from his jacket pocket and tugged them over his hands. The handbag was an imitation Gucci. The real one would have cost about four hundred dollars; this one might have been worth about thirty. When he found a packet of condoms and tubes of jellies and lubricants, he thought his instinct correct. Then he found the card that said TIA'S FLOWER SHOP.

FOUR

Hastings called his supervisor Captain Karen Brady to tell her that he wanted a couple of detectives to assist him. It was Saturday and it would mean overtime. Karen had told him last month that she wanted him to get clearance from her before authorizing overtime. Hastings thought this request was unreasonable, as neither he nor his people had ever abused it, but past experience had taught him that Karen needed to be satisfied on the little things. That way, she wouldn't question him about the bigger things.

His professional relationship with Karen was something that had to be handled delicately. Karen had never been more than an average detective. She was not dumb, but she was not particularly smart either. She was inoffensive and unimaginative and she had the administrative knack for not making enemies. The sort that appears to be everyone's friend, but at the end of the day isn't really anyone's.

But, to Karen's credit, some part of her recognized her own mediocrity. She was aware that her lieutenant would protect her to the degree that she would defer to him. Yet she could not openly acknowledge this deference. This was why every couple of months she found it necessary to assert her authority. Her latest attempt to do this was on the subject of overtime.

Now she said, "What's up?"

Hastings said, "We've got a young girl's body out here by the river."

"Dead?"

The homicide detective paused. "Er, yes."

"Who is she?"

Hastings knew that Karen was smart enough not to ask if the deceased was black or white. Not directly, anyway. But she wanted to know.

"Young white female," Hastings said. "About twenty-two years of age."

"Hmmm. Any witnesses?"

"No, ma'am."

"Suspects?"

"Not yet."

"Have you ordered a canvass?"

"Well, we have patrol officers doing that now. But I'd feel better with a couple of experienced homicide investigators doing it. At least assisting with it."

"Right, right. Well . . . is it something you *need* detectives for?"

"Yes, I believe so. It's a strangulation, Karen. There are no signs of robbery or sexual assault. Not yet, anyway." Hastings paused. "She's a college student."

"Oh?"

Hastings kept quiet.

Karen Brady said, "How long do you think it'll be?"

"No idea." Hastings said. "Maybe through the afternoon." Which probably wasn't true. But he wanted the authorization.

"Okay, George. You got it."

"Thanks, Karen. I'll let you know how it goes."

They said goodbye, then George dialed the cell number of his sergeant, Joe Klosterman.

Three rings and then Joe's voice, a tone lower than a bark.

"Speak with me," Klosterman said.

"What are you doing?" Hastings said.

"I am driving a Honda Odyssey minivan to a soccer game."

Hastings said, "Someone cut your nuts off?"

"Filial duties, homey. My daughter's playing this morning."

"At Forest Park?"

"Yeah. It's the six-year-old league. Run up and down the field, a beehive on the ball, and then someone kicks the ball ten yards wide of the goal posts and they do it all over again."

"Your son play last night?"

Joe Klosterman's son was a running back for the DeSmet High School football team. There were few prouder fathers than Joe Klosterman, five children and most of them in one sporting activity or another.

Unlike Hastings, Joe Klosterman was a man who looked like a cop and little else. He came from a long line of policemen. For Klosterman, life was a set of duties and dedication. To his family, his church, and the department.

Klosterman said, "Yeah, they played CBC. It was on television last night. Did you watch it?"

"Of course not," Hastings said. "Anne with you?"

"No. She's covering another game. Sally's in the eight-year-old league. Why, what's up?"

"I'm at the river, standing under the Poplar Street Bridge. We got a dead twenty-two-year-old girl. Karen's given me authorization to bring you guys into it."

"You don't have a suspect?"

"No. No witnesses either. Joe, it's a strangulation. A joy killing. She wasn't robbed."

"Oh. Do you have an ID?"

"Yeah. Reesa Nicole Woods. She had a student identification on her. UMSL. But we found items in her purse that indicate she was working for an escort service."

"Which one?"

"Tia's Flower Shop. You know it?"

"Not off the top of my head. You say she *wasn't* molested?"

"I don't think so. The M.E. says there are traces of spermicide, that she probably had intercourse within a few hours of her death but that it was consensual. There's a contusion to her face, like she'd been punched in the nose. That, and bruises around her neck."

Klosterman was aware of his children in the van. He lowered his voice and said, "Hands?"

"No. There are fibers. The killer may have used a scarf or a towel. Listen, Joe, I didn't tell Karen that she was a prostitute."

"Why not?"

"Well, I thought if I had, she wouldn't have authorized overtime. I told her the girl was a college student. Which is technically true."

Klosterman said, "Ah, I don't blame you."

"So if you can kind of keep that in mind . . ."

"Right. Well, have you called Howard or Murph yet?"

"No. I can, though."

"Sorry, man, I'm kind of stuck with these things for a while. Tell you what, I'll find someone at the soccer game to give Mary-Beth a ride home. Take me about an hour, hour and a half?"

"I appreciate it, Joe."

•

Klosterman arrived an hour and forty minutes later. Detective Howard Rhodes was there by that time. He was the first one Hastings could reach.

Rhodes, in his early thirties, was the only black detective on Hastings's team. He was married to a nurse who worked at Barnes-Jewish Hospital, but they didn't have any children so Hastings didn't feel that bad about asking him to come down to the river.

There was no "neighborhood" to canvass. Reesa Woods's body was bounded by the river, two abandoned buildings, and an empty street. They walked around and searched the buildings and found a couple of vagrants who said they hadn't seen or heard anything. No one had seen any vehicles.

This went on for a couple of hours, and when it was done, the detectives gathered near the county van that took Reesa Woods's body away.

The van's engine idled, smoke coming out its exhaust. The doors to the van closed, and when the body was no longer visible, Hastings realized that he hadn't eaten anything all day. He was standing with the patrol sergeant, Klosterman, and Rhodes. There was something of a contrast between them: the detectives in civilian garb, looking like civilians, the patrol sergeant, Wister, in uniform, his blue jacket and belt with holster and extra ammunition clips visible. Homicide detectives could be elitists, but Hastings gave no sign to the patrol sergeant that he wanted him gone.

Hastings said to Rhodes, "You used to work vice, didn't you?"

Howard Rhodes said that he did.

Hastings said, "You familiar with Tia's Flower Shop?"

"No," Rhodes said. "Not that name. But the way that business works, they change their names about every six months. Though it's usually the same people working them. I'd say the victim was a high-class, high-dollar model. She looks young, clean. Let me make a call here."

They stood in the cold afternoon as Howard Rhodes pulled out his cell phone. The patrol sergeant told them to let him know if they needed him for anything else and then excused himself.

Rhodes was talking now, having reached an old friend at vice, and then they heard snatches of conversation, Rhodes saying, "Yeah...I'm not surprised....Yeah, well, you deserve it, man..." and the other detectives knew that they were discussing a promotion that was up for grabs.

Rhodes shut the phone off and came back to them. "Tia's Flower Shop is one of four outfits owned by Bobbie Cafaza. You know her?"

"Never met her," Hastings said. "But I've heard of her. A madam, right?"

"Right."

"You got a number for her?"

"Yeah," Rhodes said. "Do you want to talk to her?"

"Yeah."

Rhodes dialed a number and then handed his phone to Hastings. Hastings took a breath as the phone rang, remembering that the best thing to do when informing someone of a death was just to do it, not to think too much before. The ringing stopped and he heard a woman say, "This is Bobbie."

"Ms. Cafaza? This is Lieutenant Hastings with the St. Louis Police Department. I'm afraid I have bad news."

A pause. Then the businesslike voice coming back. "Is it one of my employees?"

"Yes. Reesa Woods. She's dead, ma'am. I'm sorry."

"Oh, God. Oh...God. What happened?"

"She was murdered. And I need to speak to you about it."

FIVE

Hastings cracked the window on the driver's side and the sound of the engine filled the car as it accelerated up the ramp onto Interstate 64. Cool air flushed into the cabin and helped clear some of the mustiness out. As the car settled on a speed between sixty and sixty-five, Hastings put the window up.

Saturday and he and Klosterman were at work. Hastings was hoping to catch the second half of the Nebraska–Texas game on television today, but that looked like it wasn't going to happen. He was quiet for a moment, thinking about what was still ordered in his life.

His daughter, Amy, age twelve, was with Eileen, his ex-wife, and Eileen's husband in West County. Hastings was scheduled to pick her up tomorrow evening at six. He hadn't done any shopping, so maybe they could go out to dinner. Someplace on the Hill. That would be okay, but then he was supposed to take Carol out to dinner tonight. Dinner out two nights in a row, no, three, because they had eaten in the Central West End last night before the party, and his salary could take only so much . . . Shit. Perhaps he could persuade Carol to come over to his house and he could cook for her. He was a pretty good cook, but Carol would probably want to get out of the house, and there was that fine line between being the romantic who cooks his girlfriend dinner and being a cheap piece of shit.

Klosterman said, "Eileen have Amy for the weekend?"

"Yeah," Hastings said.

Hastings realized that he was preoccupied. Joe Klosterman and his family were fond of Amy, particularly Joe's wife, Anne. The Klostermans had invited them for dinner last Christmas after Eileen had changed her plans at the last minute and taken off for Jamaica. Amy was a tough kid, used to her mother letting her down, but being stood up on the holidays had to have hurt. At the Klostermans', Anne had spent more time with Amy than she needed to, and Hastings could see that Anne was one of those women who recognize hunger in children, who recognize a need for maternal affection and warmth. Hastings wondered if Klosterman knew how lucky he was. Probably he did.

Klosterman said, "I worked prostitution a few years ago on South Grand, before the Vietnamese moved in and the neighborhood started cleaning up. You know Melanie Chapman?"

Hastings said, "Used to be Melanie Wise?"

"Yeah, and she married Bob Chapman. Married her own sergeant, but that's another story. Anyway, I worked the detail with her. She was in her twenties then and a looker. Back then. She'd hang out on Grand near the Gravois intersection and solicit the johns. This one guy pulls over to proposition her, he's in a fucking mail truck."

"U.S. mail?"

"Yes. Wearing the uniform and everything."

"On duty."

"Yeah. He walks into the hotel room, and Keith Nichols and I are sitting there waiting for him. We put the cuffs on him, and he starts crying and he says now he's going to lose his job. I kind of felt sorry for him. Just some loser. Then I didn't feel so bad when we went to his pretrial and the guy brings his wife and she's wearing a shirt that, get this, has the Ten Commandments written on it."

"Yeah?"

"Yeah; it was kind of pathetic. But you saw that sort of shit all the time. Guy'd show up to court with his wife, show the judge that his wife was standing behind him all the way. They don't understand that that just makes the judge more pissed at them. But I gotta admit, that Ten Commandments shirt was something I hadn't expected."

"Didn't give him jail time, did he?"

"Oh, no. Six months' probation, the usual. The guy did lose his job, though."

Hastings shook his head and said, "I don't see the point."

Klosterman knew what he meant by that. Arresting men and women for engaging in the world's oldest profession. Treating what was essentially a public health problem as a criminal problem.

Klosterman shrugged. "Well, you know how it works. The neighbors see the girls on the street, trafficking, they don't like it. They call their local alderman and the alderman leans on the department to clean it up. So we go down there, make some arrests, and move it someplace else. And come on, George, if it was in your neighborhood, you'd do the same thing."

"Yeah, probably."

Bobbie Cafaza's offices were in a redbrick building on Vandeventer Avenue. Red-and-black Laclede Cabs shuttled out of the headquarters down the street.

Klosterman pressed a buzzer at the glass door at the foot of the stairwell, and when he heard a voice say "Yeah?" he said, "Police," as he looked up into a security camera.

The door buzzed open, and they walked up the stairs to the second story. They walked in and saw a carpeted room with a modest couch and table with magazines on them. Some sort of waiting room. Hastings doubted that any activity occurred here. He looked into the next room, where a woman of about forty-five was talking with four ladies wearing dresses and skirts, their ages varying from early twenties to midthirties. They listened as the woman gave them directions to a hardware convention in Brentwood and told them what to do and what not to do. They heard the woman say near the end, "...and for Christ's sake, don't act like whores." Which Hastings thought was kind of funny. One of the girls said okay, twice, and they moved out into the front room and down the stairs, talking among themselves.

Then the fortyish woman was in the room with them, giving them an appraisal.

Klosterman said, "Let me guess, the circus is in town?"

"Clowns pay better than cops," she said. "They've got better manners too."

Hastings said, "I presume you're Ms. Cafaza."

"Yes," she said.

She looked her age. There were lines in her face and it was apparent that she'd never had surgery to fix it. But her figure was good and she had a stylish carriage. Like a middle-aged Russian dance instructor. Tough and worn, but attractive too.

Hastings identified himself, showing his shield, and introduced Klosterman.

Then she said, "I feel—I feel a little guilty."

Hastings said, "Why's that?"

"Because I haven't told the others yet. I'm hoping you're wrong."

"About what?"

"I'm hoping that the girl you found isn't Reesa."

"Well," Hastings said, "it is. I'm sorry."

The madam sighed and looked down at the floor for a few moments. She put her hands on her face and then raised her head.

"Christ," she said.

Yeah, Hastings thought. Christ indeed. An attractive pimp standing before them. A young girl caught up in prostitution and her life being choked out of her before she turned twenty-three.

Hastings said, "How long has she worked here?"

"About a year. Can we sit down?"

"Sure."

Hastings and Klosterman took seats on the sofa. The windows were behind her. Through the blinds, they saw traffic on the interstate.

Bobbie Cafaza said, "Would you like some coffee?"

"I'd like some," Klosterman said.

Hastings declined. He would like some coffee, but he wasn't going to ask this woman for a thing.

She came back with a thick yellow mug for Klosterman and set it on the coffee table for him. Hastings noticed that her hands were small and delicate.

Hastings said, "Was she working last night?"

Bobbie Cafaza said, "Yes. She was scheduled to meet a client at about four."

"Where?"

"Downtown."

"What name did she use when she worked?"

Bobbie Cafaza smiled. The detective knew something about the business. "Ashley," she said.

Hastings said, "Explain to me how she worked."

"She works for me," Bobbie said. "The clients call here and I make the arrangements. She's not supposed to—she's prohibited from working independently."

"Who was she with at six?"

Bobbie Cafaza hesitated.

Hastings sighed, like he was disappointed. He said, "Ms. Cafaza, I understand what business you're in. You don't call it prostitution and I'm okay with that. But if you don't cooperate with us, we'll have to shut you down. You know that."

"Are you threatening me?"

"No, ma'am. I'm not a vice officer. I try to solve homicides. If I can do that without ruining your business, that'll be beneficial to both of us."

Bobbie Cafaza said, "Really? Are you aware of the ... extent of my clientele?"

"Let me guess," Klosterman said. "It includes the chief of police, the mayor, and some of the most powerful, respected men in the city."

Bobbie said. "Go ahead and joke. But you're not far off."

Hastings said, "Well, we'll just have to take our chances. Ms. Cafaza, do you care about what happened to Reesa Woods?"

"Of course I care. She was a good girl. You think I just traffic in people. Women's bodies. But I'm satisfying a need."

"So are drug dealers," Hastings said.

"A human need," she said. "It's natural to want a woman. You know that as well as I do."

Hastings said, "Oh, I really don't want to mince words with you. I can leave and come back with a RICO order and freeze this business up by Monday. You're a smart woman and you'll just open up another outfit in six months, but then you'll have lost six months' profit. So how about it, huh? Tell us who she was with Friday night."

Bobbie Cafaza shrugged. Hastings was leaning on her, but he was showing her respect too, in a way.

She said, "Okay. I'll give you his name and number. I can even tell you where they went. But he's an old man. And I really don't think he killed her."

Klosterman said, "But she had other clients, though. Right?"

"Oh, yes."

Hastings said, "You said she worked for you for about a year. What was her average, say, per week?"

"Between five and eight. It just depended."

"Five and eight tricks a week?" Klosterman said.

"We don't use that term."

"What do you call them?"

"Encounters." She shrugged. "Meetings."

"Meetings." Klosterman wrote it down in his notebook.

Hastings said, "What about Reesa? What sort of girl was she?"

"She liked nice things. She was professional."

"Did she have a boyfriend?"

"I don't know. I might have heard her talk with Rita about a boyfriend. But that was a while ago."

"How long ago?"

"I don't know. Maybe a couple of months."

"Do you know his name?"

"No. Rita probably would, though."

"Rita who?"

"Rita Liu. *L-I-U.* I can have her meet with you here."

"Why don't you give us her address and number instead."

"Well..."

"That would work better for us."

"Okay."

"Regarding Reesa, did she have substance-abuse issues?"

"You mean drugs? No. I don't allow that."

Hastings said, "You sure?" Using his cop's voice now.

"I know what you're thinking, Lieutenant. Most pimps use drugs to trap women into this lifestyle. Or exploit a woman who's using. That's not the way I do business. And if you understood how this business worked, if you thought about it from a different perspective from that of a puritanical cop, you'd understand why I don't want fucked-up girls working here. Besides, if she was using, I think I would have known."

"Okay," Hastings said. "Well, let's have the guy's name. And all the other people she's seen."

"How far back?"

"Since she started here."

"I'll give you what I have."

SIX

They reached the Adam's Mark Hotel clerk by telephone and were informed that Geoffrey Harris had checked out at ten o'clock that morning. The clerk told them that he presumed he had flown back to New York, where he was from.

Hastings was driving while Klosterman was the one on the phone with the clerk. He didn't like the drift of what he could overhear.

Klosterman said, "Do you know what airline he was booked on?"

"No, sir, I'm afraid I don't. I remember that he asked for directions to the Central West End."

Klosterman said, "Yes?"

"I mean, he acted as if he had a lunch date there."

"What restaurant?"

"I'm not sure."

"But he's not there anymore?"

"No, sir. He took his luggage and got into a cab this morning."

"Hold on a minute." Klosterman lowered the cell phone and turned to Hastings. "What do we do?"

Hastings exhaled. "Tell him we're sending someone to talk to him. Howard or Murph. Get Ronnie Wulf on the phone." Ronnie Wulf was the chief of detectives.

Hastings peeled off the interstate at the Jefferson Avenue exit. Made a series of turns and then gunned it hard as he put the car back on the highway and drove west toward the airport.

Klosterman was holding his cell phone now, breathing through his nose.

Then: "Chief? Joe Klosterman. Sir, I'm here with Lieutenant Hastings. We're investigating the murder of a call girl found down by the Mississippi this morning. . . . Yes, sir, that's ours."

Hastings said, "The airport."

"We believe that she was with a gentleman named Geoffrey Harris, that's with a *G*, from Westchester County, New York. With him last night. He's either left town or he's about to. . . . No, sir, we don't know what airline."

Klosterman nodded his head. "Yes, sir . . . Yes, sir, that would help us a great deal. You can reach me at this number. . . . We're on our way there now. Thank you."

Klosterman clicked off the phone. "He's calling the airport police now."

The chief of detectives had more clout than either of them and he would be able to find out which airline the suspect was on before they could. The hope was that Ronnie Wulf would find out and give them the information before they reached the airport.

He did. The call came back as they rolled up to the airport departure lots. The police light was on the dash, blinking on and off. There was a uniformed officer there, and they got out of the car as a St. Louis County car pulled up behind them, its lights on as well.

Klosterman said, "Okay," into his cell phone. Then to Hastings: "United Air. He was about to board first class, but they've delayed it."

Hastings said, "Does he know we're coming?"

"No. They just told him it was a delay."

Hastings turned to the two uniformed officers behind him. After a brief greeting, he said, "I don't want this guy spooked. Hang back and wait for my signal. Okay? As of now, he may be only a witness, and we don't want to create a stampede."

They walked quickly down the long path of one of the airport's wings, passing the gates and coffee stands. They got to the gate in question, and Hastings could see the apprehension on the ticket attendant's face. She saw the uniforms, and Hastings made eye contact with her.

The woman nodded in the direction of a man of about sixty, bald on top with gray hair on the sides. He was wearing a blue blazer and pressed white shirt.

Hastings made a signal to the uniforms and they stopped walking. Klosterman began a wide arc that would ultimately bring him behind the old man.

Then Hastings walked up to him.

The man held his raincoat over his lap. He was looking out the window, perhaps to see if the weather would prevent him from leaving town.

Hastings said, "Mr. Harris?"

The man looked up.

Hastings had his identification out. "My name is George Hastings. St. Louis police."

"Yes." Harris's voice was one of authority. Regal and British. He addressed the policeman as he would address a bank clerk.

Hastings said, "You were with a young lady last night who goes by the name of Ashley." He didn't make it a question.

Harris said, "What business is that of yours?"

"It's police business. Where is she now?"

"How should I know? What is this, some sort of attempt to extort me? If that's your game, Officer, you've picked the wrong man."

"Mr. Harris, you're mistaken." Hastings glanced over the man and saw that Klosterman was close behind him now, his pistol at his side, pointed down. No scenes, please, Hastings thought.

Hastings said, "Sir, do you know where she is now?"

"No. See here, I've done nothing improper. You want to arrest me for— Well, you've got no proof."

"No proof of what?"

"Of—well, you know. Really, this is ridiculous."

"Mr. Harris, I'm afraid we can't let you board that flight. The girl is dead and we need to question you about it. I can read you your Miranda rights here in front of all these people or we can go someplace private."

"Oh, Christ," Harris said, his regal expression crumbling.

SEVEN

Ten minutes later, they were seated in a small room at airport security. They read him his rights but did not put him in handcuffs. They told him that he could have a lawyer appointed for him if he couldn't afford one, and he shook his head during that part. And after that was out of the way, he talked to them quite freely, not so much as a man wanting to confess but as one wanting to get things straightened out.

Geoffrey Harris told them that he was an investment banker with a large house in New York. That he had started working in finance in London after graduating from the London School of Economics and had been sent to the New York office in 1991. He told them that he was married with four children and six grandchildren. He said he was in St. Louis on business.

He said, "The gentleman I worked with is named Robert Alan Gray. He is what we call in this industry a wholesaler."

Hastings said, "Selling what?"

"Financial products. They want old men like myself to buy those products. As part of the wining and dining, they basically give us a girl. He is the one who provided me with Ashley. I shall be glad to give you his telephone number. In fact, I can give you his card."

Hastings said, "Mr. Harris, you're not being honest with us."

"What?"

"We've been informed that *you* requested to see Ashley. That's what the records at the escort service indicate. Your name, not Mr. Gray's."

"Oh . . . well."

Hastings said, "You want to try again? And let me advise you of something before you go on: you've just been informed that you have the right to remain silent. Now you can exercise that right and we can make this thing a whole lot more complicated than it needs to be with lawyers and warrants and detentions. Or you can remain silent. But what you don't want to do is try to mislead us, because that by itself can be grounds for filing criminal charges. Okay?"

It took some of the salt out of this rich and successful man, and it was intended to.

"Well," Harris said. "Well, all right. I did telephone her. This time. The first time I was here, Robert set it up. And I'm confident your sources will verify that."

"But you called her the second time," Hastings said.

"Yes, I did."

"Why?"

"Well, I liked her. She seemed like a—nice woman."

"When did you call her?"

"Friday. I called the agency soon after I arrived. I had a late lunch with Robert and some others from Enterprise Finance and then we met at the hotel."

"She came to your room?"

"Yes."

"How long was she there?"

"Two hours."

"And she billed you for that time?"

"Yes. It was not . . ."

"I'm not interested in booking you for solicitation, Mr. Harris. So long as you cooperate. What did you do with her?"

"She was . . . with me for the first hour. The second hour, we just talked."

"Talked."

"Yes. I'm not so young anymore."

"You just wanted companionship?"

"Yes."

"Someone to talk to."

"Yes."

"But you were intimate with her?"

"Yes."

"Any rough stuff?"

"No. Nothing of the sort."

"From when to when?"

"From approximately four to six."

"Six in the evening?"

"Yes."

"And then?"

"Then she left."

"And you?"

"I stayed in my room. I had another drink and then I went to sleep. I'd say at around eight P.M."

"Why would you say that?"

"That's my usual bedtime."

There was a knock on the door. Hastings said, "Excuse me," and went to answer it.

It was Klosterman. Hastings went out and shut the door behind him.

Klosterman said, "We've got his suitcase."

Hastings said, "You haven't gone through it, have you?"

"No."

"Okay. I'll get his permission to search it." Hastings paused, looked off to a wall. Then he said, "Bring it in here."

"Now?" Klosterman said. "With him in there?"

"Yeah."

They went back into the security room. Harris was still in his seat, seeming unflappable. But he was English, and Hastings was beginning to think they could be a pretty tough breed.

Hastings said, "Mr. Harris, this is Sergeant Klosterman. As you can see, we've got your suitcase here. I can get a search warrant to go through this, but that would take up a lot of time. With your permission, we'd like to search it right now."

Harris waved an aristocratic hand, telling them to go ahead.

While Klosterman popped it open, Hastings sat down again. He did not want to stand over this man because he suspected that if he bullied him any more than he had, the man would clam up.

Harris had been set straight once and hopefully that would be enough.

Hastings said, "Did you rent a car while you were here?"

"No. I used a taxi."

"Do you always?"

"Yes, always."

"And you say you were in your hotel room from four in the evening until you checked out this morning?"

"I was."

"If we were to ask you to take a polygraph examination, would you be willing to do that?"

"A lie detector test?"

"Yes."

"I thought those weren't admissible in the American courts."

"They're not. But it helps us with an investigation."

"I'll take one today if you like."

"Good," Hastings said. "We'll try to make it quick." He looked over at Klosterman. Clothes were taken out of the suitcase and set on the table. Klosterman shrugged.

Hastings said, "The girl was strangled to death, Mr. Harris. And there's no evidence that she was robbed. If you're innocent of this crime, the evidence will show it. We'd like to examine some of the things in your suitcase."

"To prove I did it?"

"Well, more to prove that you didn't. The truth is, sir, we want to clear you as a suspect if you're not the killer."

"Eliminate me from the process?"

"It would help us out," Hastings said. He looked to Klosterman again and knew that they were both wondering the same thing: whether there were traces of the girl's skin on the man's ties or belts or anything else that could've been used to choke the life out of her.

Hastings said, "We'd like to do that with a certain amount of discretion, you understand."

Geoffrey Harris smiled at them for the first time. He knew a couched threat when he heard one. "I'm all for that, Lieutenant."

EIGHT

Geoffrey Harris voluntarily came to the downtown police headquarters and submitted to a polygraph examination. The test was conducted by Burl Davidson, a sergeant whom Klosterman had managed to reach by cell phone. Burl Davidson was a year away from retirement and already had set up a convenience store in St. Charles. He was a slight-looking man with glasses, and he could pass for a schoolteacher. He was an expert examiner.

Hastings and Klosterman watched Davidson do his work in another room on a television monitor. Burl videotaped all his examinations unless instructed to do otherwise. Harris was informed of this.

It took about forty-five minutes, and when it was done, Davidson removed the clips and told Harris that it was all over and he would be back in a moment.

Hastings and Klosterman watched Burl Davidson leave the black-and-white screen and a couple of seconds later heard him knock on the door.

"Yeah," Klosterman said, and Davidson walked in and sat in a chair across from them.

"Well, the results are conclusive," Davidson said. "He's telling the truth."

Hastings said, "If he's a sociopath, he could fool the machine." He was thinking of the Green River serial killer in Seattle. He too had passed a polygraph. The police released him as a suspect and he went on to murder more prostitutes. Of course, the examination had been flawed in some respects.

Davidson said, "It's possible but not likely. In fact, it's very unlikely. He exhibits no traits of your typical sociopath. Do you suspect him?"

"No," Hastings said. He hadn't, really, even before the examination. But he wanted to be thorough. He turned to Klosterman and said, "What do you think?"

"I think he's clean too."

"What did you think *before* the exam?"

"I thought he was clean," Klosterman said. "The hotel clerk says he didn't leave the hotel that evening. Their security cameras would have caught him. M.E. says the time of death was between seven and eight that evening. He didn't have transportation. If he killed her in his hotel room, he would have had to carry her almost a mile to dump her by the river. There's no way he could have transported her there. And even if he had a car hidden in the parking garage, at his age and in his condition . . . it's not possible. And his luggage has provided us no physical evidence that he strangled her. He's just a lonely old man. Her last client."

"Or second to last," Hastings said.

Davidson said, "I don't think he's a sociopath." He wanted them to confirm his opinion.

"He's not," Hastings said. "Thanks for coming down, Burl."

"Anytime, George."

Hastings went back into the investigation room and said to Geoffrey Harris, "You're free to go. We appreciate your cooperation."

"Not at all. I presume I passed your test?" A little irritation in his voice.

Hastings said, "You did. Can we offer you a ride back to the airport?"

"No, thank you. If you could telephone a taxi for me."

"Sure. Mr. Harris, did Ashley tell you where she was going? By chance, did she tell you that?"

"You mean to another appointment?"

"Yeah. Something like that."

"No, Lieutenant. She was a professional, you see. The purpose is to delude an old man like myself into thinking she's happy to spend time with him. For her to speak of other 'clients,' if you will, would dispel the charade. The sad thing is, we're grateful when they lie."

Hastings smiled. "I suppose."

Harris put his coat over his arm. "I hope you find your murderer, Lieutenant. She was a nice young lady. She didn't deserve this."

"No, she didn't."

Hastings noticed that Harris was suddenly uncomfortable. Not out of guilt but because he thought the American policeman might be expecting a handshake. Hastings was not, and he opened the door.

Harris said, "If there's anything else you need, you know where to contact me." Then he was gone.

In the hall, Klosterman said, "Well?"

Hastings looked at his watch. It was almost seven o'clock. "Oh, shit. Let me make a call real quick."

Carol answered the phone.

"Hi," Hastings said. "Where are you?"

"I'm at home. What's going on?"

"I'm still working that homicide. Ah, listen, I'm sorry, but we have to do one more thing before we go off shift."

He heard her sigh.

"I'm sorry, Carol. We don't really have any suspects and— well, I'm sorry."

"It's all right. When do you think you'll be done?"

"Maybe a couple of hours. I know we planned dinner, but—"

"Don't worry about it," she said. "Call me when you finish. If it's not too late."

"I will. Goodbye."

"Bye."

Klosterman said, "Told you not to get married."

"I didn't marry her."

"Oh. Well, I told you not to marry Eileen."

"That's right," Hastings said. "You did. What about your wife? Is she going to let you stay out?"

"Sure. You want to go talk to some more hookers?"

"I was thinking we should go to the girl's apartment. See if there's a fellow living there."

"We haven't got a search warrant." Klosterman looked at his watch. "We can call a judge, get a telephonic. But it's pretty late."

"Judge Reif will give us one. He's usually up late."

"I'll call him on the way." Klosterman asked, "You think she was killed by someone she knew?"

"Sort of. If she's a high-class call girl, I don't think she would've been standing on a street corner pitching for a job. I don't think she would have gotten into a car with a stranger. And it's usually someone they know."

It wasn't anything Klosterman didn't know. Most murdered women were done in by boyfriends and husbands, exes who didn't want to let go. He said, "Yeah, but this was a hooker, George. That widens the scope."

"I know that," Hastings said. "But let's check on what we know first."

•

Reesa Woods's apartment was in the Soulard area. It was on the first floor, a short set of brick steps leading up to the door.

Hastings knocked on the door, calling out "hello" after three raps.

Klosterman looked into the front window. The lights were out. Klosterman said, "I don't see anyone. I'll go check the back."

He did so while Hastings remained at the front door. The

apartment was one of many in a set of buildings in a row, so Klosterman had to walk all the way around the block and come back up the alley. Hastings looked into the windows. Soon he heard Klosterman's knocks on the back door. Hastings drifted down to the Jaguar parked at the curb. He knew there was no one home. He was getting cold.

Klosterman came back, holding up his arm. "Nothing," he said. "We got the telephonic warrant."

"Let's find the super. Get him to let us in."

It took some time, but they found the night manager of the complex. She let them into the apartment. It was well furnished and clean, but there were few if any signs of warmth. Above her bed was a poster of Marilyn Monroe nude. The one she did for the first issue of *Playboy*. A couple of hardback books that didn't look like they'd been read. The bed was not made. An empty refrigerator, an unopened box of Pop-Tarts in the cupboard.

They spent the next two hours going through the apartment and another half hour questioning the night manager. They didn't learn anything helpful.

They were both in lousy moods when they left.

Klosterman said, "I get the feeling she didn't spend much time there."

"Me too," Hastings said.

NINE

He called Carol from his car on the way home.

She answered the phone, "Yeah?"

"Hi. Uh, do you still want to go out for dinner?"

"Well, it's almost eight thirty. It would be nine before we sat down. I don't know . . ."

"Well, I could stop by someplace and pick something up."

"Maybe we could have dinner tomorrow night."

"I'd like to, but I'm picking Amy up tomorrow night," Hastings said. "But the three of us could have dinner."

"Well . . . let's see," Carol said. He heard her sigh. And Hastings felt it then. A funk. She had spent the day alone and he had let her down. But a girl had been murdered, and it was better to chase leads when they were hot.

Hastings said, "Do you want to be alone?"

"No. I didn't say that. Just come over."

"Do you want me to bring food?"

"No. Just come over."

"Okay."

Hastings clicked off the phone and his first thought was, Okay, but what am I going to eat?

A fine rain had begun. He turned on the windshield wipers.

Hastings drove to a Coney Island stand and ordered two hot dogs with mustard and onions and a Dr Pepper. His plan was to eat them in the car before he got to Carol's. He felt little guilt about this. It added about five minutes to his trip to her place, and his being hungry and cranky wasn't going to be good for either of them. He felt better after he ate.

Driving north on Skinker Boulevard, Hastings considered his relationship with Carol McGuire. He understood that she probably had justification to be irritated with him. He did not consider himself a workaholic, and he often got bored with people who had little to talk about outside of work. It led to even duller conversations about things like the Cardinals, but at least it was something else. In a sense, he and Carol McGuire were part of the same community. She was a criminal defense attorney who had cut her teeth in the public defender's office. They worked opposite sides, so to speak, but they knew a lot of the same people and the same cases. When they first met, it was under conditions that could arguably have been called hostile. She got a witness out of jail, whom Hastings wanted to question. Both of them thinking they needed to be adversarial to the other, but soon realizing their goals were not all that different.

Carol McGuire had been tentative with him at first. She recognized, as others had, that George Hastings could read people well enough, whether or not they were subjects in a criminal investigation, but that he may not have been the best person to read himself. In the first few weeks they started to see each other, Carol said they should remain friends. A not-so-subtle way of telling him that he wasn't going to get her in bed too soon. That lasted about six weeks, and after the first few times they made love, she asked him whether he would take Eileen back if she asked.

He expressed surprise at this, if not indignation.

"Take her back? She's married."

"I know. She left you for another man. But what if she gave that up, came back to you, and said, 'Okay, I've changed. We'll do it your way. Take me back.'"

"She's not going to do that."

"But what if she did?"

"She won't."

"But what if she did?"

"That's like asking, what if she grew wings? She's not going to do that."

"She's not going to what?"

"She's not going to—change."

Carol McGuire said, "Are you sure of that?"

"I think so," Hastings said.

"I wish you were sure."

"Come on. What is this?"

"George, can you admit some things?"

"Like what?"

"Like, you fell in love with a girl because she was pretty and charming and you hoped to turn her into what you wanted. A good wife, a good mother. A PTA mom. You thought she would become those things because you picked her."

"That I would be her Pygmalion."

Carol smiled. "Okay, she said that, not me. But was she really that far off?"

"Wait, let me understand this: you're defending *her*?"

"No, not really. This isn't really about her. You know I'm not a fan of Eileen's. I'm just saying that I understand where she was coming from."

"So she was right to leave me?"

"Oh, Jesus Christ. No. I'm saying that you and her wanted different things. She knew it, but you didn't. Her husband is an idiot, but he's far better suited to her than you."

"I don't know about—"

"George, he is. He is. This is part of the problem with you. Part of what makes you a good detective is this, for lack of a better word, arrogance you have. But it has its drawbacks too. You see Eileen with Ted and you wonder how she could go from you to him. Am I right?"

"No." But she was. And he knew it.

Carol said, "See, it's who she is. Maybe it's always who she was. But you can't see that because you get in the way. You think because she was your wife, she had the same sort of character you have. Or you could get her there. What I'm saying is, you're only seeing it through your perspective."

"So I'm the one that's delusional?"

"You were both delusional. Eileen probably always will be. But you, well . . . there's hope for you yet."

"Gee, thanks."

He had been rankled by this analysis. But in time he had grown to understand it. And as the months passed by, he had come to respect Carol in a way that he had probably never respected Eileen.

So the divorce was behind him and he had come to terms with it. But as he washed the hot dogs down with Dr Pepper, he thought now of what Claude Dwyer, his old patrol sergeant, had once told another middle-aged cop who recently got divorced. The freshly divorced cop bragged that he had another girlfriend, this one much younger and thinner than his ex, and she was moving in with him and, boy, was he getting the action *now*.

Sergeant Dwyer said, "Yeah? You want some free advice?"

"What?"

"Get a vasectomy. And I mean now."

The middle-aged cop gave Dwyer a puzzled frown, but a couple of the wiser cops laughed because they knew where the old sergeant was coming from. That is, that a man freshly divorced doesn't know his head from his ass. Particularly if he's middle-aged and a cowboy cop to boot. Dwyer knew that a man in that situation would not be himself for a couple of years and in that interval was likely to seek a quick emotional solution with another woman. *My new girlfriend's pregnant and we're going to get married and, goddammit, this time everything's gonna be just great.* From one disaster to another.

Hastings smiled at the memory. He hadn't gotten a vasectomy. Carol used the pill. And they had never discussed children.

•

Carol was watching the news when he got to her apartment. She kissed him on the cheek and said, "It was on the news. The murder."

"Yeah? Aaron give a statement?" Aaron Pressler, the department's media spokesman.

"No," Carol said. "Not on television. The newscaster just said the police were investigating it. I guess it's not that big a story. Do you want a beer?"

"Yeah, thanks. I can get it." He went to the refrigerator as she took a seat on the divan. On TV, the local PBS station was playing an old Preston Sturges film. William Demarest in a marine uniform telling small-town folk that he was at Guadalcanal and that was no fooling.

Hastings said from the kitchen, "I wouldn't say it wasn't important."

"I didn't say that."

He came back to the living room and took a seat next to her. He said, "No, you didn't. Sorry."

"It's all right. The news said she was a coed."

"They used that word? Coed?"

"Yeah, they like stuff like that. Coed murder."

"Hmmm. She was a call girl."

"She was?"

"Yeah. An escort. They probably marketed her as a college girl. It helps, I guess."

"They—the escort service?"

"Yes." Hastings put his head back and closed his eyes. It was an involuntary communication. It meant that he didn't want to talk about it anymore. Half of the first forty-eight hours gone and they had made little progress in finding the girl's murderer. Tomorrow was Sunday. He had responsibilities to his work and to his daughter. But he would think about that later.

"George?"

"Yeah."

"Do you want to go to sleep?"

"No, I'm fine. What's on television?"

"A movie. *Hail the Conquering Hero*. It's pretty good."

"Okay." He opened his eyes to watch it.

Five minutes later he was asleep. Carol McGuire took the nearly full beer from his hands and set it on the coffee table.

TEN

"Can I get you a drink, Raymond?"

Raymond Sheffield held up his glass. It was about three-quarters full.

"Oh," Carla Monroe said. "Drinking the white liquor, eh?"

Raymond said, "It's club soda."

Carla Monroe was a nurse. She was heavyset, her face almost balloonlike when she smiled. She smelled of wine. She said, "I forgot, you don't drink."

The party was at Ted Zoller's house in Kirkwood. Ted was the hospital's premier chest surgeon. He was leaving St. Mary's to take a position at a clinic in Ladue. He and his wife had invited most of the staff to his going-away party. His home was smaller than Raymond had thought it would be.

Raymond recognized about half the people at the party from work. The other half were Dr. Zoller's friends and family outside the hospital. A few of them were doctors.

Raymond made small talk with a couple of schoolteachers, one of whom had spent the previous year in China. She had brought her photos to the party, and Raymond politely went through them, asking simple questions about some of the people and places every few photos. He stopped only when Dr. MacDonald raised his voice to say that he wanted to say a few words about Ted. The guests gave him their silence and then laughed appropriately at his jokes and warm remarks for Dr. Zoller, and after glasses were raised to toast the good doctor with a great future, Dr. Zoller was forced to say something in response.

When that was done, the schoolteacher who had gone to China said to Raymond, "Are you a doctor too?"

"Yes," Raymond said.

"You worked with Dr. Zoller?"

"Yes. For a short time."

The girl was around twenty-seven, and she had healthy blond hair and a clean, athletic look. She paid little attention to her boyfriend. Her name was Tracy.

There was a pause. Tracy was waiting for Raymond to say something else.

When he didn't, she said, "I went to school with Jeff. That's Dr. Zoller's son."

"I see."

Tracy thought that she could tell him more about that. That she was the son's first girlfriend . . . in a way, though probably more of a female friend than a girlfriend. But she didn't think this man would find it that interesting. She thought, You're too old to be explaining things like that anyway. She thought the doctor was an interesting figure. He wore a herringbone jacket and tie and he looked like he belonged in the 1950s or early '60s. He was not overly handsome, but there was something interesting about him. He looked a bit like a young Martin Sheen. She saw no wedding band on the man's finger. She wondered if he was bored by her company. He didn't seem very interested in what she had to say. He seemed indifferent, in fact. Yet at the same time, he did not seem uncomfortable. She wondered if he would remain seated with her until he had to use the bathroom or if he would excuse himself before that.

Another man approached them. An older guy with a big stomach and glasses and a frog's face. He said something to the doctor next to her, but Tracy could see that it was a pretense to get closer to her.

The man sat on an ottoman and said, "Ray, you trying to keep this pretty young lady all to yourself?" Haw-haw. The doctor smiled thinly, and before he could say anything, the fat man extended his hand to Tracy and said, "Don McGinnis. How are you doing?"

"Fine."

"And you are?"

"Tracy."

"And how did you end up with Dr. Sheffield here?"

"I did— I'm here with my boyfriend. He's over there by the bar."

"Ohhh." The frog-faced man said it brightly, underlining the opportunity. Haw-haw.

Dr. Sheffield said, "Dr. McGinnis is our chief ob-gyn resident."

Tracy said, "Is that right?" Her tone polite but uninterested. She hoped he would take the cue. He didn't.

Dr. McGinnis said, "Yeah, St. Mary's is a good little hospital. It's not Barnes-Jewish, but sometimes less is more, you know?"

"Hmmm-mmm."

"A place like that, you're just a cog in a big machine."

After a moment, Tracy said, "A place like what?"

"Barnes."

"Oh. I don't work in medicine, so I . . ." She raised her hands, as if to say that he was wasting his time talking shop to her, but that didn't work either.

Another couple drifted over, the nurse who had offered to get Dr. Sheffield a drink and an intern from the hospital. A new conversation bouquet formed.

It began then. A couple of professional men, one of them in his middle years, and a woman whose best years were behind her, all of them consciously or unconsciously aware of her, young and pretty, and wanting to impress her. It had happened before. It happens to the most well intentioned of people.

The intern said that Dr. Zoller was smart, getting out of the hospital now. He didn't have the exact figures, but he was sure that the man's income would at least double. Dr. McGinnis said, sure, but there were other factors besides money to consider. He said that you could work outside the hospital system if you wanted, but then you were in the business of getting and keeping patients. He said, "Have you noticed that doctors are becoming like lawyers?"

The intern said, "How do you mean?"

"I mean," Dr. McGinnis said, "all the advertising. Look at the phone books, the billboards, the local magazines. Doctor ads everywhere. It's the sort of thing we used to criticize lawyers for. Ambulance chasers, we called them. Trolling for clients. Who'd've thought our profession would end up doing the same thing?"

The nurse said, "I don't think it's as simple as that."

"Isn't it?" McGinnis said. "Look at all the photos of doctors. They're everywhere. Like real estate salesmen. 'Introducing ten new physicians and three convenient new locations to care for you and your family.'"

The intern said, "Well, it is a business. You need patients."

McGinnis shrugged and raised his glass to tip more Dewar's into his mouth.

Dr. Sheffield said, "I think what Dr. McGinnis is saying is that something has been lost."

The intern said, "Excuse me?" having almost forgotten that Dr. Sheffield was there.

"I think what Dr. McGinnis is saying is that the medical profession is supposed to be that: a profession. Not a business."

"What's the difference?"

"There is a difference. You either see it or you don't."

"Oh, come on. Are you saying you consider this profession a calling?" The intern was smiling to himself now.

"A calling." Dr. Sheffield smiled then, just. Then he said, "It *should* be, of course. Ideally, it should be. We should be in the 'business' of healing. But are we?"

"Yes," the nurse said.

Dr. Sheffield smiled again, wider this time. He looked down.

Tracy said, "You were going to say something else."

He shrugged.

"No, come on."

"I was only going to say something about reconstructive surgery."

The intern said, "You mean breast implants." He was smirking. "It always comes back to tits, huh?" The joke brought him a couple of tired smiles but only that.

"Well," Dr. Sheffield said, "I was only going to point out that reconstructive surgery is perhaps a misnomer. A woman's face is shattered in an auto accident. We want to rebuild her face, fix the disfigurement so that she's presentable to the public. That is reconstructive surgery. That is a genuine healing. But contrast that with a woman who goes to a doctor complaining that her breasts are sagging. That there are lines developing on her face and forehead. In other words, that she is suffering from the ravages of age. Of time. Of the natural order. Do we say to this woman, 'This is nature. This is the passage of time.' That 'a struggle against time and nature is both futile and immature'? No, we do not. We take this woman's anxiety and depression as if they were symptoms of a disease. When there is no disease. There is no sickness. And in so doing, we do not heal this woman. Indeed, we exacerbate her condition. We increase her anxiety because we help foster her immature, unrealistic view of the world. We foster her childlike narcissism. When we do that, we are not healing. We are profiting from something that helps no one. We engage in something that demeans both the physician and the patient."

Tracy regarded the doctor. She said, "But if it's what the woman wants, where is the harm?"

"I've just explained the harm. Weren't you listening?"

He did not make eye contact with her when he answered her. And this did not go unnoticed. It was as if he thought she was not worth regarding.

•

On the way home, Tracy said to her date, "I don't know what I said to offend him."

The young man said, "You said, what if the woman wants it?"

"I said, I didn't see the harm if the woman wants to do it. You know, so she feels better about herself. And he got, I don't know, cold. Like I shouldn't have even opened my mouth. Up till then, I'd thought he was a nice guy. A little strange, but nice."

"He's a doctor," the young man said. "They're all assholes."

ELEVEN

Mickey Caldwell didn't know until lunchtime that his wife was going to Kansas City to visit her sister. As usual, she hadn't planned too far ahead. She just came back from book club and said, "We're going to Kansas City."

"When?"

"In about an hour. I want to see my sister."

Mickey didn't ask why. His wife's behavior had become increasingly erratic in the last year. Ever since their son had been born, she hadn't been the same. She had put on weight, which shouldn't have been that unusual. Most of Mickey's married friends made the same complaint about their wives. They also complained that they were being less frequent with the sex. They talked about going months without action from the wives.

And Mickey thought, *Months*? Try *years*. He remembered making love with his wife sometime before LSU won the BCS championship, and that had been at least two years ago. He remembered it because they had been at that game. Been at the Superdome *before* Hurricane Katrina hit New Orleans. A long time ago, and he had since stopped wondering what had gone wrong in the marriage.

Mona had put on weight, yeah. But there was something more than that. She told Mickey she didn't feel like it. Not tonight, not now . . . not ever saying, *Not ever again.* But that was the de facto reality. Mickey suspected it had something to do with all the pills she was taking. This one for depression, that one for anxiety, another one for melancholy. All these pills in different colors and sizes . . . he couldn't compete.

He believed that he had tried. He really thought he had. He had asked her if there was something he had done wrong, if she wanted to go to a counselor, if there was something he could do or change. She just looked at him blankly or denied that there was anything wrong at all. She'd once said to him, "*I* don't miss it." And that hurt, it really did. Not so much that she said it, but rather the way she said it. Like, if she didn't miss it, what else should matter? Why should it matter to him?

He had wanted to say, *But* I do *miss it. I miss you. You're my wife. I'm your husband.*

But he didn't consider himself a sophisticated man. He didn't want to seem indecent or inconsiderate. She was the mother of his child.

When a friend first suggested he go to an escort service, Mickey was repulsed. He had been raised by good Christian parents. Not just churchgoing, but decent. He knew without ever asking that his father had never even contemplated such a thing. It would have been disrespectful to his wife. His father would never even have looked at another woman. His father had stopped speaking to one of his closest friends because the man had left his wife to marry a mail-order bride from the Philippines. His father had said to Mickey, "He basically *bought* a second wife because he got tired of the one he had. A good man doesn't do that."

No, sir, he doesn't. But . . . what if he needs sex? What if his wife is denying him not just a release but intimacy? Denying him warmth and comfort? Wasn't that part of it too?

The first time Mickey dialed the number his friend had given him, he hung up when a woman answered. The second time he called, he was standing on the front porch of his home with the cell phone, and his wife pulled into the driveway in her car. He hung up again, even though he knew she couldn't hear. Later that evening she told him not to sit on the new furniture because he hadn't taken a shower after exercising. Mickey told her that he had to go the convenience store. He made the call while he was in the car.

•

Her name was Estelle and it took her about five minutes to figure him out. Nice Methodist boy of about thirty-five who had never been in the navy, never been in the Philippines, never been in Amsterdam, never been with a prostitute. Estelle knew that at root Mickey Caldwell was kindhearted and decent and was genuinely pained by the absence of sexual intimacy in his marriage. She was younger than he, but she talked him through their first time. She told him afterward that he was not the sort of man who would leave his wife and children. She told him that these sorts of arrangements had always existed and always would. That they were *good* for marriages. She told him that the five hundred always had to be paid up-front because it was better to get that sort of thing out of the way.

They met every two weeks on Wednesday nights at the Thunderbird Motel on West Manchester Road. Mickey always paid in cash and never complained.

•

Saturday nights, Mickey was usually with his family, either at home or at a friend's house watching college football, both of them being graduates of Mizzou.

On this Saturday, his wife's car was barely out of the driveway when Mickey was on the phone, dialing Estelle. When he reached her, she said she could meet him at the Thunderbird at midnight. It put Mickey in a good mood, something to look forward to as he sat on the couch and took in the game, and when Chase Daniel threw three touchdowns against Iowa State, he felt almost blessed.

He got to the hotel at eleven o'clock and quickly realized that he should've taken a nap. For he was not a night person. His usual bedtime was nine thirty, ten at the latest. He lay in the hotel bed, fully clothed, blinking his eyes at the ceiling and trying to stay awake, but by eleven fifteen he was asleep.

When Estelle came knocking, he did not answer. Not even when she called out his name.

So there was Adele Sayers—working name "Estelle"—standing alone outside a third-rate motel in West St. Louis. She muttered, "Shit." Five hundred bucks gone and she had driven all the way out here. The boy had backed out, his wife having come home early or some shit. After all the time she had spent sweet-talking him, making him feel comfortable paying for it, a phone call would have been nice.

She walked back to her car, a used Camaro, but it didn't look it, and got in behind the wheel. After turning the ignition, she settled back against the seat and felt the tickle at her neck. Then she was jerked back, the cord pulled tight against her throat. She never got a chance to scream.

TWELVE

Raymond Sheffield held the electrical extension cord tight for a full minute after the woman stopped struggling. Held it taut and then released it. He checked her pulse. None.

He had been in the car for only about a minute when she came back. He had jimmied open the passenger door and had just climbed into the backseat when he heard her walking back to the car. He'd thought she would be gone for at least an hour. An hour with whatever stooge she was lined up with.

But she came back and it had been a near thing. He had ducked down in the backseat and was unwinding the extension cord as he heard her get in, felt her weight press back against the driver's seat. When she started the car, he pounced. And soon it was over.

Well. It had turned out okay after all. She had surprised him, coming back out sooner than he had expected. But he had re-acted well under pressure. And that was a good sign.

Raymond got out of the Camaro on the passenger side. Hmmm. The car was still running. Raymond looked about the motel parking lot. Three or four cars but no one around. He ducked back into the Camaro and turned off the ignition. The engine cut.

He remained in the front passenger seat. He regarded the woman. He looked out at the parking lot, put it in context. He was hesitating . . . aware of the danger of being caught, but getting a kick out of it too. If he left now, without a memento, without a trinket, he knew that he would feel cheated. He was entitled to a prize. He took another look at the woman. Then he reached over and pulled one of her earrings off. It took a piece of her ear with it. He would wash the flesh and blood off when he got home.

Raymond closed the door and walked back to his Ford. He left the extension cord in the Camaro.

Two miles away from the Thunderbird Motel, he began to feel a certain pride. The unexpected had happened. She had come back to the car within a couple of minutes of leaving it. But he had still been ready. He had reacted not with panic but with cool professionalism. Any butcher could handle the predictable. Make an incision, remove the appendix, close, and suture. Who couldn't do that? Take a mediocrity from a med school in the West Indies, he could do it. But something more was required of the professional. A cool head. A *finesse*.

Raymond drove the Ford on Manchester to Interstate 270. He took that south to Interstate 44, past the Chrysler plant, and then south on a winding road into the hills. No one knew about the Ford except him. He had bought it with cash from some clodhopper in Arnold, and he had not told the seller his real name. The car was "unlisted," so to speak. A phantom's car.

Raymond Sheffield owned a small barn on a defunct horse farm. He had purchased the property with cash. He parked the Ford in the barn next to his Mercedes E350. The Mercedes was black. It was his "doctor's" car. Raymond backed it out of the barn, left it running while he got out and locked the barn doors. Then he got back into the Mercedes and drove back to his house in Sunset Hills.

It was almost two in the morning when he turned on his living-room light. He didn't feel tired. He went to the kitchen to make a cup of tea. While the kettle boiled, he cut pieces of sharp cheddar cheese on a wooden cutting board. Then he transferred the cheese slices to a dish and placed wheat crackers next to them.

He felt better after having a snack and tea. When it was done, he set the dish into the sink. Then he removed Adele Sayers's earring from his coat pocket, washed it in the bathroom sink, and dried it with a towel.

He sat in his reclining chair in the living room and examined the earring. A cheap piece of costume jewelry. She had not been high-class at all. Raymond felt a disappointment. Maybe it was because the earring was no longer attached to the girl. *He* would know what it was. Whenever he looked at it, he would know. But now that it was clean, it seemed inanimate. Not the prize he had thought it was. You hit a squirrel with your car, you don't mount its head above your fireplace. It's just a squirrel, for heaven's sake.

He sighed and set the earring on an end table. Maybe he would feel better about it tomorrow. Maybe he would see it and know what it should've meant; maybe the memento would come to have meaning in time.

Raymond sipped his tea and thought back to the party.

Helen Krans had not been there.

She had asked him at the end of their shift if he was going, and he had said that he probably was. She said that she had plans and couldn't go. Her disappointment appeared genuine. Raymond did not ask her what her plans were. But he knew she was going out with Harry Tassett. Raymond showed no hostility or displeasure at this. Indeed, he hadn't really felt any at that time. He believed that her relationship with Tassett—if you could call it that—would be short-lived. Tassett was an oaf. And though that probably wouldn't matter to someone like Helen Krans, she would come to see that Tassett was going to continue to chase other women and that she was just part of that collection. Raymond could recognize another predator when he saw one. Tassett was that. He was the sort that would take a certain pleasure in seducing a nice girl like Helen. But she would figure him out. Tassett made little attempt to hide what he was about, considering his lifestyle for the most part harmless. There would be a breakup, an undramatic one at that.

And Raymond Sheffield would be there when it happened.

He was being patient. For he knew how to be patient. He knew how to wait when waiting was necessary. Not that he planned to add Helen Krans to *his* collection. That would not be her role.

He planned to marry her.

He knew that in time she would come to trust him. Confide in him and be drawn to him. She was already seeing the Raymond that he wanted her to see. The decent, compassionate, thoughtful physician. She would round him out. She would be part of his daytime persona. The Dr. Sheffield persona. She would make a good wife. For who would suspect a physician? Particularly a physician who was married to such a nice, guileless girl like Helen Krans?

Raymond rubbed his eyes. He was coming down off the high now, and he found that, in spite of the tea, he was tired. He retreated to bed. He tried to read a chapter of an Anthony Trollope novel but gave up after a page. He turned off the light and went straight to sleep.

THIRTEEN

Hastings was in a convenience store buying a Sunday newspaper and a coffee when he got the call.

"Hastings."

"Lieutenant? This is Deputy Ernie Hill, County PD. We got a body here on West Manchester Road, death by strangulation."

Hastings said, "A woman?"

"Yeah. A young lady named Adele Sayers. We're reasonably sure she's a hooker. Dispatch says you investigated a strangulation yesterday down by the river. Maybe it's the same guy."

"Okay. You giving me an invite?"

"We'd welcome you."

Hastings said, "I could be there in about thirty minutes. Listen, Deputy, you got reporters there?"

"No, I don't see any yet."

"Can I ask you a favor? Tell your people not to give out any statements. Not yet."

"I understand."

Hastings got off the phone. Two prostitutes strangled in two days. Technically, it could be called a serial killing. The press got hold of that and there could be panic. Maybe they would need the cooperation of the press, but if it got out at the wrong time, the upper brass would get upset and would want someone to blame for it if the killer wasn't apprehended. Panic, fear, despair. You could tell people the facts. Tell them that out of about two hundred thousand murders committed across the nation, at most two hundred could be attributed to serial killers. Tell them that they were in far greater danger from fucked-up ex-boyfriends or estranged husbands, the everyday, commonplace monsters. Tell them, but it wouldn't matter.

Hastings hoped the murders weren't related. He hoped they weren't because if they were, they were dealing with something illogical and raw. Something unnatural. And it was this that Hastings believed people feared. Not the dumb-ass loser who drinks too much and bashes a neighbor's head against the sidewalk; not the pathetic asshole who would rather see his woman dead than free of him. Those things were common. The mass murderer was not common.

He hoped they weren't related, but he suspected they were.

•

The Thunderbird Motel was a three-quarters rectangle of rooms with red doors set against an off-white exterior. There were three county police cars and an unmarked felony car. It was early and there was no yellow tape up.

The county detectives had gotten there before Hastings. Introductions were made. The heavyset detective, whose name was Escobar, pointed through the window of the Camaro and said, "You see that? Extension cord."

"Yeah," Hastings said.

"We believe that was the murder weapon."

The girl was flopped forward onto the steering wheel.

Hastings said, "Who found her?"

"The morning cleaning woman. She told the manager and the manager called us," Escobar said. "The M.E. and the technicals are on their way."

"You've spoken with the manager?"

Escobar looked to Deputy Hill, the ranking patrol officer. Hill caught the questioning glance and said, "I did. He's waiting in the office, if you want to follow up with him."

The detectives hesitated.

Technically, it was outside the city's jurisdiction. But there was less friction between city and county on such things than there would be between city and federal. For his part, Hastings had always held St. Louis County in fairly high regard. They were a professional outfit, and that could not be said of every law enforcement agency. Good leadership and a culture that did not foster or tolerate corruption kept them clean.

Escobar was a county detective and Hastings was a municipal lieutenant. But they answered to different supervisors. Hastings held no rank over Escobar and they were both aware of this.

Escobar said, "Well, George, I know it's premature, but do you think this girl was killed by your guy?"

"I don't know yet," Hastings said. "I'll tell you what we've got downtown: a young call girl, probably high dollar, strangled by someone she seems to have willingly gotten into a car with. I don't really have any suspects. My leads are ... well, she's got a long list of clients and we have yet to go through all of them."

"Was she married?"

"No. We've checked to see if she had an estranged boyfriend. Someone outside of her work. But, again, it's early."

Early. They were nearing the end of the first forty-eight hours and they hadn't yet chased down all their leads. In fact, if someone wanted to be blunt, they could argue that they hadn't really started. A sixty-year-old man whom they cleared and allowed to get on a plane. Well, at least they knew he hadn't killed this one.

Yeah, it was still in the early stages, and now another woman had been murdered. A city with a greater population of around two million, yet both detectives were beginning to believe that there was one killer involved. And if that was true, the killer had something of an advantage over them, because he was not waiting around for them to find him. He wasn't staying still. He was looking for his next victim.

Escobar said, "What else you got?"

"Not much, I'm afraid. She worked for Tia's Flower Shop. That's an outfit run by Bobbie Cafaza. You know of her?"

"No. I never worked vice. Is she located in the city?"

"Yeah."

"We believe this girl works for an agency called Treasures. You heard of that?"

"No. You?"

"We're aware of it. It's run out of North County. Spanish Lake, to be specific. Not a madam, but a guy named Roland Gent. Ever hear of him?"

"Nope."

"He's a sweetheart. Small-timer. But smart, though."

"Anyone talked to him yet?"

"No. Not yet. Listen, George, there may be different killers here. But if not, they may want to create a joint task force. Hell, they might even want to bring the feds in, give 'em an excuse to send their behavioral-science guys out here, tell us country boys about astrology and mama complexes and that sort of shit. Why don't I call the chief deputy and you call your chief of detectives and let them decide how to proceed?"

"I'm good with that," Hastings said. "It's your county, but would you mind if I spoke with the cleaning lady and the manager?"

"Now?"

"Yeah."

•

Hastings corralled the manager and the cleaning woman in the motel's front office. Once he was satisfied that they weren't going to run off, he asked them to sit still while he made a call that he told them would take only a minute.

Ronnie Wulf answered his cell phone on the fourth ring. Hastings exhaled with relief. At least half the police officers would be in church at this hour.

"Chief, this is George Hastings. We got another dead prostitute out here on West Manchester. It's technically county's jurisdiction, but they called me because it's similar to the strangulation I handled yesterday."

"Oh, shit. It wasn't the guy you let go, was it?"

"No. That guy got on a plane yesterday, and I think this happened late last night."

Hastings heard Wulf breathe a sigh of relief. A police officer high up in the chain of command worried about being responsible for another murder. The anxiety that comes with rank.

Wulf said, "You think it's the same guy?"

"It's too soon to tell. But if I had to say one way or another now, I'd say it was. Same sort of victim. Same sort of murder."

"She was strangled?"

"Yes. With an extension cord. In her car. The way the body's positioned, it looks like the guy did it from behind."

"Her car?"

"Yeah. That's where she was found. Maybe he forced her into the car, or maybe he was waiting for her there."

"Waiting for her . . . Shit. This guy's *hunting* them?"

"It looks that way."

"There's no press there, is there?"

"No. I asked them to keep them away."

"Good. The last thing we need is to have SERIAL KILLER splashed across the local news. County accommodating you?"

"So far. Detective Escobar, you know him?"

"No."

"He suggested that we call our respective superiors and—"

"Yeah, I know. I'll call the deputy chief and we'll see where to go from there. In fact, I should probably come down there now."

"If you want, sir."

"Yeah," Wulf said, "that's what I want," and then he was gone.

FOURTEEN

As he questioned the cleaning woman and then the hotel manager, Hastings saw more and more police vehicles pulling into the parking lot. The M.E., the county evidence van with the crime-scene technicians, the navy Crown Victoria with no lights that he was fairly certain was the sheriff's, and then the unmarked Impala that was Ronnie Wulf's take-home vehicle. A yellow tape line was put up and men and women stood and talked and questioned, and Hastings was hoping it would hold out, prevent the horde from spilling into the motel lobby and overwhelming the witnesses.

The cleaning woman said that she had come to work at eight A.M. and was walking from room 4 to room 11, and that was when she walked by the Camaro and saw the woman inside. The cleaning woman was around fifty and had an accent that Hastings thought was probably Polish or Ukrainian, but then he realized that she was one of the Bosnian refugees who had come into the city ten years earlier.

"At first," she said, "I thought the lady was asleep. Too much drinking. I go past car, I go into room and clean."

"How long?"

"Thirty, maybe forty minutes. I come out, and the woman still sleeping. Only, it seemed . . . not right. I walked over to the window and knock on it. I know what she is, I want her to move on."

"You know what she is—you mean a prostitute?"

"Yes."

"How did you know?"

"Didn't you?"

"Never mind me, mama," Hastings said. "How did *you* know?"

"You can tell. Is obvious. And I've seen her here before."

"Yeah? How many times before?"

"She come, what, every two weeks. Maybe every week. Sometimes with different man. Sometimes same man."

Hastings thought about that one for a moment. Then he said, "Would you recognize these men if you saw them again?"

"I don't see them all. Just some. I come here in the morning, not at night. I not here last night. Only this morning. This morning—"

"Okay, I got it. You've seen her before in the morning?"

She seemed to think about that one. "Yes. Maybe twice."

"Twice in the morning. But what about at night?"

"I don't work nights."

"Then how do you know she comes here at night."

"I don't know. . . I hear things."

Hastings sighed. He turned to the hotel manager, who raised his hands in submission. "There's a night man. We don't look to see what's going on in the rooms. It's not our business."

"Right," Hastings said. "Have you seen her before?"

"Well, yeah."

"So you knew."

"Yeah, I knew. Look—"

Hastings said, "Sir, I don't care. I'm just asking if you know her."

"I suspected what she was, but I don't know her. We don't get a piece of it, if that's what you mean."

Hastings had not. But he kept that to himself. He said, "Well, then she was here to meet someone, wasn't she?"

"I don't know."

"Don't you?"

"I don't specifically know who she was meeting here. It doesn't go through me."

Hastings said, "It's illegal. You know that. We're going to be questioning Mr. Roland Gent. Do you know him?"

"No."

"What if he says you do?"

"I swear, I don't know him."

After a moment, Hastings said, "Well, let me see your register for last night. After that, I'll decide whether or not I believe you."

There were four names for the previous night. Two of them were still here and were being questioned by the county police. A couple on their way back to Terre Haute, Indiana, and a truck driver from Detroit. The third one was a man going west, who had listed an address in Winfield, Kansas; he had checked out through the desk at seven A.M. The fourth was a man who lived in St. Louis. He had paid with cash and left a bogus telephone number and name, but for some reason he had written in his license tag on the form.

Hastings called Klosterman and gave him the tag and asked him to check it out. Klosterman said he'd get back to him, and that was when Ronnie Wulf saw Hastings through the lobby window and waved him out.

•

The technicians and the detectives formed a semicircle around the Camaro. A contrast of civilians and uniforms, county and metropolitan. Ronnie Wulf chewing his nicotine gum, as he had been for several years, looking at the car and the dead woman, keeping the chewing to a certain rhythm, and eventually he turned to Hastings and said, "What do you think, Ace?"

Hastings said, "I think he was waiting for her in the car, hiding in the backseat. He waited for her to get in and looped the extension cord around her neck and strangled her. I believe it was premeditated. And then," Hastings pointed at her mangled ear, the bloodstain beneath it, "I think he pulled one of her earrings off."

"You think he did it after?"

"Yeah."

"Not in the struggle?"

Hastings turned to the medical examiner.

The examiner said, "It doesn't appear that it happened that way. If it had happened during the struggle, she would have been twisting her head." The M.E. twisted his head, swiveling it, in case they didn't understand him. He said, "But the tear is straight down. Like if you were ringing a church bell."

Ronnie Wulf said, "After?"

"Yeah, after." Hastings shrugged. "Who can explain why? He's a sadistic killer. But... some killers, killers who are sadists, they're known for wanting trinkets. Mementos of their work. I say this because her purse wasn't taken. And the remaining earring, which I presume matches the one that was taken, is pretty much worthless. Costume jewelry."

Wulf said, "The girl down by the river, was anything taken from her?"

"Her life."

Ronnie Wulf frowned. "Anything else?"

"No, sir. I mean, I'm not aware of anything."

"But you think we're dealing with the same guy?"

Hastings was aware of all the other law enforcement personnel around him. He wished Wulf had asked him this privately. As it was, he was onstage. He said, "I think so. But I don't have enough proof of that as of now." Hastings had already expressed this opinion to Wulf.

Wulf stopped chewing. "All right, so what *do* you have?" he said.

"I've got two high-dollar prostitutes who were both strangled within the same forty-eight-hour period. No evidence of theft. I think the man that did it—and I think it was a man—I think he was hunting them. Stalking them. And I think he did this because he likes doing it."

"And you think he's going to keep on doing it?"

"Yes, I do."

"Shit. Well, I hope you're wrong."

Hastings looked at the woman's torn ear once more. "I hope so too."

FIFTEEN

There was a bit of a *thunk* as the Ford Explorer's automatic transmission went from second to third. Not loud, but noticeable if you were listening for it. There, but then it was gone and the car went on just fine. The Explorer was coming up on twelve years old now and showed almost two hundred thousand miles on the odometer, but Tim Murphy had held extensive negotiations with his wife to get her to keep it for another two years. He swore that if it held till then, they would trade it in for whatever she liked.

She was in the car now, next to him. Murph kept looking straight ahead when the transmission made the noise. He didn't want to give anything away.

When the transmission had first gone out, Murph's wife spent the better part of two weeks hounding him to buy something new. "I *told* you," she'd say. And she'd say other things, like, *What if we'd been in the middle of the interstate, Tim? What then?* And so forth. He'd come back at her, fighting dirty, pointing to their two boys, ages six and eight, and say, "We can send them to Catholic school or we can drive a new SUV, but we can't do both." And she had said, But the damn Ford doesn't even run, so Murph had to get the thing towed to a place in Belleville where they agreed to give him a rebuilt transmission for around eight hundred dollars.

Brought it back a week later. See? Running just fine. Just remember to keep the radio turned up loud between second and third.

He was driving it now, ignoring his wife's glare, as they left Mass and he returned Klosterman's call and Klosterman asked him if he could go with Rhodes to interview a guy who had been at the Thunderbird Motel in Creve Coeur. They had found another prostitute who had been choked to death.

Murph said, "Just a minute," and put his hand over the phone. He didn't want anyone to hear him seeking permission from his wife for anything, least of all Klosterman. Klosterman was a pretty talented mimic, and Murph did not want to hear himself imitated in front of a hall full of detectives: *Huh-huh honey, ca-ca-can I go to work?*

Murph said to his wife, "I have to work. Will you be all right without me?"

Mass was over and she had nothing planned for them the rest of the day. An agreement was reached and Murph told Klosterman to have Rhodes pick him up in front of the main gate at the zoo.

They passed the St. Louis Arena, going west on Clayton Road, parallel to the interstate. Murph pulled the Explorer into the drive-through at Rico's snack shack and asked for a steak-and-cheese sandwich, fries, and a Coke. The kids carped about what they wanted, and Murph's wife scowled as Murph told them that they would eat at home and that he was picking up something because he had to go to work and eat in the car.

Murph's wife sighed "You're going to be late."

"No, no," Murph said. "I'm timing this just right."

They handed him the order through the window, and he pulled out onto Clayton Road, made the first right turn onto Hampton Avenue, and crossed over the interstate. As he made the next left and the Explorer descended the hill, he saw the Chevy Impala coming from the other direction.

"Perfect."

"Okay," his wife said. "Okay." She could give him his silly little victory. Or backhand him.

They stopped at the front gate of the zoo. Murph got out of the car with his bag of food and soda, and his wife switched over to the driver's side. She rolled down the window, leaned out, and kissed him. Closer now, she said, "Be careful, okay?" She hoped the children hadn't heard the concern in her voice. He had been shot on a case before, going to interview a witness who should've been harmless. The other detective had been killed.

"I'll call you."

•

Rhodes said, "Can you crack your window?"

"What?"

"The smell, man."

Murph said, "You want some of these fries?"

"No, I'll just smell the grease."

"Good stuff."

"How is it you can eat that sort of food and not get fat?"

"Genes, baby. I got the right genes."

Tim Murphy was a short, almost slight man who maintained the build of a bantamweight fighter. Which he had never been, but he was gifted with that air of menace and fearlessness that non-Irish cops tend to envy. People had thought that getting shot would take some of the bite out of him. It hadn't.

After he was shot, Murph's brother came down from Chicago and visited him in the hospital. His brother was a dentist. He was younger and more successful financially, and he told Murph that he was going to survive and that maybe now it was time to take a partial disability retirement and get out of this line of work. Murph said, "And do what? Go to dental school?" The brother said no, not that necessarily. But something safer and more profitable. Something with a better future. Murph told him to forget it.

Tim Murphy was not a man given to self-examination. He and his brother had grown up in a working-class, pro-union environment. And though it was the younger brother who had gone on to become affluent, it could be argued that Murph was the one who had become a snob. His identity was strongly rooted in being a policeman. Perhaps even in being an Irish policeman. It was not so much that he believed he was doing something good. He did believe that, but he knew himself well enough to know that this was not his motivation. In law enforcement, he felt a pride and a belonging and a purpose he knew he could not feel anywhere else. If that sentiment trapped him in a life that brought him the risk of being shot, so be it. He knew this was something his brother would probably never understand. He was grateful that his wife had never asked him to explain it.

Rhodes said, "What did Joe tell you?"

"He said there was another strangulation. You went to the first one, didn't you?"

"Yeah, a hooker, like this one. We don't have any leads on the first. And then they found a second one this morning at the Thunderbird Motel on Manchester. The guy we're going to see was checked in at the hotel last night. He left sometime. He used a false name and address."

"Oh?"

"But he wrote down his real tag number on the register."

"Clever."

"Yeah, a rocket scientist. Joe called the DMV and found out his real name and address. So we're going to see if he knew her. Find out what he was doing there."

"Does he know we're coming?"

"Nope."

"Good."

•

Mickey said, "We'll go the over on the Patriots. . . . Yeah, guy . . . Is Dallas giving points or getting points? . . . Huh? Romo? No, he seems to be working out. . . . Yeah, we'll see how long it lasts. . . ."

He was on the phone with his bookie. Wearing sweatpants and a ball cap at around noon, Sunday. There was an empty McDonald's bag on the living-room table, Terry Bradshaw and

Howie Long muted on the television, Bradshaw waving his arms about, Howie looking askance. Mickey's wife and kid would not return from Kansas City for hours. Sunday and he was free.

Mickey said, "No, Tiki's serious. I saw him on Letterman the other night, he said he was hurting too much. He's retiring ... yeah, fucking pussy ... shit, someone's at the door. Let me call you back."

Mickey Crawford opened the door, the cell phone still in his hand. He saw two men in sport coats and ties, civilian outfits, but right away he knew they were cops.

The smaller one held up his identification. "Mr. Crawford?"

"Yes, sir."

"I'm Detective Murphy. This is Detective Rhodes. We'd like to speak to you."

"What about?"

"It's nothing too serious," Murph said. "Can we come in?"

When he said this, he made his body language and his expression unthreatening. Detective Rhodes stood back a step. They could have been two men working for a local church.

"Sure," Mickey said. He stood back and let them come in.

Mickey was aware of the mess in his living room. He wished he had gotten dressed earlier. He wished he had taken a shower. He wished he knew what these guys wanted. Without meaning to, he heard himself apologizing for the clutter.

Murph said, "Hey, you should see my house. You married, Mr. Crawford?"

"Uh, yeah. My wife's in Kansas City. With the baby."

"How many children you have?"

"Just the one. She's two and a half." Mickey Crawford smiled and looked at Detective Rhodes. Rhodes didn't say anything.

Murph said, "So how do you like living in Creve Coeur?"

"It's okay. I guess. We bought the house about a year after we got married."

"And your wife's out of town."

"Yes." Mickey felt alarm then.

"So," Murph said, "what were you doing at the Thunderbird Motel last night?"

"What?"

"The Thunderbird Motel," Rhodes said, speaking for the first time. "What were you doing there?"

"I—I was here last night."

Murph sighed, like he was disappointed. He looked at Rhodes, as if to say, *This one's going to be difficult.* He said, "Mickey. We know you were there. Your car was there. We know."

Rhodes said, "Why don't we sit down. I'm sure there's a reasonable explanation for this."

Mickey gathered himself. Squaring his shoulders, he said, "There is. I wasn't there."

Murph sighed again and gave Rhodes another look. He said, "I guess we'll have to take him downtown."

"Now wait a minute—"

"And if we do that, it's going to become, well, a public matter."

Rhodes said, "Son, we're not your daddies. Or your priest. Just tell us what you were doing there."

"Oh, God," Mickey said. "Oh, no. I—I wasn't, I didn't . . . I was there to meet a friend."

Murph took a seat on the couch. He made a gesture to Mickey, who sat down on the chair nearby.

Murph said, "Who?"

Rhodes remained on his feet. He drifted about the room, looking and observing.

Mickey said, "A woman."

"Who?"

"Her name is—well, do you have to know her name?"

"Yes, we do."

"Her name is Estelle. She's just a friend."

"What's her last name?"

"I don't know."

"You don't know her last name?"

"No. I know it seems weird, but, oh, God." His chin was quivering now.

Murph glanced over his shoulder at Rhodes, who was walking out of the living room, toward the back of the house.

Before Mickey could say anything, Murph said, "Was she an escort?"

"Yes." Mickey's voice was on the verge of a sob.

"Tell me what happened."

And now Mickey did sob. He said, "We met, we met, I don't know, a few months ago. I called a number in the Yellow Pages and she met with me. And we, you know, met. That's all."

"You had a relationship with her."

"Yes."

Murph shrugged. No big deal. "A friendship."

"Yes."

"'Cause you get lonely?"

"Yeah. My wife . . . we don't." He paused. "We don't, not since the baby."

"I understand. Man, you're not the first. So you made friends with Estelle."

"Yes."

"And you would meet with her?"

"Yes."

"How often?"

"I don't know. Once every three weeks or so."

"At the Thunderbird?"

"Yeah, usually."

"And you met her last night?"

"No."

"No?"

"No. I mean, I was supposed to. What happened was, I was supposed to meet her. I called and made an appointment to—oh God, an appointment. If my wife—"

"Your wife's not here," Murph said. "Tell me what happened before she gets back."

"I got there at around eleven. We were supposed to meet at midnight. But I got there before she did. I wanted to watch a game on ESPN. A college football game. And I thought I'd watch it at the motel while I waited for her."

"Why not just watch it here?"

"I don't know."

"Sure you do."

"I—wait, I do know. I wanted to watch it at the motel because I was afraid if I watched it here, I'd fall asleep. And that's what happened at the motel. I was lying on the bed, watching the game, and I fell asleep. I don't usually stay up past ten."

"What game were you watching?"

"Northwestern–Wisconsin."

"When did you fall asleep?"

"I don't know. It must have been before twelve."

"Did she come?"

"If she did, I didn't hear her. I was asleep."

"You fell asleep. Then what happened?"

"I woke up. Around three o'clock or so. I was still in my clothes. And I didn't want to stay there."

"Why not?"

"It's depressing being in a motel alone. You miss your family."

Detective Murphy nodded. He saw no irony in this. "You left then?"

"Yes."

"You sure about that?"

"Yes."

"What if the motel manager says that you checked out at seven A.M.?"

"Then he's lying. Or he's mistaken. I left at three. And I didn't check out. I just left." Mickey straightened up, intuiting something now. "What's this about, anyway?"

"We'll get to that," Murph said. "You left at three and then what?"

"I came home."

"Can anyone back you up on that?"

"No. My wife's out of town." Mickey looked over his shoulder. The other detective was no longer there. Mickey said, "What happened?"

"Mr. Crawford, Estelle is dead."

"Oh, God. Oh my God. What—"

"She was strangled to death. In the motel parking lot. Didn't you know?"

"No. God, no. You don't think I—"

"I don't know yet. Would you be willing to take a polygraph?"

"A lie detector test? Yeah, I'd take one. I swear to you, I didn't, I didn't even know. Oh God. My wife . . ." He was crying now. Slumping in his chair.

Detective Rhodes returned from the back of the house. He looked at Murph and shook his head.

Later, Mickey Crawford was dressed in jeans and a sweatshirt and a ball cap. He sat in the front seat of the Impala with Rhodes. Talking with Rhodes, who he had decided was less threatening than the other cop.

Murph stood at a distance from the car, holding his cell phone. He said, "Yeah, we've set up a polygraph downtown. He's agreed to do it. He's agreed to give us fingerprints too. He's cooperating."

Hastings said, "What do you think?"

"Well," Murph said, "I guess it's possible, but I don't think it's him. We'll know more later."

Hastings said, "How could he leave the motel and not see her?"

"He says he didn't see her. Says his car was parked right in front of his room. Said he didn't see her car. Where was it, by the way?"

"It was on the other side of the parking lot," Hastings said. "It's possible he didn't see her."

"DNA tests will show if he was with her that night."

"Right. But even if he didn't have sex with her that night, it doesn't necessarily clear him. He says he never even saw her that night?"

"That's what he says. The physical evidence will confirm that. And he is cooperating with us on that score."

Hastings said, "Maybe he thinks he can outsmart us. Outsmart the tests."

"Ah, he doesn't strike me as that type, George. Again, we'll see what the tests show, the polygraph and things. He doesn't strike me as a turd. Or a lying psychopath."

"What, then?"

"I think he's a guy who's probably all right. Marriage is a little dull, his wife won't fuck him, and he got lonely for a woman. He pretended that this girl cared about him. He didn't ask much from her."

"Can he account for his whereabouts the night before?"

"Friday night?"

"Yeah."

"Oh, you mean the other girl. Yeah, I asked him about that. He said he was home with his wife, and they had another couple over for dinner."

"And you're going to check that out?"

"Yeah. We got their names and number."

"Okay, Murph. Well, keep me posted. Oh, listen, Wulf is worried about this shit getting in the press. Serial-killer scare and all that. So be careful about reporters, will you?"

"I will, George. But," Murph said, "it's probably what we're dealing with, isn't it?"

"Yeah, probably. I'll see you."

SIXTEEN

Hastings clicked off the cell phone and walked over to the county detective. *Escobar*, Hastings thought. He had heard someone call the man "Eff." Right. Short for Efrain.

Efrain Escobar leaned up against a Ford Crown Victoria, sipping a cup of coffee. Watching all the technicians at work, the brass gathering around and asking questions.

Hastings said, "Have you guys sent someone to question her pimp yet?"

"No, I don't think so."

"Why don't we do it?"

"Now?"

"Yeah. You know where to find him, don't you?"

"I think so."

Hastings shrugged. "It's your county. I'd just be riding along."

"Right," Escobar said, smiling.

•

They went in Escobar's Ford. A white slickback, no lights on top, but all the police-car goodies inside. This included a keyboard computer extending from the dashboard, standard on most county-police vehicles. Escobar would pull things up on the screen and make calls from his cell phone, and still drive all the while. Hastings sat in the passenger seat. Within a few minutes of communicating with the screen and dispatch on the radio, Detective Escobar decided that Roland Gent was likely to be at a certain address in North County.

Hastings said, "You think we'll need backup?"

"You don't know Roland, do you?"

"No."

"He's a shitbird. I remember when I used to do code enforcement, we ran into him then. That was a couple of years ago."

"Code enforcement?"

"Yeah. Metro do that?"

"What do you mean?"

"You know, to shut down crackhouses. You go into a crackhouse, it's hard to prove a criminal case of intent to distribute. Nobody knows anything. Lot of these guys, they're living in grandma's house. She comes from a different generation. A better one. Now, grandpa's dead and buried, and grandma has all these grandkids and great-grandkids, teenagers without jobs or education, and they're all living in the house. Not just them, but their friends." Escobar shrugged. It was a common dilemma. He said, "Violent, fucked up, trouble. Grandma, there's not much she can do about it. She can't control them. The neighbors, they want these places shut down. So, code enforcement teams up with county police and we'd go in and say, *Ma'am, you've got about a dozen beds or mattresses in your basement. That's too many people. A violation of county ordinance.* We threaten to shut down the house."

"Condemn it," Hastings said.

"Yeah, but it never goes that far. Once grandma gets notice of the violation, she moves the turds out. In fact, she's *relieved* we're doing it."

"Right," Hastings said.

"'Cause now she can blame the police for pushing them out. She can tell 'em, *Look, it's not my fault. It's the police.* And then they move out and she's relieved and the neighbors are relieved. It's a very effective program."

"And the guys go set up a crackhouse somewhere else."

Escobar shrugged again. "Yeah. Probably. But not in that neighborhood. You ever work narcotics?"

"No."

"It's a people-moving business. You're not going to end the war on drugs, you just need to *move* it. And people want it moved, George. They want it away from them. And it's not just the white communities that feel that way."

"Yeah, I know."

"Anyway," Escobar said, "I remember we went to one house, and we were just talking to the owner and there's really not any conflict about it. She lets us in to examine the home and everything's going fine, and then we come out and there were about a dozen people on the front lawn. Oh, shit. What the fuck is this about? And there's Roland Gent at the front of the pack. He's in front of his boys now, and he wants to show off. Jack off. He was pointing to us, saying, 'What's your name? What's your badge number?' That sort of shit. And we told him he needed to step away."

"Did he?"

"Oh yeah. He was just a big mouth."

"Anything bad happen?"

"No. We faced him and the rest of them backed off."

"Did you call for backup?"

"No," Escobar said. "We probably should have, though."

•

Escobar called for a backup this time, and it got there at about the same time they did. Two uniformed county deputies in a radio car. Escobar introduced them to the homicide detective from St. Louis metro. They agreed that the uniformed patrol officers would do a perimeter search of the front and back of the premises but remain outside for the time being.

The house was a one-story ranch style with a two-car garage. One of the patrol officers came from the backyard and gave the detectives a signal, and Escobar knocked on the front door.

A girl of an uncertain age opened it. Maybe fourteen, but no more than seventeen.

"Yeah?"

Escobar said, "County police, miss. We're here to see Roland."

"He ain't here."

"No?" Escobar said. He stepped forward. "Can I see?" He made it sound like a question.

The girl stepped back and opened the door. And then they were in.

A black man of about thirty was sitting on a couch in the next room. He was in the glare of a big-screen television. There was another girl sitting next to him. When she saw the policemen, she got off the couch and moved to the kitchen.

Roland Gent sighed. "Man," he said. "Ain't you got no respect for privacy?"

"Sorry, Roland," Escobar said. "We've got some bad news for you."

He gave them his penitentiary stare. "What?"

"One of your girls was killed last night."

"Who?"

"Adele Sayers."

After a moment, he said, "Estelle?"

"Yeah."

"You shitting me?"

"No. She's dead, Roland." Escobar's expression hardened then. "Why don't you stand up."

Roland Gent did so. And Hastings thought it was funny, the policeman's reaction. Escobar didn't think much of Roland Gent, but he wanted the man to show respect for a lady.

Roland said, "What happened?"

"Don't you know?"

"Man, I didn't—you know I didn't."

"You didn't what?"

"I didn't kill her. I don't—I didn't . . . What happened? Where is she?"

Escobar said, "Where were you last night? Where have you been?"

"I was out. I mean *out*."

"Where?"

"At a club. North Side. Man, you serious?"

"Yeah."

"Hey, I haven't even seen Estelle in, like, two months. I swear."

"Yeah?"

"She wanted to go her own way. And that was fine with me."

"Fine with you? You let your ladies quit on you?"

"Man, they want to go, they go."

Escobar said, "We think she was killed by someone she knew."

"That may be so. But it ain't me. I hear she joined some Internet service. I mean, she's working on her own, for all I know."

"What is it?"

"Huh?"

"The Internet service," Escobar said. "What's the name?"

"I don't know."

Escobar sighed. "Roland, I think you're lying."

Roland Gent frowned, shifted his body, and said, "You arresting me, or what? I'm thinking you're not. Not because I didn't do nothing, which I didn't, but because you know you don't have enough to hang it on me."

Escobar said, "What if I told you we found your prints inside her car?"

Roland Gent smiled. "I'd say you're blowing smoke up my ass. And now I know it." He seemed to feel better now, like a card-player who's just seen his opponent's tell. Roland said, "She drive a Camaro or TransAm, right? Right? I know because I remember when she got it. And I know I've never been in it. What's the game here, huh? Dead white girl and you want to hang it on a black man, right? Put it on the television so people feel better? Times change, huh. Can't beat a nigger into confessing a crime he didn't commit, so you try to con him instead."

"Oh, shit," Escobar said. Like, *Here we go.*

And Roland Gent said, "You know Mr. Jeffrey Coyle, don't you? My lawyer? Because I'm nice, I'll tell you what I'll do: I'll call him and see if he thinks it's a good idea for us to sit down and talk to you. He says it is, I'll do it. At his office. Not yours. Until then, Detective, I got nothing left to say to you."

•

They left while Roland was dialing his lawyer's number. He had had something of a victory over them and they knew it. To hang around and negotiate a meeting time with Jeffrey Coyle on Roland's telephone would have cost them too much face, and they knew that, too.

In the car, Escobar said, "Do you know Jeff Coyle?"

"I know who he is, but I never had a case against him."

"I have. He cross-examined me on a drug case. He cut me up

pretty good. Thing about him is, he's a pretty nice guy. Doesn't get mean when he questions you, but when he's finished, he's made you look like an idiot. Those are the worst ones."

"Will he agree to meet with us?"

"He might. I've done it before with him," Escobar said. "He'll agree to an interview if he's got a guy who he thinks is clean."

"Maybe," Hastings said. "And maybe he just wants to point you down a different path. A wrong one."

"Yeah, maybe. But Coyle's not stupid. He knows that can get you arrested by itself. You know, like Martha Stewart. Remember that case last year, with the school principal jacking off in the hall?"

"Oh, yeah. Mayer?"

"Yeah. Robert Mayer. A high-school principal."

"He wasn't Coyle's client, though."

"He was, actually. But not at first. Here's what happened. The principal gets caught, and the school board, superintendent—they wanted to keep a lid on it, keep it out of the papers. I mean, they had him. They had three students, two or three school-staff people, six witnesses at least, and they were solid. All that, but they wanted to downplay it. So the DA and the school district went to Principal Mayer and said, *Hey, just resign and disappear and don't ever work in a school again, and we won't file charges against you."*

"They agree to that?"

"We *thought* they did. But at that time Mayer was represented by an attorney named Garland Young, and he fucked it all up. Mayer resigns, and *after* that, Garland Young calls a press conference, invites all the local media, and they blast the district attorney, the school board, *and* the witnesses. They said it was a conspiracy, a frame-up, all sorts of nonsense. After that, the DA had no choice but to file charges. After that, someone must have gotten to Mayer and told him his lawyer was just hurting him. Or maybe someone who was paying the lawyer—someone other than Mayer—threatened to cut off the money. So Mayer fired Garland Young and hired Jeff Coyle."

"Coyle didn't walk him, did he?"

"No, he couldn't get him acquitted. Too much damage done by then. But I think the guy only got about six months, which was about three years less than the DA wanted hung on him. Coyle's smart. He knows when to use publicity, when not to."

"Does that mean he'll cooperate with us?"

"He won't try to help us," Escobar said. "But he'll cooperate with us if he thinks it'll help his client. There's a difference."

"Right."

They arrived back at the Thunderbird, and before Hastings could open the door, Escobar turned to him and said, "You think I fucked up back there, suggesting to Roland we had his prints in the car?"

"No. It was a bluff, and it didn't work. Shows he's not guilty. Or maybe it shows he's overconfident and he's lying. We'll know more later."

SEVENTEEN

By six o'clock that evening, Mickey Crawford had been cleared. There was no evidence that he had had any physical contact with Adele Sayers the night she was murdered. He had voluntarily submitted blood samples and had passed a series of polygraph examinations. The only stress he had shown was over the chance that his wife might learn that he had been with another woman.

As for his whereabouts on the previous Friday night, his alibi witnesses had confirmed that he had been at work until five thirty and then had had dinner and watched television with another married couple. Both men remembered what high school football game they had seen. This they had done independently.

Murph relayed this information to Hastings, and Hastings passed it on to the chief of detectives, Ronnie Wulf.

Wulf, as expected, was disappointed.

He said to Hastings, "Well, we've cleared *two* people now. And we've got no suspects."

"No, sir," Hastings said.

They were in Wulf's office at the downtown headquarters. It was dark outside and there was little traffic on Market Avenue. Wulf was seated behind his desk. Hastings was standing.

He said, "Murph should have his report completed tomorrow."

Wulf sighed. "In homicide, eight out of ten times, it's someone the victim knows. Agreed?"

"Yeah."

"Hell, George, you can sit down. This isn't the military."

Hastings took a seat.

Wulf said, "The question is, did this guy know them?"

"I don't know. I think he did."

"Why?"

"They're call girls. He seems to have picked them out. He seemed to have known where they were and followed them."

"What do you think of the pimp?"

"Roland Gent? I don't think he's the guy."

"Why not? Intuition?"

"Not so much intuition. Adele Sayers worked for him, but the first girl didn't. There was nothing in the press about the first murder—there hasn't been time for that yet—so he wouldn't have copied it. But we're not ruling him out. County's working up a meeting with him and his attorney."

"He lawyered up on you?"

"Yeah."

"Say you don't get anything else out of him, do we have enough for an arrest?"

"No. The techs don't have any physical evidence that he was in Adele Sayers's car. Or with her, for that matter."

"Okay," Wulf said. "Well, I've been in touch with the chief.

He wants to meet with us tomorrow morning at eight thirty. I don't know the details, but I suspect he's going to want to put together a task force along with county on this. It'll mean putting more detectives from metro on it, hopefully another half dozen or so, along with whatever county comes up with."

Hastings wanted to know who would be in charge of it, but he decided to keep quiet for the moment. He sensed—and feared—that he would be losing control of the investigation.

EIGHTEEN

Ted answered the doorbell. He was wearing a sweatshirt and a pair of jeans. He had put on weight since marrying Hastings's ex-wife. He gave Hastings a nervous hello and invited him into the house.

Ted Samster was the man Eileen had left Hastings for. A lawyer whom she was working for before becoming his lover. Hastings had suspected the affair for a while and eventually caught Eileen in a lie that he didn't have the strength to overlook. She had told him that she was in love with Ted and was planning to end the marriage because of it.

That had been a couple of years ago. Eileen was now Ted's wife, and Hastings had never confronted Ted about it. Never threatened him or punched him for making him a cuckold. Indeed, Hastings had never even really wanted to harm the man. Hastings believed that Eileen had wanted out of the marriage with him, regardless of whether or not there was a Ted Samster willing to marry her. If it hadn't been Ted, it would have been someone else.

Hastings believed that he was past being angry at Eileen. She had told him that he would be better off without her, and in time he'd come to believe that she was right. And after that, he did believe it too. So, he was past being angry at her for leaving him. But he could still get mighty irritated with her over things that related to their daughter.

Amy Hastings was not George's daughter by birth. Eileen had had her out of wedlock about five years before she met him. Hastings fell in love with Eileen and soon found that he wanted to be not only her husband but the father of her child. The formal adoption was made approximately one month after they married. In spite of all the difficulty in their marriage and the pain of the divorce, he considered himself fortunate to have gotten a daughter.

Hastings's father had been a fairly nasty piece of work. Not so much physically abusive or violent but a coward and a bully and an altogether small man. Perhaps because of this, Hastings had believed that he should avoid being a father himself. But Eileen and her daughter had made him change his mind. And, like most of life's most important decisions, it was made rather quickly.

Eileen had agreed to joint custody of Amy in the divorce. Whether she had done this out of kindness to him or consideration for Amy or for her own selfish motives was never really clear. Hastings decided that he didn't really want to know. What he did know was that Eileen had had the power to take Amy away from him altogether and had not exercised it. Whatever else could be said about her, she hadn't done that. It had made the adjustment easier.

Ted Samster was a big man, bigger than Hastings. But Ted was afraid of him and Hastings knew it. Hastings knew that he could say something to Ted to put him at ease. Something like, *Hey, forget it, man. Water under the bridge.* But some small part of him liked to see Ted uncomfortable. Even now.

Ted said over his shoulder, "Amy? Your dad's here to pick you up."

They heard her say that she was coming.

Ted said to Hastings, "You want some coffee or something?"

"No, thanks. How are you, Ted?"

"Oh, busy. Busy as usual. Eileen's at the store. She should be back in a half hour, if you want to see her."

"No, that's okay. Sorry about being late."

"No problem, man. No problem."

Amy came out to the foyer with her bag. She was thirteen now, a serious and mature girl at her age. She said goodbye to her stepfather and walked out to the Jaguar with Hastings.

In the car, Hastings said, "Sorry I was late."

"That's okay. Do we have time to stop for dinner at Regazzi's?"

"If you want," Hastings said. "I mean, if you're caught up on your homework."

"I'm caught up," she said. "I'd like some pasta."

"All right."

•

At the restaurant, Hastings ordered a small dish of fettuccine and a beer for himself, and Amy had ravioli and a Coke. He ate about half of his dish and waited for Amy to finish hers. His stomach had become sensitive over the years and he was no longer able to enjoy the things he had when he was younger. Acidic foods and drinks had been eliminated from his diet as he went from thirty to forty. No wine, apples, lemonade, bananas, tomatoes, pizza, cheeseburgers . . . it got to where he could enjoy such things only vicariously. His doctor had told him that he did not have an ulcer, just a weak digestive system. Another gift of middle age.

Still, he was grateful that he could still enjoy the occasional cigarette, a couple of fingers of whiskey. And he still liked to cook.

Hastings didn't finish his beer. He asked the waitress to bring him back a cup of coffee with cream.

Amy told him about her weekend, made a couple of mildly derisive comments about Ted. She talked about school and eventually asked him what he thought about her taking an SAT-preparation course.

Hastings said, "For college?"

"Yes," Amy said. "You took the test, didn't you?"

"Yeah, when I was about seventeen. You're thirteen."

"So. It'll help me get ready."

Hastings sighed. Not for the first time, he was struck by the competitiveness of the contemporary teenager. Worrying at age thirteen about getting into an Ivy League school. His childhood had not been a happy one, but he believed that people of his generation had had it a lot easier than Amy's. Parents of that time had been blessedly unenlightened and far less competitive and materialistic.

He said, "I'm not comfortable with that. I've told you before, you spend way too much time worrying about your future. You're a very smart girl, and you'll do fine."

"But my friends are doing it."

"Your friends are too uptight."

"They say their parents want them to."

"Their parents are too uptight, too. Look, you don't have your daddy's dumb genes. So you're going to be fine."

"I don't think you're dumb. I just don't want to get behind."

"Oh, for God's sake, Amy. You kids all worry so much. You get straight As and then you get upset because someone else got an A-plus. When I was your age, I didn't think I'd even go to college. I just wanted to get out of Nebraska. And I felt lucky to do that. Maybe one day you'll go to Harvard or Yale. Maybe not. But if you don't, who cares?"

"I care. And I'm not thinking about Harvard. But maybe Northwestern . . . Don't laugh at me."

"I'm sorry, sweetie; I'm not laughing at you. I'm not. But talking about exclusive colleges at thirteen . . ."

"Would you rather I talk about sex or drugs?"

"Oh shi— No. I just wish you wouldn't do this to yourself. You remember the Phillips kid? She had to go to the hospital after she got so thin?"

"I know."

"Now, I'm no psychologist, but I'm telling you that all this pressure to succeed can lead to that."

"Daddy, I'm not anorexic. I'm not mental either. I just don't want to end up like Mom."

"You're not going to end up like that," he said and immediately regretted it. He added, "And don't be so hard on your mother. She did the best she could."

"You don't believe that."

She was right about that. But he was not above maintaining a few hypocrisies to get through life. "I do." He paused, took a sip of his coffee. Then he said, "Did you discuss this with her?"

"No."

Good, he thought. If she had, Eileen probably would have signed her up for *two* courses. He said, "Amy, I'll think about it. Okay? If I'm persuaded that it's something that's actually helpful as opposed to something that's fashionable, I'll pay for the course. We'll talk about it next week. Deal?"

"Okay, deal."

"Good," he said. "You want to split a dessert?"

"Sure."

NINETEEN

There were about twenty police officers in the station briefing room. Some of them stood at the back of the room because there weren't enough chairs. At the front, behind the podium stood Chief Mark Grassino. Behind him were the St. Louis County sheriff, his deputy, Deputy Chief Fenton Murray, and Chief of Detectives Ronnie Wulf.

Hastings sat in the third row with Klosterman, Rhodes, and Murphy. Karen Brady sat behind them. Escobar sat with the county detectives on the other side of the room.

Chief Grassino confirmed that there was now a county/metro joint task force assigned to the Woods and Sayers murders. He said that the task force would be led by Ronnie Wulf coordinating with Detective Captain Paul Combrink of the county police. He gestured to each of them and they stood and nodded to the officers. The chief then gave the podium to Wulf.

Wulf summarized the status of the case. He pointed out Hastings and let the police officers know that he had been in charge of the case up till this point. The purpose was to signify that Hastings was his second. Hastings felt some gratitude for it, though time would tell if Wulf was merely tossing him a bone.

Wulf said, "George informed me this morning that Roland Gent's attorney has agreed to an interview at county headquarters.

The interview will be conducted by Detective Efrain Escobar of the St. Louis County Police as well as Lieutenant Hastings. This is a lead and it will be followed, but I don't want the people in this room to put a lot of stock in it. There are other leads that need to be followed. You are ordered to share any and all information and leads with each other. Any officer found to be hoarding leads or relevant information will be disciplined very harshly. Captain Combrink and I are in complete agreement on this. Our goal is to catch a monster who seems to have a taste for killing women. And I will tell you that I personally have very little patience for glory boys.

"One more thing: as most of you are already aware, we have let it be known that, at this point, we do not want media assistance. We do not yet have a profile of this killer, but we believe that he—presuming it's a he—is something of a glory seeker himself. It could be that he's seeking headlines. Fame. We do not want to encourage or reward that."

Klosterman raised his hand.

"Yes, Joe."

"Chief, I just want a clarification on the media thing. Are you suggesting that you may change your mind later on?"

Wulf said, "If it becomes apparent that there's more to be gained than lost by using the media, perhaps we'll change tactics. I'll let you know if I think we've reached that point. Again, profiling may be premature at this stage. I'm more interested in pursuing plain old leads. We're looking for evidence, not a certain personality type. Now, having said that, there are a few basic psychological things you should at least be aware of. These are of course traits that often appear in this sort of killer. One: a display of some sort of mental disorder. Two: evidence that they researched or targeted the victim. Three: evidence that they've communicated inappropriately with a person, a woman in particular. Four: they've identified with a stalker or an assassin. Often, an assassin will study the work of another assassin. One he wants to imitate and maybe improve upon. Lastly, these guys often have what's called an 'exaggerated idea of self.' They're grandiose, narcissistic."

A county detective said, "That could be said of half the people here." It got a few laughs, though not one from Ronnie Wulf.

"Again, let me emphasize, I do not want any of you putting the 'profiling' cart before the evidence horse. These are theories that can be helpful, but they do not capture killers by themselves. Any additional questions?"

Klosterman said, "Chief, police reports are public record. Now, when we file those reports on homicide investigations, there's no way to prevent reporters from reviewing them. Are we being ordered not to prepare reports?"

"No. Realistically, we've got about seven, maybe ten days before the press reviews the reports and puts it together. In other words, I am not ordering anyone here to violate policy on preparation of reports. What I am ordering all of you to do is to not personally discuss this with reporters. Casually or professionally. Our hope is that we apprehend the killer before the press puts the story together." Wulf said, "Any other questions?"

There weren't.

•

They told Roland Gent that he was not under arrest but read him his Miranda rights anyway. Told him he had the right to an attorney, the right to remain silent, that anything he said could be used against him.

After that formality, Escobar told him that he was being videotaped and audiotaped.

That was when Jeff Coyle first spoke. He said, "I pressumed that it would be. May we have a copy of the tape afterward?"

Coyle was well dressed, even for a lawyer. He had a mane of white hair and wore black-rimmed glasses. A tan Armani suit and a powder-blue shirt. He had presence, this Mr. Coyle. Hastings could see that Escobar was intimidated by him. This did not surprise Hastings. He had been in law enforcement long enough to know that police officers were often intimidated by authority figures. Even if they were mere extensions of the court. Also, police officers were better than most people at distinguishing good lawyers from hacks and acting accordingly. Coyle was no hack.

Escobar said, "Mr. Coyle, that's not up to me. The policy says we don't release it until criminal charges have been filed. If that happens, you are entitled to copies by law."

"Of course," Coyle said. "But there's no reason we can't operate in good faith in the meantime."

"I think we have been."

Coyle could say one or two words to Roland Gent right now and both of them could get up and leave, and there would be nothing the detectives could do about it. Coyle knew it and he knew that they knew it. But if they let the lawyer push them around at the start, it would never get any better. Escobar kept as silent as a poker player, and Hastings admired him for it.

Finally, Coyle made a conciliatory gesture. As if to say, *Proceed.*

Escobar stated for the record the date and the time and who was present. He stated for the record that Roland Gent and his attorney, Jeffrey Coyle, had voluntarily agreed to appear for questioning in the matter of the investigation of Adele Sayers. Escobar did not use the words *murder* or *death* or *strangulation.*

Then Escobar looked at the subject and said, "Tell us where you where Saturday night."

Roland Gent said, "I was at this club north of the Fox on Grand. It's called Torchy's City Plaza. You know it."

"When did you get there?"

"Got there around ten, ten thirty."

"Where were you before that?"

"Home. I remember 'cause I was watching the Sixers on the television."

"Who'd they play?"

"Dallas."

"Anyone with you?"

"At home?"

"Yeah."

"Linsy was with me. And Doreatha."

"They work for you?"

Coyle frowned and made some sort of grunt.

Roland said, "They're friends of mine."

Now Escobar frowned. "Counselor, I would appreciate it if you wouldn't give signals to the witness."

"We're here voluntarily, Detective. Cooperating on a murder investigation. If you intend to go outside the parameters of that investigation to attempt to obtain evidence of trafficking in prostitution, our cooperation ends."

Hastings said, "That's not our game. There's no tricks here."

"Then why ask if the witnesses work for him?"

"It's just background, I'm sure," Hastings said, giving Escobar a look himself.

"Right," Escobar said. "Background."

After a moment, Coyle waved his hand and Escobar continued.

Escobar said, "Would Linsy and Doreatha be willing to give sworn statements to that effect?"

"Sure."

"And you would be willing to bring them here to be questioned?"

"Yeah. Why not? I'm not worried, Detective. You can bring 'em here, put 'em in separate rooms, they may remember different things about what color shirt I was wearing, but they both know I was with 'em that night."

"All that night?"

"Well, till about midnight."

"And then what? Till you auctioned them off at Torchy's?"

"Shit—look, we may have parted ways at Torchy's, but I was there until it closed."

"And when was that?"

"About two. You can check with the crew there, if you want to take the time to do it. Ask for Chris Richards. He was there."

"Does he own the club?"

"Yeah."

"We will, you know. We will check all these things."

"I know you will."

"What about Friday?"

"Where was I Friday?"

"Yeah."

"I was at a party."

"Where?"

Roland looked at his attorney. Coyle nodded to him to go ahead. Roland Gent said, "Soulard. It was a party for a well-known auto dealer in the county."

"A name, Roland."

"Man . . ."

Hastings said, "Was this auto dealer a client?"

"Business contact."

"You need to tell us the name, then."

"Okay, I'll tell you the name. It was Ken Denton. Of Ken Denton Ford. And yes, I was there to provide a service."

Hastings said, "No disrespect, Roland. But I would think they'd want you to bring some girls by and leave. Not have you hang around."

"You right about that."

"So when did you leave?"

"I left about nine. I went to a club, had a few drinks, and went home."

"Torchy's?"

"No. Ralph Cutler's in West County. I like the music."

"You got people to back that up?"

"Yeah."

Hastings said, "You say that Adele Sayers and you parted company?"

"Yeah. A few months ago."

"How come?"

"I told you before."

"Tell me again."

"She wanted to move on. Thought she could do better on her own."

"You ever bring her to these parties at Ken Denton Ford?"

"I might have."

"Don't get squirrelly with me, Roland. You did or you didn't."

"Okay. I did."

"Anyone there ever get rough with her?"

"Not to my knowledge."

"She ever complain to you about people following her? A client becoming overly attached?"

"No, she did not."

"What if she had?"

"They don't want to work with a man, I don't make 'em do it."

"You sure about that?"

"Look, I ain't no street pimp. I'm a businessman. A lady want to walk out on me, she can do it. I'll replace her within a week."

"Okay," Hastings said. "But isn't that a sign of disrespect? Lady quitting on you? Leaving you?"

"No."

"What if a lady leaves you, goes back to your client base, and sets up a deal herself. Cuts you out of your forty percent. How would you feel about that?"

"I wouldn't like it," Roland said. "But Adele didn't do that. She had, I'd've known about it."

"Roland," Coyle said. He wasn't liking this.

But Roland Gent was going to continue, whether or not his lawyer liked it. He said, "Detective, the pleasure business is pretty simple. You provide a service to people who want to pay for it. Keep the girls clean, off the hard drugs, and you don't beat on 'em. Street pimp, he don't care. He thinks as far as next week, if that. But not every black man's a nigger, see? I know it's hard for you tell the difference."

"Well, I appreciate the cultural enlightenment, Mr. Gent," Hastings said. "But if you're seeking some sort of approval from me for selling women, you're wasting your time. Black, white, street, or high-rise, to me you are all the fucking same. Now I'm offering you the same deal I'm offering the white bread high-class madams downtown: cooperate with us, help us find this strangler, and you get to continue your sleazy trade. Don't cooperate, and we will shut you down."

"Hey, I'm here, ain't I?"

"Yeah, you're here. And if your alibis check out, you'll be cleared as a murder suspect. But that doesn't mean we're through with you. Not by a damn sight."

"Hey," the lawyer said.

Hastings said quickly, "We need a list."

"A list?" Roland Gent said.

"Yes. A list of customers you know Adele was associated with. We want that list today." Hastings got to his feet. "Today, Roland. Or tomorrow morning we shut you down."

Hastings walked out, leaving Escobar alone with the pimp and his lawyer.

Escobar came out a few minutes later. He said, "Hey, was that a performance?"

"Yeah, sort of."

"Well, it was a pretty good one. Coyle says he'll have a list of names for us this afternoon."

TWENTY

When it was completed, copies of the list were provided to Captain Combrink and Chief of Detectives Wulf. The names of the clients were divvied up among the detectives assigned to the task force.

Wulf congratulated Hastings on getting the list so quickly. Hastings summarized the discussion with Roland Gent and his attorney, leaving in the parts that he thought were good and bad.

Wulf, being in a supervisory position, worried about a minor detail. He said, "You didn't use the *N* word, did you?"

"No," Hastings said, "Gent did. He was just trying to bait me, maybe put me on the defensive. It didn't work. Besides, it's all on tape if he decides to make a complaint."

"Right," Wulf said. "Well, be careful, though."

"I was." Hastings felt that he knew himself pretty well and he did not believe he was a racist. Also, he felt that he'd been conducting himself professionally long enough not to be second-guessed on such things.

Wulf raised his hand. "Okay, George."

The tension passed and Hastings said, "Bobbie Cafaza, the madam, told Sergeant Klosterman and me that Reesa Woods was perhaps close friends with another escort named Rita Liu."

"Rita. Not Reesa?"

"Yes, two different girls. We were trying to find out if Reesa had a regular boyfriend."

"Bobbie Cafaza didn't tell you?"

•

"You ever see that movie *Pretty Woman*?"

Hastings said, "I don't think so."

They were in Hastings's Jaguar, driving north on Grand Boulevard. Klosterman was holding a bag of fries he'd picked up at the Wendy's drive-through.

"You remember it, don't you?" Klosterman said. "It made Julia Roberts famous. She might have been like twenty years old when she made it. You haven't seen it?"

"No, I don't remember it."

"It was a really big hit. Richard Gere plays this rich businessman who sees Julia Roberts on a street corner. She's a hooker. He pays her like five or six thousand dollars to be his girlfriend for a week or something. Yeah, I know, the plot's so ridiculous . . . anyway, she ends up helping him become a better man, a better businessman, apparently. See, she'll screw him, but she won't kiss him because, I guess, she's principled or something. Then at the end, they fall in love and get married."

"Yeah?" Hastings was only vaguely interested.

"George, you're missing the point."

"What's the point?"

"The point is, the movie glamorized prostitution. It was number one at the box office. Girls, good girls, loved it. Hell, my wife even liked it. And you know her."

"It was just a movie," Hastings said.

"Yeah, it was just a movie, another fantasy. But kids are impressionable, you know."

"I know."

"And you pick up a hooker on a street corner, she ain't gonna look like Julia Roberts, I'll tell you that."

"I know."

"More like Eric Roberts. And this nonsense about not kissing her clients, shit, you pay 'em enough money, they'll let you do anything."

"Okay, Joe."

"Pretty much horseshit, is what it was."

"Right."

Hastings had gotten used to this. Joe Klosterman was sometimes given to ranting against pop culture, Democrats, Hollywood, Al Franken, Jimmy Carter, and sometimes figures from the Kennedy administration that Hastings wasn't familiar with. Joe Klosterman liked to talk about the things that were on his mind and Hastings usually just let him do it. Klosterman thought that George Clooney hadn't made a good movie since *Out of Sight*. He thought that Quentin Tarantino was a fraud. He thought that *Dirty Harry* was a better movie than *Mystic River*, "artistically speaking." He thought that a draft would end what he thought was a stupid war in Iraq because then the chickenshit politicians' sons would be at risk of getting killed too. He thought that both the Republicans and the Democrats would fuck over the cops anytime it was politically expedient, except at election time, when they both would come hat in hand seeking endorsements from the police associations and unions. Joe Klosterman could not opine at length on these subjects at home because his wife would roll her eyes and tell him to be quiet and his kids would drift out of the room. So he did it at work. He was a good officer, a good detective, and a good man, so he was tolerated.

"Hey," Hastings said, "do you know where we're going?"

"We're going to interview Rita Liu."

"Yeah, but do you know where we're going?"

"Her apartment?"

"Yeah. She lives at Lindell Towers on Lindell Boulevard. But, Joe, get this. She's a student at Saint Louis University."

"Saint Louis U? No, that's just a cover."

"No," Hastings said. "I checked with the registrar. She's an enrolled student."

"So she's hooking to pay her way through school?"

"Yeah. Now there's a movie."

"So she really is a college girl."

"At a Catholic school, no less." Hastings shook his head in a mocking way.

"You're too cynical, George," Klosterman said and seemed to mean it.

Hastings showed his badge to the attendant in the lobby of the apartment building, and he buzzed them up to Rita Liu's apartment, which was on the eighth floor. They rapped on her door and heard a female voice ask who it was. They told her it was the police and soon the door cracked open, the chain still on the lock.

She was an almost plain-looking Asian American girl, her hair pulled back in a ponytail, and for a moment Hastings thought they had made a mistake. Wrong girl or wrong apartment. Whoever she was, she *looked* like a college student. Not at all like a high-dollar call girl.

The girl said, "Yes? What is it?"

"I'm Lieutenant George Hastings and this is Sergeant Joseph Klosterman. We're investigating the murder of Reesa Woods. We understand she was a friend of yours."

"Let me see your identification."

They showed her their badges.

She seemed satisfied that they were legitimate. But then she gave them a direct look and said, "I don't have to talk to you, do I?"

Hastings said, "Technically, you could plead the fifth. But I would hope you'd want to help your friend." He had to remind himself that this kid was almost certainly Rita Liu, no matter what she looked like.

"Help her? She's dead."

"Yeah, she is," Hastings said. "But we haven't found her killer."

Rita Liu closed the door. Hastings glanced at Klosterman, and then they heard her open the chain.

Once in, Hastings was surprised to see that it was a one-room efficiency apartment. Very small, very tidy. There was a day bed. A small chair. A bookshelf with college textbooks on it. Biology, zoology, physics . . . It was strange.

Hastings said, "You are Rita Liu, are you not?"

"I am." She looked at the detective and seemed to guess what he was thinking. "I'm not in costume right now."

No, she wasn't. She was wearing blue jeans and a baggy black pullover sweater. You could see that she had a good figure beneath that. But she wore no makeup and her hair was not styled. Her face was freckled, though this did not make her unattractive, just less exotic. Hastings guessed that she was about twenty-one. About eight years older than his daughter.

Rita Liu said, "Would you like something to drink?"

Klosterman said, "You mean, like, tea?"

The girl frowned. "No," she said, "I haven't got any tea. I've got Coke or Diet Coke."

Hastings mentally rolled his eyes. Christ, they hadn't even started the interview and Klosterman was acting like she was some sort of geisha.

"No, thank you," Hastings said, answering for both of them.

That awkwardness passed. And both of them noticed the unusual self-possession of this college girl. Though she wasn't just a college girl. She was a young woman.

She gestured to the couch and then took a seat in the small armchair, curling her legs up under her. She waited patiently while they got out their pads and pens.

Hastings said, "How did you find out about Reesa?"

Rita said, "Bobbie called me."

"Did she warn you about us?"

"Yes. She said the police would probably want to talk to me."

"Did she warn you not to talk to us?"

"No. She said to cooperate. Why? Did you think she would discourage me from helping the police?"

Hastings shrugged. "I don't know. I just thought I'd check."

"You have a distrustful nature."

"Right," Hastings said. "How long did you know Reesa Woods?"

"For about a year. Ever since she started working for the Flower Shop."

"You worked there before her?"

"A couple of months before."

"How well did you know her?"

"It's hard to say. Fairly well, I think. We worked a few trade shows together. She was nice. Trying to save some money, trying to get ahead, like most of us."

"Was she?"

"Was she what?"

"Was she saving money?"

"I don't know. I never asked her."

"Did she ever ask you for money?"

"No." Rita Liu hesitated. "No, she never asked me for money. But she did stay with me for a couple of weeks."

"Here?"

"Yes. It's small, I know. But she had a falling out with her roommates, and . . . she needed a place to stay."

"Roommates. Who were they?"

"It was a guy and a girl. I think they were students at UMSL."

"Know their names?"

"Larry and Jen. Short for Jennifer. I met them once."

Klosterman said, "What happened?"

"You mean, why did she move out?"

"Yeah."

"She never told me straight. But I think something happened with her and the guy. The guy was with the girl, but somehow got hooked onto Reesa."

Hastings said, "Did they have a sexual relationship?"

"I don't know. Reesa says they didn't. She said that they didn't do anything, but that he tried. Or that he was always staring at her. But . . ."

"But what?"

"But she may not have been honest about that."

"You mean, honest with you."

"Right."

"Would you say she was a deceitful person?"

"Well," Rita said, "we're all deceitful at times, aren't we? She probably had something going with him, Jen found out, and . . . that was it."

"Do you know if they knew what she did for a living?"

"I don't fully know. But I think they didn't. I met them once, like I told you. And Reesa told me, you know, to keep quiet about what we do. And when I met them, they just seemed sort of clueless."

"About her?"

"Yes."

"You mean, they seemed like kids?"

"Yeah."

Hastings said, "Unlike you."

She caught his meaning then and took a moment before responding. Sitting in that chair with her legs tucked up, she looked a little older and wiser now. She said, "You could say that."

Hastings said, "You're a student."

"Yes."

"At the undergraduate school."

"Yes. Are you interrogating me now?"

Hastings had his eyes down on his notepad. He raised his hand in a sort of apology. "Just background, miss. There's nothing personal about it."

"Hmmm," she said. Disapproving.

Hastings said, "Do you have friends at the school?"

"Not close friends. They're boys, mostly. And boys don't interest me."

Hastings mentally sighed. She was trying to prove something to him now. He said, "Right. But the other students, they don't know about this other life you have, do they?"

"No." She seemed proud of it. A performer, playing two distinct roles persuasively.

"Okay, let me ask you something: was Reesa Woods as good at hiding it as you are?"

"No," she said, with no hesitation.

"And apart from this Larry and Jen, you don't think there was a boyfriend in her life?"

"No, I don't."

"How about a girlfriend?"

"No. No girlfriend."

"And you don't know the last name of these roommates?"

"No," she said. "The guy, I think, works as a barback at McGill's."

"The one downtown?"

"Yes. They closed the one in West County last year. The girl may work there too, but I'm not sure."

"Apart from that," Hastings said, "any customer you're aware of that you would have concerns about?"

"Of hers?"

"Yes."

"Well, I didn't know them all. In the business, you learn not to invade another girl's turf. You know what I mean?"

"Sure," Klosterman said.

Rita Liu said, "She never complained to me about anyone. I mean, she never said that any of them scared her. They can creep you out, but making you scared is something different."

Maybe, Hastings thought. And maybe not. It was one of the problems with being a prostitute. They had to delude themselves in some way. One way to do it was to tell themselves they were able to perceive character traits that non-pros could not, but that was rarely the case. Hastings said, "Did she say anything about men who gave her the creeps?"

"Not specifically. I mean, you know, she bitched about the fat guys, the ones with bad hygiene. The usual stuff."

"What about ones getting too rough?"

"She never told me."

"What about ones getting too possessive?"

"Again, she never told me. Listen, you know how it is: most of the customers were pretty passive, suburban types. They're married, they got mortgages and white-collar careers, kids in college and so on. It's mundane, most of it. Some of them are fun. A few of them are even interesting. But mostly, it's just . . . nothing."

"Okay," Hastings said, hiding his distaste for her talk. Perhaps it would have been easier to hear it if she hadn't looked so young and normal. Easier if she'd looked like the typical truck-stop hooker, hopeless and run-down, a mere part of humanity's depressing landscape. But Rita Liu didn't look like that. It was unfair and superficial and he knew it, but it was what he thought. He said, "Ms. Liu, there's something we haven't told you."

"What?"

"There's been a second murder. Another prostitute. She was also strangled. We believe she was murdered by the same killer."

"Oh, God. Where?"

"On West Manchester Road. The Thunderbird Motel. Do you know it?"

"No, I've never been there."

"The woman's name was Adele Sayers. Do you know her?"

"No."

"She used to work for a guy named Roland Gent. Do you know him?"

"No."

The detectives could see the effect this was having on her. She was not as relaxed as she had been, though she was still trying to hide her fear.

Hastings said, "We believe this man is going to kill again. In each case, there was no robbery. Not even a rape. The fear we have is, he's developed a taste for killing women. He's chosen prostitutes for some reason. Perhaps because he believes they deserve it. Perhaps. But we don't really know." He paused, then said, "Are you afraid?"

"...No."

"Are you sure?"

"I don't know."

"Have you considered the possibility that this man has seen you?"

"Yes . . . I— Why are you saying that to me?"

"Well, I thought you should—"

"Do you want to frighten me? Or punish me?"

"Punish you?" Hastings said. "For what?"

"You know."

Hastings shook his head. "No, I don't want to punish you. I think you misunderstand me. Frighten you, yes, maybe I do. The killer, so far, has picked out his victims. We think he knew who they were. Two white, fairly high-dollar call girls. Maybe he thinks like a hunter. And the better-looking girls are, in his mind, bigger game."

"I'm not white," she said, her fear making her sound bitter. "So long as he doesn't have an Asian fetish, I'm safe."

"Yes. Maybe. Tell me something: would you feel relieved if the next victim is someone else?"

Her face contorted. "What the fuck sort of thing is that to say?"

"Okay," Hastings said, "maybe that was off base. But as of now, I'm a little short on leads. And I get the feeling you're not telling me everything you know."

"You think I'm protecting a murderer? What do you think I am? Maybe you're the one who hates women."

"No. And you don't believe that, anyway. What I want from you is cooperation. Full cooperation. Parties, places, people that you and Reesa have seen in the past few weeks. Maybe even the past few months."

"How will that help you? A lot of these men are married. You want me to ruin them?"

Klosterman said, "Ms. Liu, is it their livelihood you're concerned about, or is it your own?"

Rita Liu looked from one detective to the other. "Shit, I knew it. You've got me pegged, both of you. The nasty little whore. Look around you. What do you see? This apartment, my furniture... do you see anything lavish? Anything expensive? The people at school, they think I'm twenty-one years old. But I'm twenty-seven and it's fading fast. I've been doing things for the last few years—gross, vile things I have to work to forget about. I'm saving money, I'm educating myself because I'm trying to get out. I don't enjoy any of this. A girl I knew, not really a friend, more of a coworker, she dies, and you come here and put it on me. Why? What have I done to deserve this?"

"Ms. Liu," Hastings said. "There's no need to get upset."

"You accused me of hiding things from you. I don't know what you want from me. You want me to pretend that we were close friends? That we were sisters? We weren't."

"Ms. Liu, Ms. Liu, it makes no difference to me if you were close friends. We just want to find this man, that's all. We want this to stop. Okay?"

Rita Liu gathered herself long enough to say, "You want names and places."

"Yes."

"I'll tell you what I know, then I want you to leave me alone."

"I'll try to," Hastings said.

TWENTY-ONE

She wrote out a sort of journal for them, giving them the names of various functions they had attended over the past two months. Trade shows, parties, and the like. She escorted them to the door and did not say goodbye when they left.

In the elevator, Klosterman said, "She's scared."

"Yeah," Hastings said. "I wanted to tell her she doesn't have anything to worry about. But I really don't know that. She hasn't been threatened. Not directly, anyway. And what do I say to her? Is she any more at risk than any other hooker in the city?"

"She might be," Klosterman said, "if the killer knows her too."

Hastings said, "That thing with her getting upset, telling us she's trying to put this life behind her—was that an act?"

"If it was, it was a good one. You work crime, you meet all sorts of delusional people. The junkie who says he's going to quit using, the hooker who believes one day she's gonna be in the movies. I knew one, back when I was in uniform, she thought she should be hosting her own television show. And I don't mean a show about hookers or ex-hookers. I mean she thought she should be like Tyra Banks. She didn't just say it, she *believed* it."

Hastings said, "One of the problems with this job, people lie so fucking much you're always afraid you'll be played." Klosterman was one of the few people to whom Hastings would confess this fear. Perhaps the only cop. "Rita Liu could have been play-ing us back there. Maybe she rolled her eyes at us for being saps as soon as we left. The funny thing is, I hope she's telling the truth."

"That's not like you."

"I'm not as cynical as you think. Not all the time, anyway."

"So . . . you're falling in love with a prostitute."

"Right. Well, she's a little young for me. And the prostitution thing may get in the way of having a healthy relationship."

"Some of them straighten out, though. You'd be surprised how many of them get religion."

"About the time they're getting too old?"

"No, not always," Klosterman said. He was sensitive to Hast-ings's occasional raps against organized religion. He said, "Did Rita Liu look old to you?"

"In a way."

•

Hastings parked the Jaguar on a hill at Laclede's Landing. The Eads Bridge loomed overhead. They walked to McGill's Bar and Grill and told the manager that they needed to speak with Larry, the barback.

The manager said, "He doesn't get here until six. What's this about?"

Klosterman said, "We just need to speak to him, that's all." They didn't think the manager needed to know what it was about.

"Well, I like to know if my people are in some sort of trouble."

The manager tried and succeeded in maintaining eye contact. A man in charge. The detectives ignored this.

Klosterman said, "We need to know his home address and telephone number." The manager hesitated and Klosterman raised his voice and said, "Come *on*." And that was all it took, the manager giving Larry MacPherson's full name, address, and home and cell numbers. Hastings turned around then so that the manager wouldn't see him suppressing a laugh.

Minutes later, they were on Interstate 70 going north and then swinging west toward a large, drab apartment complex near the airport. During the drive, Klosterman called the station and gave Larry MacPherson's name to dispatch. Asked if there was any sort of criminal record on the man.

Dispatch came back and told him yes, there was. Three arrests for drug possession, the last one for intent to distribute. They said his driver's license had been suspended about a year before, but that he'd been pulled over for speeding two months ago. He'd been given a citation for the speeding and for driving under suspension. A month after that, he'd been a no-show at traffic court, so the court clerk had issued a bench warrant.

"Oh, really?" Klosterman said.

He turned to Hastings and said, "He's a wanted man."

Hastings said, "What for?"

"Failure to appear at traffic court."

"Hmmm. Well, let's hope he's home."

He was.

The apartment was on the second floor of a complex that could have been a second-rate motel in a previous life. Hastings and Klosterman walked up the stairs and got to the number they'd been given. They looked through the window and saw a young man with big shoulders and chest sitting in front of a television holding the latest PlayStation controller.

Klosterman said, "He's a big 'un."

Hastings drew breath. "Looks like he's on 'roids too." He'd seen 'roid rage in action. Steroids didn't make a man as strong or as unpredictable as PCP did, but it was in the same ball park.

Klosterman stayed by the window so he could see what Larry MacPherson would do. Hastings moved in front of the door.

"You ready?" Hastings said.

"Yeah. Go ahead."

Hastings made three hard raps on the door.

"Open up! Police!"

Klosterman told Hastings what he saw as the man turned and got up. If MacPherson had run to the back of the apartment, Klosterman would have drawn his weapon. More often than not, losers who jump bond keep guns in their bedrooms. Often more than one.

Hastings rapped the door again.

"Police officers. I said open up."

Hastings could hear Larry MacPherson coming to the door, his movements bold and quick.

Klosterman said, "George," warning him as Larry MacPherson yanked the door open.

"What the fuck do you want?" he said.

Larry MacPherson was bigger when he was on his feet. He just about filled the door frame. He did not appear to be holding any sort of weapon. But he was at least a head taller than Hastings.

Hastings said, "Calm down, chief. I'm just here to talk to you."

"You smashing on my door like you got a right to do it." MacPherson was putting his face close to Hastings's face now. Pushing him...

Hastings said, "There's a warrant out for your arrest."

"Yeah? Who's going to arrest me? You, you fucking pussy?"

Hastings felt his heart racing. He was scared and he knew it. MacPherson would know it too, in time. Hastings said, "I don't think I can."

"Why not?" MacPherson said.

"'Cause you're not wearing any shoes."

At that moment MacPherson looked down at his bare feet. His focus was still there when Hastings brought his shoe down hard on the top of Larry MacPherson's bare foot in a vicious stomp. Larry MacPherson bellowed and Hastings smashed the heel of his hand into his throat.

MacPherson stumbled back, off-balance now, and Hastings rushed him and knocked him down. He was on the floor, gathering himself to get back up and crush the smaller man, but now Hastings had his .38 snub-nose out, pointing it down on him.

MacPherson stayed on the floor, trying to catch his breath. Klosterman followed them into the apartment. Then he got behind Larry MacPherson and pushed his face into the floor, pulled his arms behind his back, and put the handcuffs on him.

"Such violence," Klosterman said, because it was past now.

"You fucking cops. You all fight dirty."

"Sorry," Hastings said. Though he wasn't.

Klosterman placed Larry MacPherson under arrest and began reading him his Miranda rights.

TWENTY-TWO

Ronnie Wulf said, "He's a big fellah."

"Yeah, we noticed that," Hastings said. "Look at his forehead. See the blemishes, the Frankenstein eyebrows. 'Roids."

Larry MacPherson was on the other side of the glass. Joe Klosterman was interviewing him. They had added a belly chain to him in case he got a mind to misbehave.

Wulf said, "You search the apartment?"

Hastings shrugged. "Plain view. We didn't have a warrant." He avoided Wulf's gaze and said, "Found a gun. That's a violation of his parole. Found a couple of bottles of cypionate and transdormal, which we think he got from Mexico. Probably selling it here. But no, we didn't find anything linking him to the strangulations."

"What about his record?"

"Drugs. Driving under suspension. No record of sexual assault."

"That doesn't clear him, though."

"No. That doesn't clear him."

They saw Klosterman stand up and walk out of the room. Then he stepped into the room with them.

"Well?" Hastings said.

Klosterman said, "Rita Liu never met this guy, did she?"

"She said she may have."

"Okay," Klosterman said. "Well, he's a shitbird, all right. He spent the first fifteen minutes talking about how much he hated you." Meaning Hastings. "Sorry son of a bitch, fucking cop, that sort of thing."

Hastings nodded. He'd gotten used to it.

Klosterman said, "Then he talked about the suspended driver's license business. He said it's his insurance company's fault because they were supposed to notify the DMV or some shit. He says he's not selling steroids. That those pills we found were prescribed by a doctor."

"What about Reesa Woods?" Hastings said.

"He says he hasn't seen her in months. He said he was working Friday and Saturday night."

"Did you tell him why you were asking his whereabouts?"

"No."

"Does he know she's dead?"

"Yeah, he knows." Klosterman frowned. "And I think he's on to us, too. I mean, the guy's a two-by-four, but he's not that fucking stupid. At one point, he asked why two plainclothes detectives are taking so much interest in a guy who didn't show up for traffic court."

Wulf said, "Get a formal search warrant. His apartment and his car too. Go to Judge Brand. He'll authorize it." Wulf did not ask Hastings how much he had searched before. Wulf knew what not to ask.

"Okay," Hastings said. "I'm going to call Murph and ask him to go back to McGill's, see if MacPherson was there Friday and Saturday."

"Good," Wulf said.

Hastings turned to Klosterman and said, "You want to stay with him?"

"Yeah," Klosterman said. "He's beginning to like me. I'm the nice one."

Good cop, bad cop. It was amazing how often it still worked. Even when the suspects were aware of it.

•

Hastings returned to Larry MacPherson's apartment with four police officers, three of them in uniform and a detective on loan from the North station. They rapped on the door, saying the standard, "Search warrant, search warrant," and they would have gone in on the third, but then a woman opened the door.

Hastings said, "Jennifer?"

A chubby girl with blond hair and bad skin. She said, "Yeah?"

"My name is Lieutenant Hastings. We have a warrant to search the premises."

"Larry's not here. Why don't you come back when he's here?" She seemed to know that it would involve Larry.

Hastings said, "He's been arrested."

"I'm not surprised," she said. "Listen, it's a bad time." She started to close the door.

But Hastings gently pushed it open. "I know," he said, "but it has to be done."

The uniformed officers followed him into the apartment and began their search. The girl didn't cry or shout. She just let her shoulders sag and stood in the middle of the room. She didn't know what she had done to deserve this. Police coming into her home without her permission. It was an injustice. An invasion.

Hastings remained close to her. Eventually, she gave him her attention. "You're not going to arrest me, are you?"

"Not planning to," Hastings said.

She looked around the apartment. Officers were opening drawers in her bedroom, looking through kitchen cabinets. Hasting could tell that she was wondering if they were going to take anything that belonged to her, if they would care if they broke any of her things.

Hastings said, "Do you want to sit down?"

"Yeah. But then they'll probably make me move," she said. "I mean, I don't want to get in your way or anything." Her tone was bitter.

"We can go sit in the car."

"Yeah? What, so you can question me?"

"As a matter of fact, I would like to talk to you. Maybe I can help you."

"Help me?" She eyed him, her expression tired and beaten. "What makes you think I need *your* help?"

Hastings moved closer to her. He didn't want the other officers to hear what he was saying. He got closer to the woman and said, "He abuses you, doesn't he?"

She didn't answer him. She looked away and Hastings detected a nod of her chin. He'd seen it before. Sometimes the victim can't help giving herself away. She's hiding it from her friends, her family, people at work. It's a lot of work, hiding abuse from people. Sometimes when a police officer just asks point-blank, it's a relief to confess it.

Hastings said, "Knocks you around some?"

"Not always."

"No, not always," Hastings said, recalling the enraged, bowed-up figure he'd punched in the throat. "Sometimes he's nice, right? Probably after he's been mean. Tells you he's sorry. That he needs you. That he loves you. That he won't ever do it again. Am I right?"

"It's none of your business. I can handle it."

"No, you can't. You can get used to it, but you're not ever going to handle it. Why don't you come outside with me? We can have some privacy."

She walked out to the balcony with him. She lit a cigarette.

Hastings said, "He's in police custody. He can't hurt you now."

She snorted. "Yeah? For what? Driving without a license, right? He'll be out in the morning. And you know who he's gonna call to bail him out, don't you?"

"Maybe," Hastings said. "Maybe he'll get thirty days in county."

He wanted to say that maybe he'd get a whole lot more. Say two consecutive life sentences for murder in the first degree. But he didn't know that. "How long have you been with him?"

She shrugged. "About two years."

"Did he always take steroids?"

"No. That started a few months ago."

"Did it change him?"

"... Yeah."

Hastings said, "It's nothing to be embarrassed about."

She snorted again, as if she felt patronized by him.

"It's not. You feel ashamed, but it happens to a lot of women. In a way, men too."

"Men too, huh? God, I wish that were true."

"What I mean is, people tell themselves it's not that bad. They just sort of condition themselves to it. They get used to it. What I'm saying is, you're not a bad person."

"Gee, thanks, Officer."

"What I'm saying is, you don't deserve this."

She shrugged again.

Hastings said, "You thought about leaving?"

"Sure. But where would I go? He'd just find me."

"He threaten to do that?"

"Not in so many words."

"He threaten to kill you?"

"No."

"Ever?"

"No."

"You sure about that?"

"Yes. I'm sure."

"There was another girl living with you," Hastings said. "Her name was Reesa. Do you remember her?"

Jennifer was looking at him now. "Yeah. What about her?"

Hastings thought then, She doesn't know. She doesn't know that Reesa Woods is dead. Though she could be conning him.

Hastings said, "What happened to her?"

"I don't know. She lived with us for a while. Then she moved out."

"How come?"

"I don't know. She moved on. Got her own place, I guess. Why?"

"How did you know her?"

"We worked together."

"Where?"

"At—at Lady Godiva's."

"A strip club?"

"A *dance* club. What's this about?"

"I'll get to that," Hastings said. "Were you both dancers?"

"That's none of your fucking business, but, yeah."

"You still there?"

"No. I quit. I'm working at Famous-Barr now. I sell clothes. Look," she said. "Are you trying to get off or something, asking me about when I was a dancer?"

"No."

"Why all these questions about Reesa?"

"Don't you know?"

"No, I don't."

"She died. Friday night."

"What? What happened?"

"She was killed. Murdered."

"Oh, God." She placed her hands on the railing of the balcony. She took a few breaths. Then she looked at him. "Larry? You think Larry did it?"

"I don't know yet," Hastings said. "What do you think?"

"I think you're fucked. Larry wouldn't murder anyone. And he had no interest in her."

"He wasn't attracted to her?"

"No." She was offended by the suggestion.

"He never made a play for her?"

"No."

"How do you know?"

"Because she would have told me."

"Yeah?"

"Okay," she said. "Maybe he liked her. Maybe he would have liked to fuck her. I don't know. But nothing happened between them. I *know* that."

"How do you know?"

"Because I would've known. We were living in the same apartment together. If they had done it, I would've known. You can tell. A woman can always tell."

"But he wanted to, didn't he?"

"I don't know."

"Yes, you do. You know."

"Okay, maybe he did. He's not perfect, you know."

Right, Hastings thought. He said, "But she wasn't interested, was she?"

"I don't know. I guess not."

"Did it make him angry?"

"Yeah, maybe. But he didn't—look, he didn't do what you think he did."

"I haven't said anything," Hastings said.

"I don't want to talk to you no more. I don't think I like you. You acted like you cared about me, cared about what he was doing to me. But all you care about is Reesa."

"Reesa's dead, Jennifer."

"I know that," she said. "Okay? I know that. What do you want?"

"Tell me where he was Friday night."

"He was at work. He works at McGill's."

"Saturday night."

"The same place. He's a barback."

"When did he leave for work Friday?"

"I don't know. I was at work until six thirty. He was gone when I got home. Saturday, I worked until eight. He was gone when I got home that night too."

"When did he come home?"

"Saturday?"

"Yeah."

"I don't know. I was asleep."

"Did he wake you?"

He meant, wake her up to use her. Or hurt her.

"No," she said. "He didn't wake me."

"What do you know about Reesa?"

"We worked together. She quit, I stayed."

"Did you know . . . ?"

"That she became a hooker? She never told me, but yeah, I figured it out. All of a sudden she had all this money. At first, I thought she'd fallen in with a coke dealer or something. Or maybe she was dealing herself. But I figured it out."

"Did you ever talk to her about it?"

"You mean, tell her to stop? No. I didn't care, really. It was her business."

"What did Larry think about it?"

"I don't think he knew. He's not the brightest guy."

"He's hit you before, hasn't he?"

"Yes."

"Has he ever put his hands around your neck?"

"I don't know. I don't think so."

"What do you mean, you don't know?"

"No. He never tried to choke me. He may have, you know, grabbed me by my throat once or twice. But—"

"When did he do that?"

"I don't know. Maybe a few weeks ago. Look, I told you, he wouldn't do this. I know him. He ain't like that. Seriously, do you think if I believed he killed those girls, I'd be telling you this? You think I'd want to protect him?"

Hastings had no doubt that she would, love could be a sickness, but he said, "I don't know."

"I mean, if I thought he had done that, I'd want him in jail for my own sake. Wouldn't I?"

"Maybe."

"*Maybe*? My God, do you think *I'm* some sort of monster too?"

TWENTY-THREE

It was a three-story gray-stone town-house on Pershing Place, off Euclid Avenue in the Central West End. Walking distance to the Chase Park Plaza and Forest Park. The real estate market had faltered in the past few months, but Marla still believed she would get the asking price, which was a million seven. Her latest showing was at seven thirty in the evening, a bond salesman and his wife, transplanted from New York to St. Louis so he could manage the sales department at Edward Jones. The husband was younger than Marla expected, maybe less than thirty-five. Rich, though. Very rich. The bonuses they paid on Wall Street alone could pay for this house. Marla was friendly to the man, but not too friendly. She could see that the wife was intimidated by her and she didn't want to alienate *her*. You don't sell the wife, you don't sell the house.

Marla was older than the wife. Forty-two, but she still had the model's figure and she knew it too. The bond dealer's wife was frumpy and getting heavy, and her hair was cut like a boy's. Marla liked to be looked at and she caught the husband ogling her at least twice, but she hoped the bond dealer wasn't getting any ideas that would spoil the sale.

She was wearing a Donna Karan outfit. Tan skirt and jacket over a dark brown silk blouse. Her chest was nicely tanned.

The short-haired wife was sighing and *hmmm*ing and saying, "I don't know . . ." but Marla was an experienced Realtor and she knew that the lady liked the house. And she was right to like it. It was reasonably priced and was in one of the higher-prestige neighborhoods in the city.

Marla said, "In Manhattan, you would have to pay about three million for something like this."

"More like five," the wife said, not making eye contact with Marla when she corrected her. "And you'd be in Manhattan."

Marla smiled over the comment. *Bitch,* she thought. Probably pushed her husband to get out of New York so they could live in a better place to raise their children. But she wasn't going to let these Midwest yokels forget that she was from New York. No sir. They've got the money, Marla thought. They have the money.

The husband looked past his wife's shoulder and gave Marla an apologetic smile. Marla smiled back at him. A moment of conspiracy. But Marla cringed on the inside. The husband was not exactly ugly. Not hideous, just sort of doughy and unappealing. Probably one of those types who hadn't been with a girl till his twenties, but then got rich and somehow believed he was entitled to beautiful women. Now he was all but winking at her. *Hey, it's the wife, heh-heh. What are you going to do? Heh-heh.* He was a prospective buyer, not a prospective lover. Men like this never seemed to figure out the distinction.

The wife looked at the husband, not catching him leering.

The wife gave him a tired "let's go" look and they began moving toward the foyer.

At the front door, the husband said, "We'll be in touch. You know we like it. I just have to talk to her, that's all."

"I understand," Marla said. "I do have to show it to another couple tomorrow. No pressure, though."

"Of course not," he said. He hesitated, then extended his hand. Marla shook it, conscious of the man's wife getting into the Lexus on the street. The wife wasn't looking up at them. She seemed preoccupied with getting home or to a restaurant where she could rag on someone there.

The husband held Marla's hand a tad longer than necessary. Then he released it and walked down the stairs. "I'll call you," he said.

"Okay," Marla said, her sales voice doing the talking.

She went back into the house and made sure all the lights were turned off and the doors were locked.

Then she called her office and told her assistant that Anderson, the customer, would likely make an offer tomorrow and that he was to be forwarded to her immediately. She told the assistant this even though Anderson had her cell number. He might call for a social reason as well. But the goal was to get him to sign on the line that was dotted. After that, if he persisted in this delusion that there was some sort of romantic connection between them, she would graciously but promptly disabuse him of it.

She clicked off the cell phone and climbed into her Range Rover. For Sale signs were in the back. She put the key in the ignition and turned.

Nothing.

She tried again.

Nothing.

"Oh, shit," she said. Sixty-thousand-dollar SUV and it wouldn't start. "Unbelievable," she said. "Un-fucking-believable." Her language was coarser when customers weren't around.

She was still trying when a man walked up on the sidewalk. He was wearing a Burberry raincoat and an Irishman's flat hat. He slowed his walk, hesitated, and then walked over to the driver's window.

Marla opened it.

"You need a jump?" the man said.

"I don't know. It just won't start. It's never done this before."

The man smiled. He seemed sympathetic. Marla noticed that he was well dressed. He said, "I'm not a mechanic, but I think it's probably your battery." The man pointed to a late-model Mercedes and said, "That's my car there. I've got jumper cables." He paused then said, "If you want to try that."

"Okay," Marla said.

She watched the man walk back to the Mercedes and pull it forward so that it was parallel to the Range Rover. Marla stepped out of her vehicle as the trunk of the Mercedes flipped up. She was standing next to him as they looked into the empty trunk.

Marla said, "Where are they?" Meaning the cables. But then her consciousness went black as the man brought down something hard on the back of her head. She fell halfway into the open trunk. Then the man took her by the legs and shoved the rest of her in. Then he closed the trunk.

TWENTY-FOUR

There was a photograph of Ronnie Wulf with the mayor and the Missouri candidate for the Senate behind Wulf's desk. It had been taken on a golf course, a fund-raiser of some sort. It made Hastings uncomfortable for some reason. He was a former athlete, perhaps even arguably a retired one, but he had never seen the appeal in golf.

Wulf was sitting behind his desk, reading Hastings's latest report. Attached to it were supplemental reports written by Detectives Murphy and Rhodes.

Wulf looked up from it and said, "Well, what do you think?"

"We don't have any evidence linking him to it."

"He knew Reesa Woods. You know he's violent, abusive to women."

"That's evidence that he knew Reesa Woods and that he roughs up his girlfriend. It's not evidence that he strangled these two women."

"Have you looked hard enough?"

"We're still looking at it."

What he was trying not to do was make the facts fit the profile of Larry MacPherson. Hastings didn't really know what Larry MacPherson's psychological "profile" was, and he wasn't sure it would make much of a difference if he did.

Wulf said, "Don't you have a gut feeling?"

"No," Hastings said. "And to be frank, I'm not sure I'd want to trust it anyway. Sometimes gut feelings can have shit for brains."

Wulf didn't seem amused by this. He seemed disappointed. He said, "Detective Murphy's report indicates that MacPherson showed up for work Friday night at seven P.M. Reesa Woods's approximate time of death could have been as early as six fifteen P.M. He could have killed her and gotten to work in that time."

"I understand that—"

Wulf went on. "It also indicates that MacPherson left work at approximately eleven thirty P.M. on Saturday night. Which would have given him time to kill Adele Sayers."

"Yes," Hastings said, "it's possible. But it's not likely."

Wulf looked directly at him as he said, "It's not likely." As if the statement was weak.

Hastings felt he was being interrogated now. Pressured to agree. He didn't like it one goddamn bit.

He said, "Chief, he would have had to book it pretty quickly from Laclede's Landing to West County in order to kill Adele Sayers. Very quickly. The evidence shows that Adele Sayers was murdered from behind in her own vehicle. That is, that the killer followed her to the Thunderbird Motel and waited in the car for her *before* he killed her. It's not likely that MacPherson would have had the time to do that."

"You feel sure about that."

"You want me to say what I think, or you just want me to agree with you?"

"Take it easy, Lieutenant."

"Yes, sir." Hastings raised a hand in conciliation. "I'm not trying to be difficult. I think the guy's a fucking nasty piece of work. He likes to beat up his girlfriend and take a lot of steroids. But that describes about a quarter of the people we deal with on a daily basis."

"That makes him incapable of murder?"

"Plenty of people are capable of murder," Hastings said. "Him probably included. But we're dealing with something that's . . . uncommon."

"And you think Larry MacPherson's common?" Wulf put a not pleasant emphasis on the last word.

"In a way, yes."

Wulf leaned back and seemed to think for a moment. Then he said, "You went to behavioral-science training in Quantico, didn't you?"

"Yeah." It was a one-week course.

"I understand you're skeptical of this psychological-profiling business."

"I am."

Wulf said, "How come?"

"Oh, I don't know."

"Don't you think those guys at FBI know what they're doing?"

Hastings sighed. "I suppose they do."

"George, I remember when I was younger, first became a detective, I had some backup role on an FBI case. I didn't like the feds, thought they looked down their nose at me. I understand how it is. But you've got to get past that."

"Look, Ronnie, I don't have a chip on my shoulder."

"Don't you?"

"No. I worked that case last year with them and we got along okay."

"Not at first, though."

"Maybe not at first. Some are okay, some aren't. It's just that I don't think profiling is a science. Even if I did, even if I thought that Larry MacPherson 'fit' the profile of a serial killer, it wouldn't be enough to make a case on its own. There has to be evidence that he did it. Evidence beyond just being a guy who beats up his girl-friend."

"Okay," Wulf said. "Well, you're entitled to your opinion, George. No one's denying that."

"It's not an opinion," Hastings said. He couldn't stop himself from saying it. And he liked being patronized less than he did be-ing bawled out.

Wulf gave him a brief glare. Hastings did not think he was be-ing insubordinate, but it was clear that Wulf thought he was pushing it.

"That'll be all for now," Wulf said. He didn't say anything else.

•

Driving home, Hastings thought it was ironic. He had been try-ing to caution his superior about the dangers of giving too much significance to intuition. *I know he's the guy. I feel it in my bones.* Horseshit. Intuition was not evidence. Intuition could lead to false arrests. Maybe he shouldn't have made that remark about guts having shit for brains. Where had he heard that in the first place? ... Right. Klosterman had said it. Funny when Klosterman says it to him. Not so funny when he says it to the chief of detectives.

And now the irony was that Hastings was having his own intuition about his place in this investigation. Specifically, he was intuiting that Ronnie Wulf was going to take him off it. Not officially, of course. Ronnie Wulf was smart, politically. He would not be the sort that would create unnecessary drama by saying, *You're off the case, Detective!* He would just sort of quietly exclude Hastings from things. Meetings would take place and Hastings would not be asked to come. Additional reports or tips would come in and Hastings would not be apprised of them. He wouldn't be fired or removed. He would just be left out of the loop. The investigation would continue without him. Which would be the point.

Christ, Hastings thought. For what? For not going along with Wulf's theory about Larry MacPherson? For not wanting to charge MacPherson with the murders of Adele Sayers and Reesa Woods? There simply wasn't enough evidence to put it on MacPherson. That was the logical, by-the-book, law-and-order conclusion.

That's what was so perplexing about it. It was not that Wulf was taking the correct, "official" position and that Hastings was rebelling because of a "gut feeling." If anything, it was the opposite. If there was an "establishment" position in this stupid pissing contest, Hastings was the one taking it.

But Wulf's in charge of the investigation, Hastings thought. You're not.

This was why he was still a lieutenant. And it was also why Karen Brady was a captain. Karen's lack of intellectual curiosity and her determined willingness to get along with her superiors got her promoted. Karen didn't intimidate anyone.

Well, he could go in tomorrow morning and apologize to Wulf. Tell him that he'd meant no disrespect, it had been the end of a long day, blah, blah, blah. Do that and maybe Wulf wouldn't cut him out of the loop. In short, go in and eat shit.

Maybe he could do it. But then maybe that would just make it worse. Above all, he did not want to acquiesce in charging MacPherson for these murders. Did not want to go along with it. Not yet, anyway. If he did that, he wouldn't deserve the rank he had now. He wouldn't deserve to work in homicide at all. If he had to, he'd examine every scrap of evidence himself. And if at the end of the day the facts showed that MacPherson had killed those women, Hastings would give Wulf a full-blown apology.

But he doubted it would come to that.

He wasn't sure why he was so sure of this. Maybe it was because MacPherson's girlfriend seemed so utterly convinced that MacPherson was not a monster. Which would not be conclusive on its own. Girlfriends and people in general tend to see what they want to see. But it was more than that. Hastings had looked into the eye of MacPherson and had seen a 'roided-up man-child. A violent con and a loser, yes, but a fool too. And Hastings had trouble believing that the real killer was a fool.

TWENTY-FIVE

"Lew speaking."

"Mr. Llewellyn?"

"Yes."

"Cliff Llewellyn?"

"Yeah. What can I do for you?"

"You're the man that wrote the story in yesterday's paper, aren't you?"

Llewellyn sighed. He was approaching fifty and felt older. "Which one?" he said.

"The one on page twenty-three in the metro section. 'Police investigate woman's murder.' Rather prosaic headline, don't you think?"

"Right." Llewellyn started to hang up on the crank. But he stopped when the voice spoke again.

"Don't hang up," it said. "Don't do that. I can help you."

"How?"

"Let me ask you something, Mr. Llewellyn. Do you not see that the murder of Ms. Sayers is connected to the murder of the other woman? The one named Reesa Woods? The one who called herself Ashley?"

The crime reporter stayed on the line. He said, "The police reports don't indicate that."

The man said, "They don't, do they? I see the police are hiding things from you. Well, Mr. Llewellyn, far be it from me to tell you how to do your job. There's a connection between the two, I assure you. A connection that I believe will demonstrate that this story does not deserve to be relegated to the back pages."

Llewellyn said, "Who is this?"

"Call me Jim."

"Jim. Jim what?"

"Springheel Jim. Now listen to me because I'm only going to tell you this once and then I'm going to let you go. In the central downtown library there is a book on the third floor entitled *When Terror Walked in London*. It's an old book; I don't think anyone's checked it out in years. In that book, you'll find a letter that I believe you'll find very interesting."

The expression on Llewellyn's face was changing now. He couldn't help himself. Coworkers near his desk were taking notice.

Llewellyn had been the crime reporter for the *St. Louis Herald* almost twenty years. Had seen all manner of brutality and violence. He wanted to remain skeptical and detached at this moment. But he was frightened too.

Llewellyn said, "Are you telling me you killed those women?"

"Boy, you like to go straight to the point, don't you? Right for the jugular. Like Mike Wallace. Are you taping this?"

"No," Llewellyn said. He wasn't either. He hadn't been ready for this.

"You should be. It's an exclusive. It could make you famous. But I'm afraid I must go."

"Wait a minute. *Wait.* I need to know more."

"I will not spoon-feed you. You have what you need now. Don't be greedy. Oh, and, Clifford? It's three now." Springheel Jim allowed himself a chuckle. "Bye-bye."

•

Raymond Sheffield hung up the phone and walked back to his car. And indeed there was a spring in his step. He wondered why he hadn't done this before. Before it was fun, before it was a kick. Killing the girls and dodging the police had been something. But it was too easy. It was like watching a top-notch football team take on the army. Score 77 to 3 or something embarrassing like that. There was no challenge there. No excitement. And he was entitled to excitement. He was entitled to respect. He had earned it.

A tree falls in the woods and nobody hears it, does it actually make a noise? Indeed, does it even fall? Does it matter if it falls or not? It has to matter. It has to mean something. If it doesn't mean something, it doesn't mean anything. It must have significance. It must achieve notice.

He felt so much better now. He felt better that the pieces were connected. The death of two prostitutes was meaningless unless they were connected. One prostitute dead, who cared? But two by the same killer, now *that* was something to write home about. And three women, well...that was an achievement. Surely the journalist would see that. If he had any artistic sense, he would see it. If he was more than just a hack, surely he would see it. Oh, don't let him be a hack, Raymond thought. Please don't let him be a hack. He had been generous with the reporter. He had pointed him to a letter that he had placed in a library. A letter that he had stored in a book about Jack the Ripper, no less. Which was obvious and clichéd, but, oh, why not? Why not give the masses something to latch on to? Something old, but something new too. Something fresh.

Yes. *Fresh* was the right word. Something new, bold, and exciting. Something fulfilling. Something not yet perfect. But getting there.

Tonight, he had killed the woman with a dumbbell. That had been a mistake. He had intended only to knock her unconscious with it and then strangle her when he got her out of the Central West End. But he had brought the weight down too hard and too quickly and it had killed her. It messed up the symmetry of his work. He wanted them all to die by strangulation. His signature, his calling card. It just didn't have the same effect if one was bludgeoned to death. Raymond had always admired the big-game hunters of Africa, true professionals, who refused to use machine guns to bring down their prey. You don't use a machine gun to kill a leopard. It was unsporting, they'd said. Unsporting, yes, but vulgar as well. Messy and lacking in finesse.

They would say all sorts of things about him, he knew. They would try to diagnose him with their pedestrian psychology.

Loser, they would say. Lacking what they called "affect." *Probably works at a bowling alley or a factory. A misfit living in his mother's basement.* They would say such things about him to comfort themselves. They would say such things because they wouldn't know what else to say.

He had seen the real estate lady's picture in the paper last week. She was with her husband, one of the owners of the Lacey Park Cancer Clinic. Dr. Benjamin Hilsheimer was his name. The two of them standing next to another couple at a fund-raiser for multiple sclerosis, as if any of them gave a damn. Typical society function. Dress up and smile for the cameras. Right away, Raymond had been drawn to her. Tall, red-haired woman of forty or so. With her surgically implanted bosoms and her long legs, she still looked good. She looked very good. And what was she doing with this Dr. Hilsheimer? This gray-haired old goat who was at least twenty years older than her? Really, what was she doing with him? And where did she get the nerve to list her profession as "Realtor" when obviously she was little more than this old goat's concubine?

Now she was dead, disposed of in woods twenty or so miles north of the city. He had not buried her. She didn't deserve it. She had cheated him by dying too soon. He propped her up against a tree in a seated position. *Hiya, sailor!* He debated undressing her or pushing her skirt up to make her appear ridiculous. Expose her for what she was. But he decided that that would detract from the effect he was seeking, and took only her turquoise bracelet to remember her by.

On the way back to the city, he told himself not to let her get him down. Okay, so he had not done a perfect job. He had muffed it. He had screwed up the conclusion, the finale. But the process was better. It was better this time, it was more satisfying, because he had tricked her. And she had not been just some low-rent escort. She was above ground, a woman with her picture in the paper. A middle-class trollop, trying to marry her way up.

And how wonderfully susceptible she was! She had seen his Mercedes, had seen his expensive clothes, and that was enough for her to let him get close. Maybe she thought she could even spirit a few bucks out of him at the end. Line up a future client. Can I show you a house, Doctor? *Is that what you thought, Ms. Hilsheimer? Did you take* me *to be such an easy mark? Did you underestimate me, like all the others?*

Easy. It had been so easy. He could do anything. He believed that he would have made a good spy or maybe even a good actor. Playing the butler in a murder mystery, wearing white gloves as he wrapped his hands around lovely white necks.

Raymond suppressed a laugh.

He felt better now. He had cheered himself up. And remembering the phone call to the reporter made him feel better still. Now let it work, he thought. Raymond smiled to himself. Shakespeare. He knew his Shakespeare. He wondered if he should've said that to the reporter. Maybe the reporter would have gotten it.

TWENTY-SIX

The assistant managing editor looked skeptical.

He was about ten years younger than Llewellyn. He was thin, and he wore a trimmed goatee like many men his age. He had a degree in journalism from Columbia University and an MBA from Washington University. He was inordinately sure of himself. His name was Mitchell Coury, and he didn't like his first name shortened.

He said, "A serial killer? I haven't heard of that."

Llewellyn said, "He said the murders of the two call girls are connected. One Friday and the other Saturday. This past weekend."

"You wrote a story on it?"

"On the second one. You know, I just reviewed the police report."

"All of them?"

"No, not all of the police reports."

Mitchell Coury frowned. "And you say you asked him if he did it?"

"Yes."

"And he said no."

"No, he didn't deny it. He didn't admit it either. Well . . . I think he did admit it."

Coury sighed. "Sounds like a crank."

Llewellyn said, "That's what I thought too." Though he didn't. Not entirely. Llewellyn was afraid of Coury in the way that middle-aged men sometimes become afraid of younger men in the workplace. Finding a new job or a new career at fifty is a frightening prospect. Fate or nature or some angry god had made Mitchell Coury his boss.

Llewellyn said, "Should we call the police?"

"Why?" said Coury.

"Well, I mean, it might be important."

"A crank?" Coury sighed again, pushing the older man. "I just don't see why he'd call here."

"Maybe to get attention."

"Yeah, that's what I'm worried about. He calls up here, jacking around, and I'm supposed to send you on some sort of treasure hunt. I don't see the point." Coury said, "Do you *want* to go to the library?" He said it like it was a waste of time.

Cliff Llewellyn wanted to call the police. A crank, maybe, but the guy had sounded creepy. He could want attention *and* be a killer. He wanted to tell Mitchell what it was like to be on the receiving end of that call. That it wasn't cowardly to be afraid about something like that. To trust a rational fear.

He said, "Mitchell, I think we should take it seriously. I mean, it's up to you. But I . . ."

"So you *do* want to call the police."

"Well—yeah."

"Okay, Cliff. If that's what you want."

Mitchell Coury left Llewellyn alone. He seemed not to want to be around if things became embarrassing. Llewellyn mentally shrugged his shoulders, resigned himself to the situation, and picked up the telephone.

●

It was Escobar who called Hastings.

Hastings was cleaning up the dishes after dinner. He had made a pasta dish with Italian sausage and some spring peas and an egg-cream sauce. Amy said it was a little bland and Hastings told her to use more salt and pepper.

Hastings shut off the water when Amy brought him the telephone. She told him it was a Detective Escobar.

"Yeah?" Hastings said.

"George, Escobar here. Hey, we got a call from a reporter at the *Herald*. He said a guy called him claiming that he killed the two girls. He said he left a letter for the reporter in the downtown library."

"Who's the reporter?"

"Cliff Llewellyn. You know him?"

"Yeah. He's all right."

"I talked with him on the phone. I'm headed down to the library with some other guys. Llewellyn's going to meet us there. You want to come?"

"Yeah. I've got my daughter here . . . let me drop her with some friends and I'll meet you there."

"Good. Listen, George: Llewellyn said the caller told him, 'It's three now.'"

Hastings looked over the kitchen counter at his daughter. She was doing her homework, but *Dancing with the Stars* was on the television.

He said, "Three?"

"Yeah," Escobar said. "I don't know if I should hope the guy's a crank or if it's an honest-to-God lead."

"I know what you mean," Hastings said. "I'll see you soon."

•

There were at least two dozen police officers in and around the library. A good many of them were not in uniform, searching for a suspect who perhaps wanted to view the investigation in process. Library staff members were stopped and questioned along with library patrons, many of whom were homeless people looking for a warm place to be for the day. Protests were made, voices were raised, people were delayed. No suspects were held.

When Hastings arrived, a technician from the crime scene unit was already there. They had cordoned off the shelf holding the book *When Terror Walked in London.* Llewellyn was there with a younger guy, and Hastings saw right off that this guy was going to be a problem.

The guy said his name was Mitchell Coury and he was the

managing editor of the *Herald*. He said to Hastings, "Are you in charge?"

"Excuse me?"

"Are you the lead detective on this case?"

"No," Hastings said. "Would you mind stepping back?"

Mitchell Coury said, "Do you have a search warrant?"

"No. This is a public place. The staff has agreed to cooperate with us. Are you speaking on their behalf?"

"I'm the one that received the call," Coury said.

"Yeah?" Hastings said, a little hardness in his voice.

"Well, actually it was Mr. Llewellyn here. But I'm speaking for the paper."

"That's good to know," Hastings said, and walked past him

The technician's name was Curtis Nyguen. Hastings had worked with him before. Nyguen looked at Hastings and said, "Okay?"

"Yeah, go ahead."

Curtis Nyguen pulled on his latex gloves and removed the book from the shelf. He opened the book and went through the pages and soon found a sheet of paper with words typed on it. He placed the paper in a see-through plastic bag and sealed it. He paged through the book twice more and did not find anything. Then he placed the book in a separate container.

Nyguen said, "You think he used gloves?"

Hastings said, "If it's our guy, yeah. He seems to be pretty smart. But you're going to dust these shelves, aren't you?"

"Yes. And our people will take the letter and the book back to our lab."

Hastings nodded.

Then he looked at the letter.

Greetings, my children.

You may have read about the murders of the ladies of the night, to wit, Ms. Reesa Woods and Ms. Adele Sayers and, the latest addition, Mrs. Marla Hilsheimer, who's not technically a prostitute but cut from the same cloth as the other two. Let me assure you that the demise of all three of these women was all my doing. Reesa was found by the river, where I left her. Ms. Sayers is missing an earring, which I have decided to keep. Mrs. Hilsheimer is somewhere north of the city, waiting to be discovered by the authorities, who may get around to finding her if they put all their small minds together. When she is found, it will be noticed that she is missing the bracelet which was on her right wrist. Unfortunately, she was not strangled like the others, but we can't win all our battles.

You may wonder, Who is this? Is he something we can understand? Is he a product of our times? A product of our society?

The truth is, you cannot know. You want to know, but you can't. It's not in you or the pedestrians at the police department to know. It's not in you to understand. It's only in me.

Yours truly,
Springheel Jim

TWENTY-SEVEN

Wulf wanted to know why he hadn't called him immediately.

Hastings said, "Detective Escobar called me first. It was a tip. But we weren't sure it was anything legitimate until we checked it out."

"And now?"

"We think he wrote the letter."

"You think who wrote the letter?"

"The killer."

"That's your theory," Wulf said.

"It's my thinking, yes." Hastings said, "Detective Escobar thinks so too."

Wulf looked away. Since Escobar didn't work for him, his viewpoint didn't count.

Hastings saw that Wulf was pissed off. He wanted to have the killer in custody. He wanted it to be Larry MacPherson because they already had MacPherson in the county lockup and that would make things easier for everyone. Hastings didn't blame Wulf for being angry, generally. But he suspected that Wulf had found out about the letter from his counterpart at the County Police Department, rather than from his own people. This had cost Wulf some face on top of being wrong about MacPherson's being the killer.

Hastings said, "I'm sorry I didn't call you right away. I didn't know it would turn out to be something key."

"You still don't know that."

Christ, Hastings thought. He said, "Perhaps not. But it's been confirmed that Marla Hilsheimer is missing."

Wulf shrugged.

And Hastings said, "And the thing about the earring. The earring belonging to Adele Sayers. Springheel Jim made a mention of that. That detail wasn't available to the public."

Wulf still wanted to fight him for some reason. He said, "It could have come from someone who had access to the task force's documentation," still wanting to fight him.

"It's possible," Hastings said. Though he didn't think it was possible. "But it's not at all likely. But putting the earring aside, how could he have known about the disappearance of Marla Hilsheimer?"

"You're presuming she's dead?"

"Yes, sir. I'm presuming he killed her."

"And you want to tell this to her husband? Her family? Are you that sure?"

It was a shitty question. An unfair one, geared to emotions. Hastings said, "I can hope that I'm wrong. But if you order me to give my opinion to the family, I will." Hastings hesitated, then he said, "Listen, do you think we should fax a copy of the letter to the FBI's Behavioral Science Unit?"

Wulf seemed to consider this. The lieutenant was asking his

opinion. It was intended to flatter him, though Hastings hoped that Wulf would not detect it.

He didn't. Wulf said, "Yes. Do that." Some of his authority had been regained.

Hastings figured that it would take the FBI profilers at least two days to render an opinion on Springheel Jim's letter. Yes, it was written by the killer. No, it was not. Perhaps it may have been. Whatever their finding would be was of little importance to Hastings. He thought it was written by the killer, and that was all that mattered to him.

Hastings was familiar with the Green River serial killer investigation. There were few homicide detectives who weren't. In that case, the killer had sent a letter to the local newspaper. The Seattle task force forwarded a copy to the FBI's Behavioral Science Unit. After review, the FBI said that the letter had "no connection with the Green River homicides" and that the letter was a "feeble and amateurish attempt to gain some personal importance by manipulating the investigation."

They were right about the letter being an attempt to gain some personal importance, but they were wrong about it not being written by the murderer. Gary Ridgeway, the Green River serial killer, later testified in court that he *did* write and send that letter. And that after he wrote it, he'd gone on to kill several more young women.

Hastings had had no role in that investigation. It was in another city and it was before his time. He had no reason to think that the FBI analyst had acted in bad faith or was incompetent. To his way of thinking, it was the culture in law enforcement that was probably to blame. The overconfident belief in the all-knowing profiler.

But for whatever reason, men like Ronnie Wulf seemed to take comfort in sending things to the FBI. Perhaps it was because Wulf actually believed the feds were expert in making such determinations. But Hastings had worked in law enforcement long enough to know that that would only be part of it. FBI assistance would take some political heat off the chief of detectives and, by extension, the Metropolitan Police Department itself. Whether FBI assistance was helpful or not, Wulf would be better able to claim he'd done everything he could.

Which was fine with Hastings. He had no personal beef with Ronnie Wulf. The existence of a random killer loose in the city frightened people. And the longer the killer remained at large, the more police officers' nerves became frayed and department morale declined. Wulf was in charge of the task force, and he had to answer directly to people that Hastings did not. And it was obvious that the investigation was wearing on Wulf, making him irritable and at times even petty. Hastings had to remind himself that Wulf was essentially a good man and that he probably had not wanted to be put in charge of this.

Now Hastings could see that Wulf's anger was off him. At least at this moment. Hastings said, "Is there anything else you'd recommend?"

"You've interviewed the reporter?"

"Yes. I spoke with the one that spoke with Springheel Jim."

"Did he tape the call?"

"No. But I summarized what the reporter remembered in my report. The reporter seemed to believe that the caller was an educated man."

"Why's that?"

"He used a couple of big words. *Prosaic* being one of them."

"Prosaic."

"Yeah. It means ordinary. Common—"

"I know what it means. So we're dealing with a college-degreed murderer, huh?"

"I don't know," Hastings said. "I do think he's smart though."

"No prints on the letter or the book?"

"No."

Ronnie Wulf sighed. "No, there's nothing else I can suggest. Just go back to work."

Hastings left Wulf's office and started his drive home. It was almost midnight. Hastings cursed to himself. Earlier, he had dropped Amy off at the McGregors', neighbors who had a daughter Amy's age. Hastings liked Terry McGregor, the kid's mom, but found the husband pretty tiresome. If he picked Amy up now, he would likely wake up the parents, inconveniencing them even more. Terry was a good lady and she had never once complained about having Amy over. But sometimes Hastings feared that he was taking her for granted.

He thought back to what he had said when he left Amy there hours ago. Something to the effect that he should be gone for only a couple of hours. And Terry McGregor had said not to worry because it was perfectly fine if Amy stayed the night. A casual offer inconsiderately accepted.

Shit. Well, he would drive by their house on the way home. If a light was on, or the flashing light of a flickering television screen, he would give a couple of soft knocks on the door. If not, he would have to let Amy stay the night and then pick her up early in the morning.

There was no light on, though, flickering or otherwise. And Hastings drove home alone, feeling like a crappy parent.

He unlocked the door to his condo and walked to the kitchen. There was too much on his mind to go straight to sleep. He made himself a whiskey, two fingers on ice, and a splash of water on top. He left the television off and put a George Jones record on the turntable.

Alone now, and he would still be alone if Amy were down the hall asleep in her bedroom. But he felt better when she was in the house with him. He felt more secure, more complete. He did not believe he was the sort to mope over the past. But tonight he thought about the past. He thought about what his life would be like if Eileen hadn't left him. They would still be a family, and he wouldn't have to feel shitty for dropping Amy off at a friend's and taking advantage of a decent, generous woman whom he didn't know well enough to be taking advantage of. It would be different if Eileen hadn't left. Maybe not better and almost certainly not happier or calmer, but they would be a family under one roof.

A family. He wondered, not for the first time, if he could round out the circle. He wondered if Carol McGuire could fill that role. Not just as a wife but as a stepmother. He feared that he knew the answer. Carol had always been nice to Amy. Had never said an unkind word to her or about her. (Though she'd said plenty about Eileen.) But, though there was nothing negative on Carol's part regarding Amy, there had been nothing positive either. Not much concern either way. She had once said to him, "You need to take better care of *yourself.*" And Hastings had not liked that, had not liked that at all. It was not so much the words she had used as the context in which she'd used them. In that conversation, he had taken Carol to mean that he should pay more attention to himself than he did to his kid.

But he had chickened out of that conversation. He had an *idea* of what she had meant, but he wasn't entirely sure. She could have meant that he should eat better or exercise more or get more sleep. It may not have been a suggestion that he give less of his time and less of himself to his daughter. He could have asked Carol to explain her comment then, to elaborate. But he hadn't. He had let it drop. Perhaps to avoid conflict. Perhaps because he didn't want to know the truth.

He wondered about it from time to time. And when he did, he wondered if he and Carol McGuire would go further in their relationship. Whether they were building to something or if they had reached their zenith. He wondered if what they had now was enough for him. He'd never asked her if it was enough for her.

Eileen, Amy, Carol, Terry McGregor. Hastings was a cop, an ex-jock, a die-hard Nebraska college football fan, a hunter and an outdoorsman and a country music fan. A man's man, by God. Yet his personal life was wrapped up with women and girls. He had no son. His only close male friends were the police officers he worked with. His relationship with his father had been terrible. His mother had been a sweet and gentle soul, and he had spent much of his childhood protecting her from his father's petty cruelty. He wondered if there was some sort of connection there.

And he wondered about Springheel Jim.

What had *his* childhood been like? Had it been normal? Had it been unhealthy? Had abuse or neglect played a part in making him a monster? Had there been some concrete incident or series of incidents that caused him to hate women? To look upon them with nothing but contempt and callousness and a complete absence of empathy? To see them not as women or as human beings but as objects to fulfill his dark, pitiless fantasies. Was there a cause? Or did he just exist?

Hastings did not like to think about this man. He did not want to contemplate this beast at the same time that he contemplated people he cared about. Women he cared about. This beast who looked upon women as not quite human.

If you were not a psychopath, it was difficult to get at. It was difficult to understand. It was difficult to get into the killer's head, because he thinks in ways normal people are not capable of thinking.

The most hardened policeman will weep at the sight of a child's corpse at the scene of a traffic accident. Will wince if he sees the accident happening. Shoulders hunch as the vehicles collide because the normal person hopes that no one will be hurt. *Please, God, don't let someone die. Please let it be all right.*

But the psychopath doesn't think that way. He is not affected. He lacks the capability to feel the affect. To him, death and cruelty and destruction are mere images. It's not in him to feel.

No, Hastings thought. That's not entirely true. They feel, all right. They feel the thrill and joy of being wicked. For them, it is liberating. And they feed on fear. The fear can be almost intoxicating.

That's why you wrote that letter, isn't it? Hastings thought. You wanted attention and you wanted to brag and you wanted to show the police and the press how smart you were. But you wanted to create fear too. Like a cat batting at a mouse. You want to feed on that, don't you?

He was vain, this killer. He had placed his letter in a book about Jack the Ripper. *Look at me! A modern-day Jack the Ripper, see? Ha-ha!* He liked being clever. Apart from creating sensation, Springheel Jim wanted to let the public know that serial killers were by no means a recent creation. They had been around for centuries. Indeed, the FBI had taught Hastings that the medieval myths of vampires, demons, and werewolves stemmed not just from German folklore but from actual gruesome murders. Even back then, people could not comprehend that human beings could commit such atrocities. It had to be attributed to the supernatural because it could not be comprehended that a man could do such things. The existence of Stoker's Dracula was easier to contemplate than history's Vlad the Impaler.

It was these thoughts that put the minor issues with Ronnie Wulf in perspective. Wulf was getting worn-out. Maybe it had something to do with age too. Maybe Wulf had liked the thrill of pursuing the enemy, the chase, when he was younger, but now he was getting leaned on from people above him. Or maybe he was just tired. It could happen to the best of officers. Maybe it would happen to Hastings one day as well, and he too would seek refuge in an administrative position.

But not yet, Hastings thought. Not yet, Jim.

TWENTY-EIGHT

His letter was in The *Herald* the next morning.

The police had not encouraged that. Indeed, Lieutenant Hastings had told the managing editor that publishing the letter would reward the killer. But Mitchell Coury had said, "*If* it's the killer. But you don't really know, do you?" Hastings would have liked to find a way to stop the publication, but he was too busy working the case and updating Wulf to do anything about it.

So it was a front-page story, and the full letter appeared on page 5.

•

Raymond Sheffield bought a copy in the lobby of the hospital and read it in a stall in the bathroom. It brought a smile to his face. A smile, then a laugh, and he wondered for a moment if there was anyone else in the restroom to hear him. He was still for a minute or so and concluded that he was alone. With some effort, he stuffed the newspaper into the trash bin on his way out.

His thrill renewed when he went into the locker room and saw Ogilvy reading the story. Yes, yes, he was reading it; he had it open to the page. Raymond remembered his discipline. Don't crow about it, he told himself. Don't brag. Not to these fools. He could look at Ogilvy and smile and say, *Reading the lowbrow rags, eh, Ogilvy?* Or something else clever. Watch the slob lift his stupid fat face and say, *Huh?* No. He would resist that. Not that there was a risk of giving himself away. Not to Ogilvy anyway: Ogilvy was too stupid to figure it out. No, he would resist it because it would be too obvious, too pedestrian. Better to wait.

And he was glad he waited, glad he resisted, because sure enough Tassett came in and Ogilvy looked at him and said, "Have you read about this?"

And Tassett walked over and looked at the paper and took in a few lines and said, "Huh. Fucked-up, man."

And then Raymond had to say over his shoulder, "What's that?"

"There's a serial killer on the loose," Ogilvy said. "He's killed three women."

"Oh, that's terrible."

"Three?" Tassett said. "No, it says two."

"He's claimed he killed another one," Ogilvy said. "The police confirm that she's missing. They haven't found her yet."

Raymond kept his face turned away from them. He hung his sport coat in his locker and removed his white smock and put it on. They will, he thought. They'll find her today if they try. He hadn't buried her. He hadn't even tried to hide her. He wanted her to be found.

Tassett seemed unconcerned and blasé about it all. But Ogilvy was looking up and down from the newspaper. Perhaps to himself, he said, "How do you explain something like that?"

Tassett said, "What?" He didn't know that they were still on the subject.

"How do you explain something like this guy?" Ogilvy said again. He was directing the question to Tassett, but he seemed disturbed enough that he would have taken an answer from Raymond, whom he had never really liked.

Tassett turned and said, "You mean, clinically?"

"Yeah, clinically." He would take anything. Raymond knew that Ogilvy had a wife and daughter. He had a dog too, and he probably wondered if she would bark if someone tried to break into their home. Raymond also knew that Olgilvy's wife was a graduate student at Washington University and that she walked alone to her car when she went home at night.

Tassett shrugged. "I don't know," he said. "Maybe you don't."

They finished dressing and then walked out. Neither one of them said a word to Raymond.

Raymond hesitated for a moment. Ogilvy had left the newspaper on the bench. Raymond wanted to walk over and read it again. But he didn't.

•

In the hall, Helen gave him a bright good morning. She asked him how his weekend had been, if he enjoyed the party. Raymond gave her the right answers. The weekend was nice, the party was pleasant, but he was tired after working that long shift and so forth and so on. They spoke briefly about the weather and work and where they would go for Thanksgiving vacation.

Helen said that her family was in Virginia but that she wouldn't have time to go that distance.

Raymond said, "Are you scheduled for Thanksgiving day?"

"Sort of. I come on at midnight."

"Ooh."

"Yeah, I know. It sucks. How about you?"

"Me? I don't think I'm scheduled until that Friday."

"No," Helen said, "I meant how about your plans for Thanksgiving?"

"Thanksgiving?"

"Yes. Are you going back to Boston?"

"No. There isn't time for that."

"That's where your family is, though. Right?"

"My parents are dead."

"Oh. I'm sorry. And . . . no siblings?" Helen Krans was starting to regret that she'd gone down this conversational path.

"No." He waited to see if she would ask if he had children. He was ready for it.

But she took whatever signal he was sending and accepted it. She looked up at the room where they had booked a diabetic coma a couple of days earlier. "Busy day today," she said. And that was that.

•

Later that day, Raymond was sitting alone at a table in the cafeteria when Tassett approached him. Tassett did not ask but merely sat down opposite him.

"Hi, Raymond."

"Hello."

"Listen, I'd like to ask you a favor. Helen said you're on shift the Friday after Thanksgiving and she's on Thursday. Thanksgiving. Could you switch shifts with her?"

"Switch shifts," Raymond said, "so that I work Thanksgiving, you mean?"

"Yeah."

"Why?"

"Well, I've got that Wednesday off and Thanksgiving, and we'd like to spend a couple of days in Chicago."

After a moment, Raymond said, "Chicago."

"Yeah. A two-day trip." Tassett smiled. "We could use the break, man."

"Why are you asking?"

"Well, I figured you didn't have anything—"

"No. Why are *you* asking?"

"She didn't want to ask you."

"So she sent you to?"

"No," Tassett said. "This was my idea."

Raymond studied the young man sitting across from him. He wondered what it would be like to shoot him in the face.

He said, "No."

"No?"

"No," Raymond said again. He returned his attention to his food.

TWENTY-NINE

Escobar called Hastings to tell him that they had found Marla Hilsheimer's body in the woods north of St. Charles.

Hastings said, "Has her husband been notified?"

"Yeah. I spoke with him on the phone. George, I asked him if she had been wearing a bracelet. He said she had a lot of jewelry, and he couldn't be sure what she was wearing the day she went missing. But one of my guys checked with the staff at her office, and they said she had been wearing some sort of turquoise Indian thing."

Hastings asked for directions and then told Escobar he'd meet him there.

Klosterman was with him as they drove out to the site. When they arrived, Mr. Hilsheimer was there, an older man in a high-dollar camel coat, his strong face twisted in grief. Hastings took him in view and reminded himself that somewhere was a man who had taken pleasure in inflicting this pain.

There was a single dirt road that brought them to the edge of the woods, vehicles from the County Police Department and St. Charles PD and a few unmarked cars. The officers had to walk through wet ground to reach the body of the woman.

Hastings and Klosterman conferred with the county medical

examiner. They were informed that she had died of a blow to the back of her skull and that the time of her death was likely between six and eight P.M. the night before.

Escobar left Mr. Hilsheimer and came over to talk with them. The detectives made sure that the next of kin were not within hearing distance before they began a discussion that could be construed as clinical.

Escobar said, "There was no bracelet found on her. And we seem to have confirmation that she was wearing one yesterday at work."

Hastings said, "So Springheel Jim was probably the killer."

"Looks that way."

Klosterman said, "She worked at a real estate office?"

"Yeah."

"No part-time . . ."

"No," Escobar said. "She wasn't a call girl. I guess she could pass for one. She's pretty."

Hastings said, "She's a prize."

"Pardon?"

"A prize," Hastings said. "He's picking out attractive women. To him, maybe they're all whores."

"Killing them because he likes them?" Klosterman said. "Because he's attracted to them?"

"You could call it an attraction, but when I say prize, I mean, you know, the way a hunter gets points. A ten-point buck, that sort of thing." He said to Escobar, "Have we got any sort of foot-prints?"

Escobar sighed. "I don't know, George. We've had about twenty officers walking all over the place."

"Well, that's fucking great."

"It happens."

"I know it happens. It doesn't mean it's okay."

After a moment, Escobar said, "She had an appointment yes-terday in the Central West End. She was showing a house on Pershing Place to a couple that are moving here from New York. They told our officer that they left her between six and seven P.M. And as far as we know, that's the last time anyone saw her."

"What time does she usually get home?"

"Her husband said it varies. Sometimes it's late. She usually calls him, though."

"Was the Pershing Place house her last scheduled showing?"

"Yes."

"So he abducted her there." Hastings turned to Klosterman and said, "Pershing Place off Euclid? That's a bunch of row houses, isn't it?"

"Yeah. Million-dollar ones. But . . . it would have been dark. You want to check it out?"

"Yeah," Hastings said. He turned to Escobar and said, "The vehicle's still there?"

"Should be."

"I'll have my techs get on it. Will you fax me a copy of the husband's statement as soon as you can?"

"Sure."

Klosterman said, "I'll see if I can get the keys from the husband."

•

Klosterman called the crime scene unit from the car. The techs weren't there yet when he and Hastings got to the Central West End. The street was tree lined and they could see the gray-stone townhouse with the For Sale sign in front, the Range Rover in front of that.

Klosterman touched the keys in his pocket, and Hastings remembered the way the old man had handed them to him without saying a word, Klosterman saying, thank you, sir, but not telling him he was sorry because he'd probably heard it too much for it to mean anything now.

Hastings parked the Jaguar across the road, and they got out and pulled on their latex gloves. They approached the Range Rover. Klosterman pressed the locking device on the keys and heard the car lock.

Up close, Klosterman said, "I just locked it."

"Yeah?"

"I mean, it was unlocked. She left it unlocked."

"Or he did."

They opened the front door and did a cursory search for bloodstains. They didn't find any. Her work materials were on the front seat. Sales sheets, listings, contracts with the company's banner across the top. A briefcase on top of them to hold them in place. They didn't look like they'd been pushed around.

Hastings said, "There doesn't seem to be any sign of struggle up here."

"Or in the back," Klosterman said. Though he had only glanced back there. He would leave the thorough examination to the techs.

Hastings said, "Did he grab her before she got in the car?"

Klosterman shook his head. "No. Her stuff is in the vehicle. She must have gotten in first. He could have been waiting for her in the back, like he did with Adele Sayers. But there's no sign of a struggle."

"She got in and then she got out." Hastings looked at Klosterman and said, "Hand me the keys, will you?"

Hastings put the key in the ignition and turned. Nothing. He tried again and there was still nothing, so he leaned forward and pulled the release lever for the hood. He got out of the vehicle and took a look at the engine and the battery and saw what he thought he might see.

"Shit," Hastings said. "He disconnected the battery. Waited for her to try to start the car and then came along—"

"And probably offered to help," Klosterman said.

"Knocked her on the head and then took her away."

"In a neighborhood like this," Klosterman said, looking down the street at the wealthy homes and the well-kept trees and high-dollar cars, "maybe he found a way to blend in. Put her at ease."

"Maybe."

Yeah, maybe. For this was a sadist and a psychopath they were dealing with. The psychopath likes to deceive, likes to trick. He likes being clever.

And Hastings couldn't help wondering what Marla Hilsheimer thought in her last few moments. *Goddamn car . . . oh, good, here's someone who might help . . . looks harmless enough . . .* Seeing a man, not a monster. Seeing what she wanted to see and not what he was. Seeing what *he* wanted her to see.

And what do you hope for now? Hastings thought. They had nothing. They knew it and he probably knew it too. What do you hope for? That he just gets tired and stops? That he decides to give humanity a break and stay in for a few nights? That he retires? That the merciless somehow finds mercy? What do you hope for?

Hastings remembered the time he had taken Amy to the Chicago Field Museum of Natural History and they had seen the man-eating lions of Tsavo. Stuffed and mounted there since 1924, they seemed unimpressive. Though male, neither of them had the shaggy, virile mane that you see on the MGM roaring lion. They were four feet at the shoulder and weighed about five hundred pounds apiece, but they still looked a little scrawny.

Yet, between the two of them, they had killed 135 railroad workers in Uganda in just a few months, and that was the conservative estimate. They worked mainly at night, unafraid and undeterred by campfires or thorn *bomas*. Every night for three weeks straight, they stalked, they killed, and they remained at large. At one point, fifty shots were fired into the darkness at the sound of a roar, but they made no purchase. It was at this time that the natives, and not a few Englishmen, began to think that they were dealing not just with a couple of man-eating lions but with demons. Colonel Patterson himself, the supervising engineer, later wrote that he saw a pair of eyes glowing at him in the dark. People later remarked that this would not have been physically possible, as there was no outside light to reflect the glow. But Patterson was there among the heat and the darkness and the sound of a man screaming as he was dragged off into the bush.

The guide at the museum said, "Don't let the appearance fool you. They didn't have manes, but these were tremendous animals. They were in great condition." There was admiration in the guide's voice then. Even Amy noticed it, and Hastings felt some comfort at her recoil.

When they left the museum, she asked if the lions *were* demons.

And Hastings had said, "Of course not, sweetie. They're just animals that formed a taste for people. A lion's not capable of being good or evil."

"But why did it take so long to kill them?" She wasn't sympathetic to the lions. Perhaps they weren't pretty to her. They were a hard, dark force of nature.

Hastings said, "That was over a hundred years ago. They didn't have the technology we have now. Infrared lights, that sort of thing. As far as seeing eyes glowing in the night, well, fear and darkness and heat can mess up your perspective."

Hastings wondered about that conversation now. Wondered if he'd been wrong. They had technicians and infrared lights and task forces now. And yet they had nothing. There were still eyes glowing in the darkness. Seeing, stalking, and planning.

THIRTY

There were three car wrecks that night. Four people were brought in by ambulance, two by their own vehicles. The two that drove themselves weren't particularly injured but were seeking documentation to strengthen a lawsuit. The ER staff was used to such things. Three of the people brought by ambulance had legitimate injuries, one of them requiring sutures to the forehead and one with a dislocated shoulder.

Helen Krans attended the dislocated shoulder. A young man of about twenty-five, shot up with morphine so that he wouldn't feel too much pain, but his arm was still out of the socket. Helen and a nurse wrapped a sheet around his torso and then another nurse held the sheet tight on one side as Helen tugged on his arm on the other side. It took three good tugs—the guy crying out groggily during this—but the arm went back in on the third try and everyone seemed to feel better.

Helen went on break after that. She took the stairs down to the back entrance of the hospital, passed a couple of paramedics by an ambulance, and lit a cigarette.

She was not the only doctor on staff who smoked. Her habit during college and medical school had been roughly half a pack a day. But it had been increasing lately and she was aware of it.

She knew it was related to stress and work, and she told herself that she would cut it down when her residency was finished.

Helen Krans was aware that her life consisted mainly of work. She had no husband and no children. She was having an affair with Harry Tassett, but she didn't think of him as a boyfriend. Nor did she think of him as a "friend with benefits," because she thought that sort of phrase was vulgar and insulting to all parties involved. He was her lover, for the time being, and nothing more. She enjoyed Harry's company. He was fun in bed and he could be funny, and he was not the sort to get heavy. As she saw it, they were serving out some sort of term in life—residency—and helping each other through the loneliness that comes with it.

She was aware that some people thought she was aloof, perhaps even mercenary. This didn't bother her though. For she knew herself, and she did not believe that she was cold or unfeeling. And she had never had much patience for professional women who went "girly" over men. Professionalism meant a great deal to her. It was more important to her than a man.

She was one of three children born to well-intentioned parents. Her father had been a flight officer in the navy, and he too had put a great deal of stock in professionalism. He was a good egg, but he spent little time trying to tell his children to be generous or moral or upright. Rather, he stressed to his two sons and daughter the importance of being good *at* something. In his way, he was something of a feminist. He did not presume that his daughter should strive to be merely a good wife and good mother.

When Helen told him that she wanted to be a doctor, he encouraged her in a way that could not be called patronizing. He supported her decision just as much as he would have had she been one of his sons. He did not create for her a different standard.

Helen in turn always worked hard. She graduated at the top of her class in college and got accepted into medical school. Being attractive, she was often approached for dates. Those she liked, she would go out with. Usually, the relationships would last for only a couple of months because the men would compete with her on one level or another. Or, upon finding that she was a little smarter or more competent than perhaps they were, they would move on to someone else.

She was a secure person and did not try to intimidate the men in her life. At least, she didn't think she did. She did not try to one-up people in general. But as she went further in her ambitions, she learned that men liked to feel needed by a woman. And she was not especially good at accommodating this. She didn't care to try to be, either. To start with, she knew it would have been contrary to her nature. Also, she knew that her father would recoil if he ever saw her "dumbing" herself for a man. He would not tolerate that.

She saw her parents infrequently. They lived in Norfolk now, and she didn't get much time off. Her relationship with her father was one of mutual respect and fondness, but it was not one given to long heart-to-heart talks. Her mother was starting to ask questions about marriage and family. Helen would say, invariably, that she was working too hard to think about such things now.

Which was true. She *was* working too hard to think about it now. Perhaps marriage and a family would come later. But when it did, the timing would be of her choosing.

Her cigarette was coming to its end now. She was aware of someone approaching her. Harry.

"Hey." He drew up next to her. He was wearing his sheepskin jacket, which he looked good in. He said, "Well, I tried."

"You tried what?"

"I tried to get Raymond to switch shifts with you. So we could go to Chicago."

Helen frowned. "Why did you do that?"

"Because I wanted you to come with me. You said you wanted to go."

"I said I'd go if I could. I didn't want you asking him to switch shifts."

"It's no big deal."

"If I'd wanted that, I would've asked him."

"I was just trying to help. Sorry." He was pouting now. Jesus.

"Harry, I know you meant well. But it makes me look weak, you doing that."

"How?"

"It just does." She sighed. "What did he say?"

"You know, he got pissed. Like I'd offended him just by asking."

"He said no?"

"Yeah, he said no."

"Well, I don't blame him."

"Why not?"

"He's full-time staff, Harry. He's not on the same level as us. You belittled him by asking that."

"Jesus, I didn't think it was that big a deal." Harry Tassett put his hands in his jacket pockets. "Is he sweet on you or something?"

"Oh shut up, Harry. He's a good physician."

"I didn't say he wasn't. You want me to go up and apologize to him?"

She knew that he didn't mean it. She could fuck with him a bit by saying yes, but she wasn't in the mood right now. She said, "No. Just don't say anything more. He'll forget about it soon enough."

She could see that he wanted her to give him some sort of sign now. A touch or a smile to put him at ease, maybe let him know that they could fool around after their shift. But she didn't feel like being all that generous now.

Harry. Maybe he meant well. But maybe he didn't. She was aware that Raymond Sheffield had something of a crush on her. She was not comfortable with this, partly because she wasn't at all attracted to him and also because she thought he was a little on the creepy side. She was glad that Raymond was a good doctor because his competency made it harder to feel pity for him. She did not like to pity people.

She wondered now if Harry had spoken to Raymond not so much because he wanted to take her to Chicago for a couple of days but rather to ward Raymond away. *She's taken, pal. She's with me.* Had he spoken to Raymond as a favor to her, or rather to stake a claim on her? This would have been wrong on a couple of levels. First, she wasn't Harry's to claim. Second, and more important, the notion that she could conceivably bed down with Raymond was repellent to her. Did Harry actually worry about that?

Shit, she thought. Never mind. She hadn't gone into medicine to be wrapped up in this sort of nonsense.

"It's getting cold," Helen said. "Let's go back in."

They went back into the hospital, two figures walking hunched against the cold, visible to one standing at the window on the sixth floor. In sight until they walked under the cover of the ambulance sally port.

Raymond Sheffield kept looking out the window for a few moments after that, his hands in the pockets of his smock fingering a small piece of metal, his forehead almost touching the glass. At that moment, he was unaware of his reflection, his head outlined and glasses shining back their own reflection, hiding his eyes.

THIRTY-ONE

Hastings ordered a cheeseburger and fries and handed the menu back to the waiter, who then left them alone.

Carol said, "Why didn't you order the rigatoni? It's great here."

"I'm not in the mood for it."

"We're at one of the best Italian restaurants in the city, and you order a cheeseburger and fries. You're going to hurt their feelings."

"The red sauce upsets my stomach."

"You and your stomach. You can't drink wine? Not even a little?"

"Not even a little," Hastings said. "I'll watch you drink yours. Maybe you'll spill a little on your lovely white blouse."

"Then I'll throw the rest on you." She paused and looked at him. Then said, "How are you?"

"Pretty beat."

A moment passed. "I read the story in the newspaper. The letter. Was that the real deal?"

"We're not sure," he said without looking at her.

Carol said, "It is, isn't it? The killer wrote that."

"I think he did, yes. I wish I didn't."

"Why?"

"Because it's what he wants. Credit. Attention. He's winning."

"And you're losing?"

"I don't look it at it that way."

"I'm sorry. I know you don't. Sorry."

Hastings waved it away. Carol trafficked in human misery too, defending criminals and seeing destruction and waste. Most of them were guilty of the crimes charged against them, but she believed the devil himself was entitled to due process of law. Like many criminal defense lawyers, she used gallows humor to deal with grief.

But she knew Hastings too. Knew that his ego was part of what kept him going.

She said, "It's scary, a person like that."

"Did you ever defend it?" Hastings said. "Did you ever represent a person like that?"

Carol knew that his question was not judgmental. He rarely judged her.

She said, "I don't think so. And I've defended some pretty bad apples. Particularly when I worked for the public defender. Most of them were poor and stupid and Latin or black. They never had anything."

"Did you sense . . ."

"Sense what? Evil?"

"Yeah, maybe."

"I don't know. Maybe. Once in a while. Depravity. Moral depravity, sure. But you know how it works."

"What do you mean?"

"What I mean is, I never asked myself if they were guilty. That's not my role. My role was to give them the best legal defense I could." She smiled at him. "Should I apologize to you for that?"

"Never."

"Anyway, I never thought of it that way. I believe in the system."

"Due process."

"Well, if we don't have that, all you have to do to put someone in prison for life is arrest them. And you don't want to live in a country like that."

"We don't?"

"I don't and neither do you. So shut up."

"Do you believe in monsters?"

"Monsters?" Carol waited to see if there was a joke.

"Yeah," Hastings said. "Monsters."

"You mean like human monsters?"

"Yeah."

After a moment, Carol said, "Yeah."

Hastings was surprised. She knew that he had always considered her a bleeding-heart liberal, unwilling to accept the existence of evil. But she had never been as simple as he thought.

Then she said, "But, George, who is it that determines if someone is a monster? You?"

"Yeah, maybe."

"Is this something you can see?"

"I wish."

Carol smiled, shook her head. "You cops . . ."

"What about us cops?"

"You're so black-and-white. This guy's a turd. This guy's a scumbag. This guy's a gangbanger."

"We're simpleminded."

"I didn't say *you* were."

"But Joe is? Murph?"

"No. Stop doing this."

"Okay."

"All I meant was, you guys have a tendency to brand people. Not all of you, but a good many of you."

"What do I call this fellow?"

"It seems like he named himself."

"Yeah. That he did. But what would you call him?"

"A sociopath."

"A sociopath is someone without a conscience. This guy's something more than that."

"Well, yeah. God knows what made him like that."

Hastings said, "Maybe nothing made him like that. Maybe he just—is."

"George, come on. Nobody comes out of the womb 'like that.' He obviously suffered some sort of trauma."

"We don't know that."

"It's usually the case."

"No. I think it's something we'd like to believe is usually the case. So *we'll* feel better. Safer. But what if they're just born?"

"That's what you'd like to believe."

"I'd rather not, actually."

"Yeah, you would. You'd like to believe that because it's easier for you to believe it."

"And your beliefs. Don't they make things easier for you?"

"No, not necessarily. Not always. I'm not simpleminded either."

"No. But you are cute."

"Don't patronize me. Not now."

"Sorry."

"And show a little compassion."

"For who? The killer?"

"No, not the killer. But for the guy who had the shit beat out of him since birth. Who's only known poverty and cruelty. Who has nothing to lose."

"Well, maybe I would if I had the time. But I'm pretty busy dealing with the victims these folks leave behind. The *girl* who's getting the shit beat out of her now. The women getting killed."

"I see. So I have no compassion for them."

"No. I know you do. We just see it differently, that's all."

"I know it's just liberal dogma to you, George. But environmental forces make these people."

"Why can't nature make these people? Just as nature sometimes produces a three-legged frog?"

"Because we're not frogs, goddammit. We're talking about a human being here."

"Are we?"

"Oh, shit, George. Don't you see where that thinking takes

you? You start dehumanizing these people you're chasing, you might just as well exterminate them like bugs. You speak of monsters, fiends . . . these are people."

Hastings didn't say anything.

Carol said, "You think this killer is an aberration. I agree with you. But then you suggest that he just *exists*. That he was a monster from birth. That's just too . . . cold."

"Nature can be cold."

THIRTY-TWO

Raymond finished his shift at eleven o'clock and drove home. He poured water into the kettle and cut some slices of apple and set them on his cutting board. While the kettle boiled, he read again his letter in the newspaper. It brought a satisfied smile to his face. But it was fleeting.

He was wondering about Helen Krans.

The events of the day had knocked his thinking out of whack. He had supposed that she was having some sort of relationship with Tassett. He had convinced himself that she was a modern woman and that she could live how she wanted to. He believed that he had convinced himself of that. But he had managed to think that she was not a bad woman. He had placed her in a certain compartment. But she didn't seem to fit there. Not anymore.

What was she doing with Tassett? Tassett was only screwing her. Did she think of him in a similar way? A pig to fill the void? Why had she sent Tassett to tell him that she wanted to go away for the weekend? Did she think so little of him?

Helen was supposed to be different. A physician who admired his work. A professional. Not just another slut on her back, spreading her legs and telling her idiot boyfriend to put it in, put it in, put it in.

No, he thought. She was nice to me. She's better than that.

Isn't she?

Or was she laughing at him? Saying unkind things about him to Tassett. Maybe Tassett teased her about him. Told her that Dr. Sheffield was after her and what did she think about *that*? Did Tassett tell her to close her eyes and think of Dr. Sheffield? What things did they do? What did they say about him?

Raymond reached into the pocket of his jacket and touched the small piece of steel, making sure that it was there. It made him feel better when he touched it. He took it out and placed it on his kitchen table.

It was a small, black hairpin.

She wore hairpins at work. She was like that. Not fancy, not taking the time to have her hair done because she was a professional and she didn't fuss much with her looks. Though she was attractive, to be sure. She would put her yellow hair up with hairpins, clipped at the top of her head. They would fall out here and there as her shift progressed. People joked that some of her pins could be found in the patients.

Raymond had found this one on the floor of the operating room where she had attended the young man's dislocated shoulder. It must have been knocked loose while she tugged on his arm.

After he found it, Raymond's first impulse was to bring it back to her. Tell her he'd found it and thought that she might want it back. Might want it back after it had been on the floor in an emergency room ward.

An offering.

And maybe he would have given it to her. Maybe he would have given it to her even after she'd sent Tassett to tell him she wanted to switch shifts. *Go ask Raymond. He's got nothing going on. Ask Raymond to stand by while we rut like animals....* Maybe even after that he would have taken the pin to her, and she would have smiled at him and cleared up the misunderstanding. Told him that the thing with Tassett was over. Or had never been.

But then he had seen them through the window. And after seeing that, he had reached into his pocket and touched the hairpin, and when he felt it, he felt comfort. For a moment, he felt peace. He had a part of her now. But only a part.

There were things in his past he liked to remember. Things he liked to take out and look at again. His work on Ashley was one of those things. A killing that he'd created. *His* creation, his work. He liked to think about that. He liked to think about the beginning, the middle, and the end. Sometimes he would start out by thinking of the end. The last moments of her life, and then he would go back to the beginning, where he had picked her up. Sometimes it was fun to do it that way. Explain the beginning after the end. He liked to play it different ways. It was his work, after all, and he felt entitled to move it around when it suited him.

But there were also things that he did not like to remember. He was getting better at sorting out the memories he liked and the memories he did not. He was getting more and more control. But he was not there yet. He had not yet reached perfection. Some of the bad memories would come upon him, and he could not stop them from coming. Like the times after his parents divorced and his mother would come home with a man she had picked up at a bar or a party. Sometimes the man would be surprised to see a little boy sitting alone in front of the television. And his mother would say, "He'll be fine." And then she would take the man by the hand and lead him off to her bedroom. Later, Raymond would listen for sounds—silence, muffled conversation, more quiet, laughter . . .

His mother had not abused him. Indeed, she had seemed like an older sister to him. Later, he would decide that she was silly and frivolous and girly. A nonentity.

His father had remarried, a less pretty, more stable woman with her own children. Raymond's stepmother had tried to take to him but, like most grown-ups, had trouble doing so. Raymond remembered overhearing her tell his father, "There's something missing from him." A disagreement over a toy led Raymond to slap his eight-year-old stepsister across the face, hard enough to knock her to the ground and fatten her lip. The parents tried to mediate the "problem," but the swollen lip was visible evidence that couldn't be ignored. Raymond was no longer allowed to be with his stepbrothers and stepsisters. His father had tried to spend time with him alone after that, but the visits grew less and less frequent and eventually ceased.

Other bad memories would surface at times, and he had to concentrate to suppress them. He had to will them away. The bullying at school. The cruel laughter. The dismissive glances. The invisibility. He had hated the bullies, but more than that he envied them. And he knew he would have done worse if he had their power.

The dreams began about the time he reached puberty. Dreams that he knew were different from other boys'. He didn't dream about cars or sports or amusement parks. He didn't dream of girls he knew from school being naked and doing things with him or to him. He dreamed about a pretty girl at school being naked and covered with shit and dirt, all her black hair shaved off and dozens of sharpened pencils driven into her head. He would wake from these dreams startled but not frightened. He knew even at that age that he should not discuss the dreams with anyone. As he got older, the dreams became more vivid and detailed. And in time he came to realize that the dreams were fantasies.

In college, Raymond had sat in a classroom once while a student argued with a psychology professor. The professor had been lecturing that bad parenting makes bad children. A student asked if the reverse was also possible—that bad children could make bad parents. The professor got upset and told the student that that sort of thinking was fascist and reactionary. The student seemed to take some pleasure in rattling the professor.

Raymond would remember that exchange from time to time. He would forget that the offending student was a young woman.

THIRTY-THREE

They were in a cramped conference room, Hastings, Klosterman, Rhodes, and Murphy. Hastings put Springheel Jim's letter on top of the viewfinder, and it came up on the large monitor screen.

Hastings knew that all of them had already read the letter. But he wanted an open exchange of ideas. He had his own impressions, but impressions weren't evidence and they could be misguided, like anything else.

He didn't want the entire task force in on this. It could be argued that he was having a secret meeting, away from the scrutiny of the masses. But there wasn't time to be careful of protocol.

Hastings waited as the detectives reread the letter. Then he said, "My thinking is, the guy's educated."

Klosterman said, "Why?"

"He uses words like *demise* and *pedestrian*. And he talks about us having small minds."

Rhodes said, "I don't know, George. I was in the navy and I met guys who'd never gone to college, and they could finish *New York Times* crossword puzzles in about ten minutes. You don't have to be college educated to write. Or use words."

"Okay." Hastings considered this. "But were they older or younger?"

"Usually older. Been in the service for a long time."

"So they'd read a lot."

Rhodes shrugged. "There isn't much else to do on a ship, when you're not on duty."

Murph said, "Okay, if he's not educated, he reads a lot. But then what?"

Hastings said, "He says we're pedestrians. It's not enough that he does these things, he has to let people know he's smart. Smarter than the rest of us."

"So smart he writes letters to newspapers?"

Klosterman said, "He's boasting. He wants to taunt us."

"He wants to be noticed," Rhodes looked at the other detectives. "He wants credit."

Hastings looked at the letter again. With his pen, he pointed to the references about Adele Sayers's earring and Marla Hilsheimer's bracelet. Hastings said, "He's keeping trophies."

Klosterman said, "That's not unusual. For a sadistic killer, it's not unusual."

"If we knew who he was," Murph said, "we could get a warrant to search his house and probably have enough to convict him right there."

"If we knew who he was and had cause to search." Hastings took the letter off the viewfinder. He replaced it with a sheet of paper with three names written on it. They were:

1. Reesa Woods
2. Adele Sayers
3. Marla Hilsheimer

Hastings said, "We know that he targeted these three women. We know that he knew who they were and where they would be. So. How? How did he know about them?"

Rhodes looked around the room to see if anyone would speak first. Then he said, "I checked out Adele Sayers. After she left Roland Gent, she set up her own Web site. I checked that out. It's fairly typical. Her face is blanked out; you can just see her body. It could be that the killer found her through that Web site, not through Roland."

Rhodes showed them what he had downloaded. The Web site was listed under "Estelle" and it was broken into a few subcategories: contact, biography, gallery, "donation" rates. There was a section that said she expected her clients to be gentlemen, that she preferred that they be professional businessmen, that she showered before each date and expected them to do the same, that drinking was fine but drunks were not. Another paragraph stated that there was a two-hour minimum and that for the sum of two thousand dollars, you could get eight hours to "learn the art of stimulation." Her stats were given: weight, height, hair color, breast size, and shoe size. There was also a pair of shoes in one of the gallery photographs. The biography declared that she was drug- and disease-free and that she looked for the same. At the end of the contact subsection was a paragraph stating that this was not an offer for prostitution but that anything that occurred during their time together was a matter of personal choice between two or more consenting adults of legal age. That all donations were for Estelle's time and companionship only and that she would not discuss or agree to any type of solicitation. Further, that any attempt to compromise her position on these issues would result in termination of the date and forfeiture of all donations.

Murph said, "They always give out information about shoes. A lot of shoe fetishists out there."

Hastings said, "Where's her computer now?"

"I checked with Escobar. He said her apartment is sealed."

"Okay, but did county take the computer?"

"Yeah."

"Good. Can you follow that up, examine the hard drive?"

"Yeah."

Hastings said, "Well, let's walk through this. I see her image on the Internet. Her face is blanked out, so I don't know what she looks like. I contact her via e-mail. And then what?"

"Maybe she gives you her cell number," Murph said. "After you come to an agreement on money."

"Maybe. Or maybe she agrees to meet you."

Rhodes said, "They can be pretty cautious, some of these girls. Adele Sayers, Reesa Woods . . . they want 'professionals.' Guys who are clean, have money, and aren't going to beat them up." He shrugged. "But I don't know if he had been with her."

"You mean," Hastings said, "he could have contacted her just to find out what she looked like. Just to find out who she was. And no more."

"Yeah."

"Why do you say that?"

Rhodes said, "Because he didn't have sex with her. Or with Reesa Woods or with Marla Hilsheimer. There was no sexual contact. Not every psychopath is a sexual sadist. And vice versa."

"So what?" Klosterman said.

"So, maybe he contacted her, agreed to meet with her, and showed up . . . just to see her."

"To see her," Klosterman said.

"To see what she looks like. So he would know where to find her. So he could follow her later."

"To the Thunderbird Motel," Hastings said.

"Yeah," Rhodes said. "We know she didn't go there to meet with him. Mickey Crawford admitted *he* was there to meet her. So the killer followed her there."

Hastings said, "The long and short is, you believe that he looked at what you looked at." Hastings gestured to the Internet downloads.

"Yes."

Hastings was thinking in terms of prizes again. For a few moments, nobody said anything.

Then Murph spoke. "George?"

"Oh, sorry," Hastings said. "Let's wrap this meeting up. Howard, check out that computer. Find out who contacted her. Murph, go with him. Joe, come with me for a minute. I want to check something."

A few minutes later, Hastings was at his desk, in front of his computer. He googled Marla Hilsheimer and found the site of the real estate company she worked for. She was dressed professionally, looking smart and cute in front of a house that she had sold.

Klosterman was standing behind Hastings's chair. "I don't see anything about donations," he said.

Hastings shook his head. "That's not what I was thinking." He turned around. "How did he know about her? How did he know about Marla Hilsheimer?"

Hastings clicked on another site. An article in the *St. Louis Post-Dispatch*.

And there she was.

Pictured at a society function, standing next to her much older husband. She was wearing a black cocktail dress that accentuated her ample bosom. She was a looker, all right. A woman of forty that younger and older men would be drawn to. A trophy to her husband, if you wanted to be uncharitable about things. A prize.

The detectives were quiet again. The whir of the computer the only sound.

Klosterman said, "You think he saw her in the newspaper?"

"Yeah," Hastings said. "I think he did."

THIRTY-FOUR

Hastings was alone when he returned to the Thunderbird Motel. He parked the Jaguar in the spot where they had found Adele Sayers's Camaro. He walked away from the car and looked at it from different points around the motel parking lot. He stood in front of the lobby and looked at the car, pretending it was hers.

The medical examiner had said that there were no traces of semen in her at the time of her death. Mickey Crawford had said that he was asleep in his motel room when she came knocking. She had knocked on the door of that room on the other side of the parking lot. He followed her here, watched her get out of the car, Hastings thought. Jumped out of his car and got into hers while she was still in sight. Her back would have been to him. It would have been dark, but all she would have to do was turn around to see him.

Quite a risk he was taking. He didn't wait until she got into the hotel room before he got into her car. Why didn't he wait? Was he too anxious? Did he get off on the risk? Did he perhaps want to be seen by her?

If she turns around and sees you, what do you say? Do you introduce yourself, show her that you're harmless? Deceive her the way you deceived Marla Hilsheimer?

Were you bored? Was that it? Did you want to change it up to keep it interesting?

Or did it make you feel clever to get inside the woman's car? To hide and wait for her to come back so you could spring? ... Maybe the fact that she returned to the car early made it more fun? An unexpected kick.

Hastings pulled out his cell phone and called Rhodes.

"Howard?"

"Yeah, George. I've got the computer. I'm at county with it. Escobar wants to keep it here for the time being, but he's letting me look at it. The e-mails for the last three weeks have been tracked and identified. Except one. It's from the county library. Here in Clayton."

"He used the computer at the library?"

"Yeah. You can use it without having to leave an identification."

"Shit."

"Yeah," Rhodes said. "I still don't know if he went to Harvard or not, but he's smart."

"You guys going to check out the library?"

"Yeah. We're going in about ten minutes."

"Keep me posted."

"Will do."

Hastings drove downtown.

He parked near the Adam's Mark Hotel. He took the elevator up to the room Reesa Woods had shared with Geoffrey Harris. Hastings stood in the hallway for a few minutes, looking at a closed door. A maid came down the hall with her cleaning cart. She looked at him curiously, and he said hello and took the elevator down to the lobby.

In the lobby, he asked for the desk manager. It was not the same guy they had dealt with before, but Hastings referenced himself and the man cooperated with him. They went back up to the room, which was vacant and clean. The desk manager remained in the room with the detective. Hastings looked around, trying to feel things that probably couldn't be felt. The manager grew uncomfortable with the silence and said, "We've got this reserved for this evening. But we don't expect the guest to check in until four o'clock or so."

Hastings nodded at this. A moment later, he said, "Okay." And they both walked out.

The desk manager said, "Was there anything in particular you were looking for?"

Hastings shook his head. He had little idea, really.

The elevator doors opened at the mezzanine and two men got in. They had name tags dangling from their necks. They were well-dressed men, wearing slacks and expensive golf shirts. The tags read, NATL.

After a moment, Hastings asked, "What's that acronym?"

The smaller guy said, "National Association of Trial Lawyers."

"You're here for a convention?"

"Yeah. Some genius said we should have it here instead of Vegas."

"It's what happens when you let women plan it," the other lawyer said.

Hastings smiled with them and they got off the elevator in the lobby.

The desk manager turned to him and asked if there was anything else he could do. Hastings told him that there wasn't and thanked him for his time.

On his way out, Hastings looked around the lobby again. His gaze took him to the escalator going up to the mezzanine. He wondered why the lawyers hadn't just taken that. Conventioneers. As Klosterman had once said, if you want to bring convention business to the city, you've got to have two things: casinos and pussy.

Hastings went back to the desk manager.

THIRTY-FIVE

The campus was different now. It was hard to believe that it was twenty years since he had last been here. Twenty years earlier, there hadn't been all these walls and modern buildings and humanistic, erotic art that seemed out of place. Twenty years earlier, it had looked like what it was: an unassuming midwestern Catholic university.

George Hastings at eighteen. From no place, Nebraska, to a university in the biggest city he had ever seen. There on a baseball scholarship, and it had taken him some time to stop believing that he was too dumb to be there. Maybe they accommodated athletic-scholarship recipients at other universities, but they hadn't been too generous to him. He was expected to take nine hours of theology and six hours of philosophy along with everyone else. Even if his major was communications, the standard for most academically challenged jocks.

Those courses were a vague memory now. He remembered one of them involving circles inside other circles and discussions of fire, air, and water, and he never did figure any of it out, but somehow got a C anyway. Being a baseball player at the time, he was actually somewhat proud of this. Until he later learned that just about everyone else that ever took the class got an A or a B.

Now he sat on the wall that he had sat on in his youth and

wondered how he had ever managed to fit in at a place like this. He wasn't meant to be a professional baseball player. Maybe he wasn't meant to be a college graduate either. But a talent for the sport had gotten him the college degree. And then, lacking any sort of trade skill, he had become a policeman. Not out of any thought-out ambition, but mainly because he didn't know what else to do.

Getting nostalgic in your middle age, he thought. But watching the girls and boys go by, he thought, Nostalgic for what?

The kids dressed differently now, but they looked the same. Now they looked like kids. To him they did, anyway.

When he first picked out Rita Liu from the crowd, he was not sure it was her. Again, she appeared younger than her actual years. Younger and not so shiny, as call girls often appear. She blended in. Maybe better than he had.

Hastings remained where he was, seated on the brick wall in the quad. A grown man out of his element, his legs folded, his sport jacket and sidearm covered by an overcoat.

He locked his eyes on Rita Liu. She noticed him, first with curiosity, then with anger.

She walked over to him. Now she was standing before him. Her face was weighted and she no longer looked like a kid. "What do you want?"

"I just want to talk."

•

The waitress brought her a cappuccino and the detective a large mug of coffee with a little container of milk and a spoon. Hastings poured the milk into his coffee, then stirred it. Gray light filtered in from outside. Students murmured at other tables.

Hastings said, "This used to be a bar."

"Yeah?" Rita said. "When was that?"

"Years ago."

"You didn't go to school here, did you?"

"I did, actually."

She looked at him for a moment. Then said, "That's funny."

"Yeah, isn't it."

"I suppose you don't think I belong here either."

"Why would you think that?"

"Because of what I do."

"You're a student," Hastings said. "This is a school."

She looked at him for a moment. She had been around, and she thought that he might be playing her. Being a smart cop now instead of a mean one. It also occurred to her that he could have meant what he said. "Is that how you think of me? As a student?"

"How do you want to be thought of?"

"As a lady."

"You are."

"And what are you? A social worker, now? Maybe a minister trying to reform the bad girl?"

"I'm trying to find a killer. Before he kills again."

"I see. He's going after respectable women now. I suppose that changes things, doesn't it?"

"Like it wasn't important before?"

"Was it?"

"Knock it off. You know it was. Let me ask you something: did you ever hear of Gary Ridgeway?"

"No."

"He was a serial killer in Seattle. They caught him a few years ago. He admitted to killing forty-eight prostitutes. But some say he may have killed around seventy." Hastings leaned forward, conscious of the other students sitting nearby. He said, "Most of those girls were streetwalkers. Poor, black, with drug addictions, some of them with children to support. He'd pick 'em up, take him to a hotel or to his house, and strangle them. Just like that. You think they deserved it?"

"No." Her face contorted. "Why would you ask me that?"

"Do you think *you* deserve that?"

"No."

He said, "What happened then, happened. Maybe it was because the community didn't have much interest in helping the police. My own view is that the police probably did everything they could. But I'm biased, being a policeman myself."

"So you don't think the community is anxious to help find a whore-killer? Is that what you're trying to say?"

"This can be a sick world, Ms. Liu. There are people who are attracted to monsters like this. They can draw admirers. Women have married them even while they're sitting on death row. They become celebrities. That's what this guy wants, I think. He wants to be known. Appreciated. Admired. Maybe he'll kill another real estate saleslady or maybe he'll stick to call girls. Because let's be frank, who's going to remember the name of his next victim? Particularly if she's a hooker. He, in contrast, will be remembered. And he knows it."

"Why are you doing this to me? Haven't I given you everything you want?"

"I don't know," he said. "It's not because I think you deserve it. Maybe you don't believe me when I say that, but it's true. I think I'm telling you because I have a feeling you're one of the few people that can help me. And there's a difference between cooperating in an investigation and helping."

"What, am I supposed to atone for my past sins? Is that what this is about?"

"No."

"Because I don't owe you that."

"What about Reesa Woods?"

"I told you before. I hardly knew her. You came to me thinking I would want to help because she was a close friend. But I wasn't lying to you. I really didn't know her that well."

"I know."

"You know? *You know?*"

"Yes."

She stared at him. He was like a man confessing to her. Coming to her openly and honestly. He had admitted that there had been little or no friendship between her and Reesa. He was trying to appeal to her as a human being. Because he thought she was one. And maybe something else, too.

She said, "It's not my problem."

He shook his head. "Maybe not, but you didn't tell me everything."

"What are you talking about?"

"The Adam's Mark Hotel. You were there."

"What?"

"I spoke with the desk manager. I asked him if Reesa had ever been a guest at a convention at the hotel. He said he wasn't sure but he thought so. Then I asked him if he remembered an Asian girl being there too and he said he did."

"Did you show him a photo of me?"

"I don't have one. I described you and he remembered you." Hastings leaned forward. "Look, stop lying to me. You and Reesa were there together. You worked a party together. He didn't remember which one, but maybe it was more than one. But you didn't tell me about it. You didn't tell me you were at that hotel. Why did you keep that from me?"

"You don't know—"

"You want, we can go down there right now. You may look plain and collegiate, but he'll recognize you. You want to go? Come on, let's go."

"Okay," she said. "Okay. I was there. Once in a while, I'd go there."

"Why didn't you tell me?"

"Look, we were freelancing, okay? Bobbie didn't know about it."

"Bobbie, your boss at the Flower Shop?"

"Yes. If that got back to her, she'd fire me. Maybe do something worse."

"Was Reesa freelancing too?"

"Yeah. A little. Not as much as me."

"Are you sure?"

"Yes."

"Because the man Reesa was with before she got killed was lined up through the Flower Shop. I know that's true."

"So what if it was? We used that hotel a lot. It's safe and it's clean. What I'm saying is, we'd sometimes go to conventions without clearing it with Bobbie."

"And cut her out of her fee?"

"I guess."

"Did Bobbie ever find out?"

"No. I told you, that's what I'm trying to prevent."

"You should have told me about this before."

"Now you're angry at me? Why? What does it change?"

"Young lady, you keep things from us, we may miss an important lead. And that's another day this fiend has to roam the streets and find another victim. And you dare to sit there and tell me *we're* not sympathetic."

"I told you, I could lose my job."

"A job? A job. How many more women have to die so you can remain comfortable?"

Tears were coming down her cheeks now. She folded her arms and called him a fucker under her breath.

"What?"

"You," she said. "You're a bastard. What you're doing is not . . . right."

Hastings said, "How many times did you do this? How many times did you crash these conventions?"

"Me or both of us together?"

"Both of you together."

"Twice. Two conventions. Any more than that, Bobbie would have been onto us."

"Tell me about them."

"One was a group of manufacturers. They were mostly from out of town. I went with one upstairs; Reesa went with another guy from Wisconsin."

"Wisconsin?"

"Yes."

"Was that the only time she was with him?"

"As far as I know."

"What about the other one?"

"It was a local thing. A pharmaceutical company sponsored a wine-and-cheese event. They sell their drugs to doctors and clinics. They want the doctors to be happy. I didn't seal any deals that night."

"What about Reesa?"

"Yeah. Some doctor. I think he was Jewish."

"These were local doctors?"

"Yes."

"A doctor you think was Jewish."

"She was talking with two guys. Sort of between them, you know, working them. And then she went up to the room with the older one. His name was Tim or Ted or something. Ted . . ."

"Go on," Hastings said. "Go back to it. Picture it. Picture yourself there . . . Are they wearing name tags?"

"Yes, he's got a funny name. I heard her call him Dr. Z."

"Z. Can you remember the rest of it?"

"I'm trying . . ."

Hastings said, "Keep going," as he went to the counter and asked for a copy of a telephone book. The barista gave him one, and he brought it back to the table. He turned to "physicians" in the Yellow Pages and went to the end. There were four physicians under Z.

Zanovich, Zarrinkameh, Zink, and Zoller.

After a moment, Rita Liu put her finger on the name Zoller.

"You think that's it?" Hastings said.

"Yes." she said. "Yes. I think that's it."

THIRTY-SIX

Hastings called Klosterman from his car. Police officers are supposed to advise dispatch of their whereabouts so that the department knows where they are in case of emergency. The rule does not apply very strictly to homicide detectives, who can operate on a more laissez-faire basis, but it is a good practice nonetheless. If he found Dr. Zoller at his clinic, it was not likely that the doctor would inject him with an overdose of morphine and then take off for Switzerland. But if he did, Klosterman would know where to find him.

He summarized his interview with Rita Liu to Klosterman.

Klosterman said, "What do you think?"

"I don't know. It's something we didn't know before. It happened a week before she was killed. Reesa Woods is dead, so we can't get her account of what happened after they went upstairs."

"A doctor, huh? You think he'll condescend to see you?"

"I'll persuade him. How're things there?"

There was a pause and then Klosterman lowered his voice. "Karen seems to have taken a sudden interest in the case."

"You think Ronnie's trying to squeeze me out?"

"Maybe. Listen, George. He came to me and asked where you were on the case. I'm not saying he was going behind your back or anything, but . . ."

"He's going behind my back."

"Well, I don't know if I'd put it that way. But he's getting nervous. I used to work under him years ago and he was okay. But..."

"Yeah, I know. He's okay," Hastings said. "Did you put him at ease?"

"I think I did. You know how it is, now the guy's killing randomly. He's not just limiting himself to prostitutes anymore. The public's scared and they're leaning on the brass."

"Yeah, I know." Hastings was aware that Ronnie Wulf might replace personnel on the investigation just so that he could tell his superiors he was doing *something*. It was a common, unfortunate practice in administration. He wasn't even sure he could blame Wulf for falling prey to it. He imagined that Karen Brady was second-guessing him now, coming up with ideas that probably weren't very helpful. Maybe she'd find out about the "secret" meeting he had had with the members of his own team and demand to know why she hadn't been advised of it. As if she would have been interested in coming anyway. When administration wanted to come after you, they could always come up with something.

Ah, fuck it, Hastings thought. He had just lectured a call girl on being more concerned with her career, such as it was, than with preventing the deaths of more women. If he ignored or pissed off his superiors, they would find a pretext to take him off the investigation. But if he paid them too much heed, he would thwart himself. He couldn't go through an investigation continually asking himself, What will Wulf think? What will Karen say? It would make him weak and ineffective and, ultimately, useless. In a sense, he'd be taking himself off the case. And maybe they'd find the killer without his help. Maybe he wasn't as necessary as he thought he was. But he would have to sort that shit out later.

He said, "Joe, just try to keep them . . . satisfied. Okay?"

"I got your back, buddy. Call me if you need anything."

•

The Brentwood Surgical Clinic was near the Galleria mall near the intersection of Brentwood and Clayton. It was a pretty green-and-white building with high-dollar vehicles parked on the side. Hastings remembered coming to another doctor's office not far from here on another case. This had been a couple of years ago. That doctor had murdered two people.

He showed his police identification to the receptionist in the waiting area. The receptionist was a tough-looking girl with a New Jersey accent and she said, "What's this about?" in a blunt voice, and Hastings almost found himself developing a fondness for her.

He told her that it was about a homicide investigation and that it was very important that he speak to Dr. Zoller as soon as possible. Hastings read the girl's name tag and said, "Destiny, I'd like to do this discreetly, without having to bring a lot of uniformed officers and police vehicles around. I assure you it won't take long."

The girl, whose full name was Destiny Fisher, said, "Homicide? Who got killed?"

"You don't need to know that. If I have to come back here later with more guys, are you going to take the responsibility?"

"Maybe I will," she said. Then she actually smiled at him and said, "Hold on a minute."

Dr. Zoller was not quite as cool.

He tried a couple of psych games that professional men sometimes deploy to try to intimidate cops and other little civil servants: leading the cop into his office, sitting behind his desk surrounded by his diplomas and other signs of power and status, acting like he was in a hurry, and so forth. But he was scared and Hastings knew it.

Dr. Zoller said, "So what can I do for you?"

"I'll come to the point, Doctor, as I know you're very busy. We have evidence that you were with Ms. Reesa Woods a couple of weeks ago. You may have dealt with her in her professional capacity, wherein she goes by the name Ashley."

That was enough. Dr. Zoller was probably a good man overall, and it's not easy to be nonchalant when a policeman confronts you with evidence of soliciting a prostitute.

Zoller said, "Ah..."

"She was a prostitute," Hastings said.

"Uh, yes. I may have—"

"You did," Hastings said.

There was silence in the little office then. Hastings allowed it to fill the room with discomfort as he stared patiently at the little man.

"Ah . . ."

"Ashley's dead, Dr. Zoller."

"I . . . I didn't know."

"It was in the newspaper."

". . . Was it?"

"Yes."

"I—I didn't know. Listen, Lieutenant, I'm a married man. . . ."

"Of course, sir. I'm not interested—not at this time—about whether or not you violated the laws of public decency or other such things." Hastings remembered the language from the call girl's Web site. He said, "After all, donations to a lady friend from a gentleman are private business, are they not?"

"I . . . I suppose so."

"And what two consenting adults do in private should remain private, don't you think?"

"Yes."

"But this young lady was murdered."

"Last Friday—"

"Excuse me?"

"Last Friday," the doctor said. "Wasn't it last Friday?"

"Yes. It was."

"I was with my wife and family last Friday. My son had a football game. I swear—"

"Football game?" Hastings was not on solid ground here. He

had not advised the man of his Miranda rights. But he had not arrested him either. Hastings said, "Who's your son play for?"

The question could be considered conversational.

"Vianney," the doctor said.

"Who did they play?" Just chatting now.

"Country Day."

"What was the score?"

"Score? Oh, God, I don't know. My son's team won. He didn't get to play till the second half. He complained about it—"

"Other people can confirm that you were there?"

"Yes. Definitely. Yes—oh God. Shouldn't I have a lawyer here?"

"Should you?"

"I don't know."

Hastings said, "Dr. Zoller, are you under the impression that you're a suspect in a murder?"

"No! I mean, God—I'm not, am I?"

"No. But you're a witness."

"Because I— Look, maybe I should have a lawyer present."

"For what? Diddling a call girl?"

Dr. Zoller mumbled something that trailed off.

Hastings said, "I told you, I don't care about that. But you knew this young lady was murdered." Hastings was using the principal's tone of voice now. The tone that police and prosecutors can use on the most powerful of people. *You should know better, mister.* And it seemed to be working on this man.

"Well—"

"And you didn't contact the police. Did you?"

"I wasn't aware that I needed to."

"You didn't want to help?"

"I've got . . . I'm married."

"You're married with children and you've got a good practice and probably a lot of nice things. House, cars, boats, and what have you. Your wife finds out you misbehaved, she may file for a divorce. And then you've got a rather large mess on your hands. Am I right?"

"I . . . don't . . . It's possible, yes."

"It's very possible, isn't it?"

"Yes."

"And you don't want that." Hastings was counseling him now. In a way.

The doctor's voice was distant, barely audible. "No," he said.

"I understand that. Believe me, I do. You want to talk about messy private lives, take a look at your average cop."

The doctor smiled uneasily.

"Always getting in trouble over—well, you know." Hastings smiled but resisted a wink.

Dr. Zoller stared at him.

"Anyway," Hastings said, "like I said, I can sympathize. And there's no reason for these sort of indiscretions to come out. I mean, you are cooperating, after all. Right?"

After a moment, Dr. Zoller said, "Yes. Right." He spoke quickly after he figured things out.

"Good, I'm glad to hear that." Hastings gave the fellow a moment to breathe. Then he said, "You met Reesa at the hotel, correct?"

"Yes."

"Was there an Asian woman there as well?"

"Yes. She was pretty, but I . . . I was talking with . . ."

"Ashley," Hastings said. "You knew her as Ashley."

"Yes."

"Who saw you with this woman?"

"Uh . . . well. There was Dr. McGinnis. He was there. And Dr. Sheffield. Wait, Dr. McGinnis left early. Raymond met the women. He spoke with the other one for a while."

"With the Asian girl?"

"Yes."

"Do you remember what name she used?"

"No."

"Okay. You said something about Raymond. Raymond who?"

"Raymond Sheffield. That's Dr. Sheffield."

"What did he do?"

"He was with me when I met Ashley. He was talking to her for a while. But he got put off or something. I don't know."

"What do you mean, he got put off?"

"It's hard to say. I mean, I've only known Dr. Sheffield for a short time. He's a younger man and I don't think he's been with a—"

"A call girl?"

"Right. I don't think he's done that. If you saw them together, you would have thought that he thought she was just a girl at the party."

"But you knew better?"

"Yes."

"Did this Raymond Sheffield seem angry at the girl?"

"Angry? I don't know. I never considered it. He only talked with her for a little while."

"And then what?"

"Then I talked with her and we—we went upstairs."

"And he knew it."

"Well, I presume he did. I never discussed it with him afterward. I mean, what was there to brag about?"

Hastings was a bit surprised by this. Zoller may have had weaknesses, but self-delusion was not one of them.

Hastings said, "What did he do?"

"What did he do? I don't know. I guess he left."

"He ever say anything about it to you afterward? Like, how was it? Or, you dirty dog . . . ?"

"No."

"Nothing?"

"Nothing."

"He never showed any interest himself?"

"In Ashley?"

"Yes."

"No. I mean, he was talking to her. But no. He never asked for her number."

"He never asked you?"

"No."

"Do you know if he asked her?"

"No. I don't know."   .

"I have Dr. McGinnis. I have Raymond Sheffield, who, as I understand it, is also a doctor. Is there anyone else you know that was at this event?"

"No. That was all. I mean, apart from the people from the pharmaceutical company."

"You say you haven't known Dr. Sheffield very long. What about Dr. McGinnis?"

"I've worked with Don for several years. He's a good doctor."

"What about Dr. Sheffield?"

"Young, but very competent."

"Is he a local?"

"No, actually. He moved here from Boston."

"Is he married?"

"No."

"Ever been?"

"I don't know. Lieutenant, I'm not sure I'm comfortable answering questions about Dr. Sheffield."

"Well, it is a murder investigation."

"I understand that, but Dr. Sheffield is not some sort of derelict. He's a respected physician."

"Right," Hastings said. "Was he ever married?"

The doctor gave up. "I don't know. We didn't discuss our private lives."

Hastings said, "You said a Dr. McGinnis was there, but he left early?"

"Yes."

"Did he meet Ashley?"

"No."

"Just you and Dr. Sheffield?"

"Yes."

"Does he like women?"

"Dr. Sheffield?"

"Yes."

"I—are you asking me if he's gay?"

"No. I asked if he liked women."

"I don't know, sir. I have no reason to think that he doesn't like women, no."

Hastings said, "Do you have a daughter?"

"I don't think that's particularly pertin—"

"Do you?"

"Yes."

"How old?"

"She's in college. Brown, to be exac—"

"Would you feel comfortable if your daughter were dating Dr. Sheffield?"

"No, I would not. I don't think this line of questioning is very professional, sir."

Hastings let the man's indignation exhale. He found that it was often useful to stand back from such things. He was quiet for a couple of moments. Then he said, "Why not?"

"I don't know," Dr. Zoller said. "I just wouldn't."

"I understand," Hastings flipped through his notes, half of the action being pretense, then said, "Well, I guess that's all I have for now. I appreciate your time."

Dr. Zoller got to his feet. He still seemed upset.

Hastings said, "You understand, of course, that this is a homicide investigation. I have not suggested that your colleague, your former colleague, is a suspect. Nevertheless, we don't want the investigation compromised. Okay?"

"You mean you don't want me telephoning Dr. Sheffield to tell him what you asked me. Is that it?"

"That's it exactly."

"And if I do, I suppose you'll ruin my reputation with all this business of ..."

"No, sir. I have not threatened you. Don't accuse me of that. But I assure you it's not in your interest to impede this investigation."

"Really? Well, I may call *my* lawyer."

Hastings pulled out a business card and handed it to Zoller. "If he has any questions, he can reach me at this number."

This took some of the fire out of him, as Hastings suspected it would. He did not begrudge the doctor. He supposed if someone ever brought his daughter into an interrogation, he'd probably get upset too. But Dr. Zoller was hardly the first white-collar professional to try to rattle him with lawyer threats, and he wouldn't be the last.

Out in the reception area, the girl whose tag said Destiny flirted with him, saying, "You weren't too rough on him, were you?" She spoke quietly, having fun but not wanting to lose her job over it.

Hastings held his hands up. "Kid gloves, sis. Kid gloves."

"I'll bet." Warmth in her tone now, but it could cool down anytime.

Hastings hesitated for a moment, wondering if she liked him enough to help him. She was waiting for him to say something, he saw. He said, "Could I ask a favor?"

"What?"

"Would you call St. Mary's Hospital for me and find out what hours Dr. Sheffield is working?"

"Today?"

"Yeah."

She gave him a steady look, one that said that she knew he was requesting something dubious, but she picked up the telephone.

Minutes later, he was in the car. He checked his watch and dialed a number. Klosterman picked up the other end.

"Joe. Raymond Sheffield, M.D. He's an ER physician at St. Mary's. Find out what you can about him. Check with DMV, find out what kind of car he drives."

"Okay."

"Do the car thing first. Call me as soon as you have the tag and model."

THIRTY-SEVEN

Rita Liu said, "I have to work."

Hastings said, "You mean *work*?"

"Yes."

"You feel comfortable telling me that?"

"You know everything there is to know."

He was standing in the girl's apartment. She was in a black cocktail dress and her hair was put up. When she opened the door, he didn't recognize her. The transformation was startling. She was model pretty, magazine pretty.

Hastings said, "Look, it's important. Come with me, look at a man. Tell me if you remember seeing him before. It'll take an hour at most."

"My date is in a half hour."

"Reschedule it."

She hesitated.

"Come on," Hastings said. "Please."

She glared at him, sighed, then walked over to the telephone.

When her customer picked up, Hastings heard her use a voice and a tone that was new to him. A seductive, sort of smoky tone. Playful and soft and enticing. It was like she had walked onto a movie set and a director had yelled "action." She was in character, and Hastings had to admit that it was a good performance.

He heard her say, "Now stop . . . You know I want to see you. You *know* I do. . . . All right . . . Nine o'clock, then." There were a couple of beats and then she gave the guy a throaty laugh and said goodbye. She hung up the phone and turned back to Hastings.

"Are you at least going to drive me to this fucking place?" she said. The sexy mama was off the clock.

•

As Rita sat in the passenger seat of his Jaguar, wearing a black raincoat over her dress, she crossed her legs. She had good posture, Hastings thought. She had a certain poise. She looked like a lady.

Hastings drove the car fast, pushing it hard by vehicles treading along in the slow lane. If Destiny Fisher was right, Raymond Sheffield would be ending his shift in twenty minutes. But he could leave early, and Hastings didn't want to miss him.

They got to the hospital parking lot. It was flat and outdoors but bigger than Hastings would have liked it to be. He drove up and down the rows of cars, looking for the black Mercedes that Klosterman had phoned him about. He found it a couple of minutes later. The tag matched what he had written down. Hastings put the Jag in park, walked over to the Mercedes, and looked at the tag again. He looked into the windows of the car. He saw nothing of interest. He walked back to the Jaguar and opened the trunk. From the trunk he removed a long, steel-cased police flashlight. He walked back to the Mercedes and shone the beam on the tires.

There, between the treads. Mud.

Hastings felt his heart pounding.

It didn't necessarily mean anything, he thought. It *could* mean that the car had been used to transport Marla Hilsheimer's body out to the woods. But it could also mean that the car had been driven down a dirt road in the country. Or through a puddle at a Wal-Mart.

He shone the light along the car's lower chassis. There was no mud along the sides. But the car looked like it had been washed recently. He could get the mud off the roof and sides, but he couldn't get all the mud out of the tire treads.

Hastings took a pen out of his inner jacket pocket. He pried some of the mud loose from the tire and placed it in a plastic Ziploc bag. Maybe it would help.

Now he was standing at the back of the car, looking at the trunk. It was a newer Mercedes and no doubt it had a burglar alarm. Even if it didn't, he would probably have to break the lock to get the trunk open, and he didn't have a warrant to search the car. He walked back to the Jaguar.

Inside, he said to Rita, "Have you seen that car before?"

"No."

Hastings drove down a few car lengths and then backed into a space. He cut the engine.

Five minutes went by.

Rita didn't say anything.

There was some lighting on the lot. Enough to give the employees of the hospital some illusion of security. Hastings hoped that they were close enough to the man's car and that there was sufficient light for Rita to identify him. If she could identify him. He didn't want to move the car closer because he didn't want the doctor to know they were there.

Rita said, "How long do we have to sit here?"

"It might be just a couple of minutes. It might be longer, though." He hoped that Sheffield hadn't left with someone else.

Rita sighed. "I rescheduled the appointment. I didn't cancel it."

"Hmm-hmm."

She gave him a side glance and shook her head. She murmured something.

Hastings said, "What?"

"Nothing."

"No, you said something."

"I said, 'You too.'"

Hastings chuckled. "What do you mean?"

"You're using me. Like the others. That's what I said."

"I'm investigating a murder and you're a witness. There's no need to be self-pitying about it."

Now she laughed. "Is that what you think? That I'm self-pitying?"

"I don't know."

"Well, don't flatter yourself. Whatever you give me, don't give me pity. Don't ever give me that."

Hastings looked at her.

No, not a girl. He had seen her perform tonight, telling her client on the phone that she was looking forward to seeing him. *"Now stop . . ."* Flattering the man, playing a part. Patronizing someone who wanted to be patronized. She was good enough at it that it made Hastings feel sad. What had happened to her, that she could do that?

"Okay," Hastings said.

She seemed to like this answer. She gave him another look and then glanced out her window. She said, "Hastings."

"Yeah."

"What's your first name?"

"George."

"Maybe you're okay, George. Maybe."

"You mean, for a cop?"

"For a man."

"Hmmm," he said, his tone skeptical.

Rita said, "We're a little alike, you and I."

"Are we."

"In a way. You don't really trust people. You're kind of mercenary. Were you ever with a hooker?"

"Every payday."

She laughed and said, "That's cute. Cops are the worst, you know."

"How's that?"

"The worst hypocrites, I mean. They judge us, bust us, lecture us—say things like, 'Where are your parents? What would your mama think?' Then they hit on us, ask for freebies."

"Any cop caught doing that would be terminated. Besides, how would you know? You've never been arrested."

"If I had, you'd probably use it against me, wouldn't you?"

"I use whatever I can."

"I'll bet you do." She returned her attention to the window. Then said, "Well, at least you're honest."

They sat in silence. A minute passed and then another.

A car started on the other side of the parking lot. Hastings looked at it in his rearview mirror.

Rita said, "George—"

"Hush," he said. He saw someone coming.

A man in a raincoat and a flat hat. He came into the glare of one of the overhead lamps. His face was partially hidden by his cap, but Hastings saw that he was wearing glasses.

He touched Rita Liu on the arm.

She leaned forward.

The man walked to the Mercedes. He removed his hand from his coat pocket, and the car's alarm made a *thweep* sound, then the doors unlocked and the inside light came on.

He got into the Mercedes and started it. The rear lights came on and the car backed up. The man drove past them and then circled around the lot to go out the exit.

Rita said, "That's him."

"That's the man you saw at the hotel?"

"Yes."

"The same man you saw speaking to Reesa?"

"Yes. It's him. I'm positive it's him," Rita said. "Look, I want to get out of here. Now."

Driving back to her apartment, Hastings said, "I appreciate you doing that."

Rita Liu grunted. She was smoking a cigarette, the window cracked so that the fumes could wisp out.

"Rita?"

"What?"

"I want you to be honest with me. Are you sure you've told me everything?"

"About what?"

"About the night you met Dr. Sheffield. The night you and Reesa were with Dr. Zoller."

"Yes."

"Yes, you're sure?"

"Yes. I don't care if you believe me or not. I'm telling you the truth."

"Okay. Can you tell me something else?"

"What?"

"Are you frightened?"

"Yes."

"More so than before?"

"... Yes."

"How come?"

"Because I think he killed her."

"You think Dr. Sheffield killed Reesa."

"Yes."

"Why?"

"I told you, I've told you everything I know. I didn't see anything. I don't know anything." She turned to look at him. "Really, I don't."

"So it's an intuition?"

"Don't make fun of me," she said. "Don't."

"I'm not. But—tell me why you think he killed her."

"I don't have reasons. I'm sorry, but I don't. It's a feeling. I should have felt it before. I was there when she met him; I should have known. There's something off, something not right..."

"Something not right about him?"

"Yes."

"But you can't look at a man and say he's guilty of murder. You can't just see it in his eyes. It doesn't work like that."

"You need evidence, right?"

"Right."

"Well, that's your problem. But I know what I feel, and I don't want to be anywhere near him."

"We don't know that he's the guy."

"And you, you bring me back to see him. Why? Did you think I'd enjoy being involved in the pursuit? That I'd get a kick out of it?"

"No, I didn't."

They were near her door now, the lighted entrance to her apartment building in view.

"Leave me out of it," she said. "Do you understand? I don't want anything more to do with this."

She slammed the car door and walked up the steps.

THIRTY-EIGHT

Ronnie Wulf said, "Do you think the girl is keeping something from you?"

Hastings said, "I doubt it."

"But you don't know."

"Do you mean, does she know that Sheffield did something more and she's not telling me? Something like that?"

"Yeah."

"Again, I doubt it."

"So you trust the girl?"

"Yeah. I think so."

Wulf sighed. "She's a hustler, George. They lie all the time."

"I don't think she's lying. Not about this. She was frightened, Chief. She wasn't faking that."

"But if she doesn't know anything, how could she be frightened? How could she know enough to be scared?"

"It's a fair question, Ronnie. But . . . I don't know. You asked us not to hoard leads. You asked us to share information."

"I know. But is this a lead or a theory?"

"You asking me?"

"Yes, I'm asking you."

"It's a lead."

"Then follow it up."

"Okay," Hastings said. "Look, we found out Sheffield was married. While he was in medical school. They divorced shortly before he moved here. Her name is Cheryl Jensen. She's in Boston. I think it might help if we talked to her."

"An ex-wife? I don't know."

"It's worth an interview."

"Let's say he is your guy. What if you talk to her and she calls him and warns him you're after him?"

"I've thought of that. But I think the interview is worth that risk. Besides, we can warn her not to do that."

"What if she's loyal to him? Ignores the warning."

"I'll be subtle."

"I don't know, George. An ex-wife? If you think it's a good idea . . ."

"I do."

"And then what? She tells you she was married to a monster, likes to kill women?"

"It beats doing nothing."

Ronnie Wulf looked at him to see if he was being insolent. But then he realized that they both were tired and out of sorts.

"Okay, George. Make the call."

THIRTY-NINE

"Ms. Jensen?"

"Yes?"

"Cheryl Jensen?"

"Yes. Who is this?"

"My name is Lieutenant George Hastings. I'm a police officer in St. Louis, Missouri."

"How did you get my phone number?"

"The phone company gave it to me. They usually cooperate with us."

"You're not going to ask me for a donation, are you?"

"To what?"

"A police union or something like that."

"No. I'm investigating a matter in St. Louis that involves people working at St. Mary's Hospital. These include your ex-husband."

"Raymond?"

"Yes. Raymond Sheffield. You were married to him, weren't you?"

"Yeah . . . What's this about?"

"I'm afraid I can't discuss it. But we're interviewing a lot of people. Just getting background on witnesses. Nothing special." Hastings was quiet, waiting to see if the woman would push him.

Then she said, "Well, I'm in the grocery store right now. Can I call you back later?"

"No, I'm afraid that won't work for me. Listen, I promise I won't be long."

"Well, all right. What do you want to know?"

"How long were you married to Raymond?"

"About three years."

"When did you divorce?"

"We separated, gosh, almost three years ago. The divorce was granted about a year and a half ago. A couple of months before he moved to St. Louis."

"What do you do now?"

"I work at Cambridge Bank of Massachusetts."

"Doing what?"

"I help them sell their financial products. It's called financial planning."

"Did you go to school for that?"

"I went to college, but I didn't study business or banking."

"What did you study?"

"Arts and sciences."

Hastings hesitated.

And the woman said, "Well, it was a two-year program. Suffolk Community College."

"Yeah?"

"Yeah. I was going to finish, do four years. But then I met Raymond and he was going to medical school, so I quit and got a job at the bank. The bank's been pretty good to me."

"Sounds like you like the work."

"I do. The people are great."

"Did you go straight from high school to college?"

"No. After high school, I joined the army. I was in four years."

"Did you like that?"

"Not really. Lot of dirtbags in the army. Sorry."

"That's okay."

"I mean, some of them are good people, serving their country. But some are just dirtbags."

"How so?"

"Well, I had one sergeant tell me he could get me transferred to West Germany if I'd be his girlfriend. And he was *married*."

"That's not nice."

"No, it wasn't. And he was black, too."

"Oh," Hastings said.

"Sorry. That must have sounded terrible. I'm not prejudiced. I mean, I try not to be."

"Of course," Hastings said. "So you got out after four years."

"Yeah. I'd had enough."

"When did you meet Raymond?"

"About a year after I got out."

"How did you meet him?"

"I was at a club with some girlfriends and he started talking to us and . . . I don't know, we just started talking. He seemed nice. He didn't drink. He wasn't loud. He didn't, you know, come on too strong."

"He was a gentleman."

"Yeah. I was used to bozos getting drunk and saying, 'Yo, Cheryl. Take your top off.' And he wasn't like that. And he didn't, you know, push things."

"You mean he didn't try to rush you into bed?"

"Not at all. He wasn't pushy like that."

"That's good."

"He was nice. Always polite. Always asked me how my day was. Attentive, thoughtful. You know."

"Sure." Hastings paused. "Old-fashioned, you mean?"

"Yeah. That's what he was. Old-fashioned."

Hastings wondered if she had been raped while she was in the army. Or if she had been otherwise abused. He said, "Did you both want to wait until you were married?"

He bit his lip after, fearing that she would say he was getting too personal.

But she said, "Well, I don't think I did. But he wanted to. Like you said, he was old-school."

"Okay. So you did wait?"

"Yeah."

"I know you're divorced now, but I presume you were happy at first."

"Yeah. I thought so. I quit school and started working full-time at the bank. And he was in medical school. He studied a lot. Usually, at night, he'd go to the library to study. So sometimes I wouldn't see him until late."

"How late?"

"Sometimes pretty late. Midnight, maybe even later. Usually I'd be asleep when he got home."

"Oh."

"Well, it was okay. I mean, I knew his schoolwork was important to him."

"Did you and he socialize with the other medical students?"

"A little. Not much, though. I felt out of place."

"Why?"

"Oh...I don't know. They'd all been to college, even the wives of the other students. And, well, I just felt uncomfortable."

Hastings said, "Well, I'm sure Raymond wouldn't have married you if he thought you were dumb."

"No, I don't think so. I just felt out of place. And I guess I was hurt."

"Why?"

"Because he didn't make much of an effort to help me fit in with them. To help me feel better about it. Like what you said. About not marrying me if he thought I was dumb. He never said anything like that to me."

"Perhaps he was preoccupied with his studies."

"Maybe. But he could have been nicer."

"Made you feel more appreciated?"

"Yeah. Something like that."

"But he must have liked you if he married you."

"That's what I thought. At first. But after a while, I started to wonder why he *did* marry me."

"Why's that?"

"Because—well, I don't know."

Hastings said, "You can tell me."

"Well, he never would say much to me. I mean, after we were married. Before, a lot. But not really after we were married. Even when he was home. He'd come home and I'd cook dinner for him, and we'd sit at the table together and he . . . he just wouldn't talk to me. Just sit there in silence. It was like I wasn't there. Once, I was trying to talk to him and he said, 'Excuse me, I'm eating my break-fast now.' Eventually, I started to ask him if I'd done something to make him mad. He'd just look at me and shake his head. And that was *it*. It gets in the air, something like that. It hangs over you."

"What?"

"You know. Bad feelings. Anger."

"I'm sorry."

She went on as if she had not heard him. "You know what made it worse?" she said. "What made it worse was when we were at some sort of party or someplace in public, he *would* talk to me. You know, the way a husband speaks to a wife he cares about. He'd do it in public but not in our home. Now what was that about?"

Hastings thought, He was performing. Playing a role. Hastings said, "I don't know."

"I mean, you hear stories about guys getting married so their wives can put them through medical school. But . . ."

"Do you think that's what he did?"

"I don't know. It's not like he got any money out of me. But after all that, I never knew why he married me."

"Did he abuse you?"

"Abuse me—you mean like hit me?"

"Yeah."

"No. He never did anything like that. He wasn't physical."

"Were you intimate?"

A pause. Then she said, "You mean like in bed?"

"Yeah."

Hastings readied himself to tell her that everything she said would be held in confidence. An old trick. But before he could say anything, she answered him. The human need to unload can be powerful.

She said, "No. Not very much. He was weird that way."

"What do you mean?"

"I don't think—I don't think he liked it very much. He had trouble . . . sometimes he couldn't . . ."

"Couldn't get an erection?"

"Yeah. I mean, I'm no supermodel, but I've got a good body. It'd never been a problem before. I mean, with me and other guys."

"I understand."

"Sometimes I think he did the weird things to cover that up."

"What do you mean 'weird things'?"

"Oh . . . it's kind of embarrassing."

"It's just us here."

"Well . . . one time he put on this Oriental mask. He was naked except for this mask. I guess he thought I'd like it. But I didn't. I didn't like it at all."

"Did it frighten you?"

"Yeah. A lot. So I told him to stop it. To take it off. And he got really mad. He said I was provincial or something."

Hastings said, "Prosaic? Did he call you that?"

"Yeah. That was the word. I'd never heard it before. He was always using these big words, you know, showing off. He never called me stupid. I mean, he didn't use the word *stupid*. But he was all the time letting me know I was. And I didn't *know*. I don't know anything. I'm not smart. I don't know what to say at parties when his friends are bringing up books and movies I never heard of. I told them I liked *Gone with the Wind* once and they all looked at me like I was retarded."

"Him too?"

"Yeah. Him too."

"Who filed for divorce?"

"I did. But I think he would have if I hadn't."

"Why?"

"Because he didn't like me. He not only didn't love me, he didn't even like me. Why would you marry someone you don't even like?"

"I don't know." Hastings said, "Did you ever ask him?"

"I did, but he wouldn't give me an answer."

"You said he never abused you."

"Yes."

"Was that the truth?"

"Yes."

"Were you ever scared of him?"

There was silence. And Hastings was afraid he'd lost her. "Ms. Jensen?"

"Once," she said. "I had this squirt gun and I squirted water on his face. Just, you know, horsing around, trying to have a little fun. And he got so mad. He ran over to me and grabbed me by the shoulders and screamed into my face, *'Don't you ever do that again!'* I'd never seen him like that. I don't think I've ever seen anyone like that. I didn't know what I thought he would do then." Her voice broke. "I don't want to talk about this anymore."

"Okay. Ms. Jensen, if—"

But she had clicked off the phone.

FORTY

Klosterman said, "You're not going to get a search warrant based on that."

Hastings looked around the room and let his eyes rest on Murph. "What do you think?"

"I think Joe's right," Murph said. "Judge Foley might have authorized one for you. But she's on the appellate bench now."

"What about Judge Rief?"

"No way. We don't have cause."

They needed a search warrant to search Raymond Sheffield's house, to see what was on his personal computer, traces of a note from Springheel Jim. To see if he had earrings and bracelets and other little trophies of his night work. A search warrant properly and timely executed on the man's premises could sometimes make the case by itself. Presuming he was their guy.

Rhodes said, "Do you think he's the guy, George?"

"Yeah, I think he is. There's the mud on the tires. And Rita Liu seems to think so. And the conversation with the ex-wife."

"That's not much," Klosterman said. "He said the word *prosaic* to her. It's not much, George. And the hooker? What, she had a bad feeling about him?"

"Intuition, she says. Or she just got scared when she saw him."

"Did he look scary to you?"

"No," Hastings said. "He seemed pretty average. But, shit, none of it means anything. We can't eliminate him as a suspect because I think he looks normal, and we can't arrest him because she thinks he's a killer and his ex-wife said he used big words and wouldn't make love to her."

"What about the call girl? Does she really *know* anything?" Klosterman said.

"She knows she saw him in Reesa's proximity before she was murdered. She saw him again, with me, and got scared. Why? I don't know."

Murph said, "Some of these call girls, they're kinda nutty. I remember this one I hauled in once, she thought my patrol car was haunted. Said that somebody died in it."

"Somebody probably did," Klosterman said.

Rhodes said, "Say you do go to a judge and ask for a warrant; won't he ask if you're putting the cart before the horse? I mean, we haven't even interviewed the guy."

"No, we haven't."

After a moment, Murph said, "You worried he'll lawyer up on you?"

"A little," Hastings said. "Also, if we interview him, he's likely to go back to his home and clean it up. Presuming he's the guy, he's operating on the notion that we're not going to find him. He believes he's pretty smart. Remember his letter. He says he's something we cannot comprehend. Because we're too dim. Too parochial. And in a sense, he's right. We *are* pedestrians. We can't comprehend him. We're constrained by sanity and conventionality."

"Or humanity," Rhodes said.

"But maybe that can help us, George," Murph said.

"What do you mean?"

"Being smarter than you, maybe he won't need a lawyer. Won't want one. As far as he's concerned, he can handle you on his own." Murph smiled. "What are you, after all, but an idiot cop?"

Hastings looked to Klosterman.

And Klosterman said, "Good point."

"Okay," Hastings said. "But if I talk to him, he'll know we're onto him, and he'll go clean his house, and then we'll lose evidence against him. We don't have any direct witnesses."

"We got Dr. Zoller and Rita Liu," Murphy said.

"That's not direct," Hastings said. "Neither one saw him commit a crime."

"So what then?" Klosterman said.

Hastings said, "If I don't talk to him, I don't have enough probable cause to get a search warrant. If I do talk to him, he'll clean up his house, and then a search of it won't help me get a case against him."

Murph said, "We can smother him. Twenty-four-hour surveillance. Do it for two, three days, see what he does?"

Hastings said, "I don't know if the chief would authorize it."

"Why?" Murph said.

"Because it's not his idea," Klosterman said.

"All right," Hastings said, "that's enough of that." The mild insubordination was quelled, and Hastings said, "The bottom line is, we don't have enough now. I'm going to have to talk to him."

"Where?" Murph said.

"His house."

"An ambush interview?" Klosterman said.

"Yeah. I'll go alone in my car. You guys follow in a separate vehicle. I'll be wired. I want the interview taped, but I also want to be able to call out for help in case I see him go for the kitchen knives."

It was a joke, he guessed. But he was scared too. Maybe it was because of the mud he'd found on the tires of the Mercedes. Or maybe it was the discussion with the ex-wife. The mention of the Oriental mask... Or maybe Rita Liu's intuition was spilling over to him.

FORTY-ONE

You're running, he thought. Running from the pain this silly little bitch has inflicted on you.

His shift had ended and Helen Krans had been approaching him. To say what, he didn't know. That she wanted to explain Tassett's request to him? To explain that she meant no offense to him? To say maybe they could have a cup of coffee together? Not outside the workplace, of course, but inside, where it would be safe and professional and no one would think much of it.

Maybe she would do that, and he wouldn't know what to say. He wouldn't know what to say to the bitch. He had learned to control himself over the years, learned to channel his gifts. But he wasn't ready to be so angry, so infuriated at her. He wasn't ready for it. He had to dart away from her, pretend that he hadn't seen her. He flushed with humiliation.

Control. He must control himself. The where and the when had to be up to him. He could not let external factors control it.

Now in his car, he looked down at the speedometer. He was going seventy miles per hour in a fifty zone. His heart skipped and he lifted his foot off the accelerator.

It was happening again. His anger was unchanneled. He was acting impulsively, and that was not acceptable. It was not smart. It was not adult. It was impetuous, and being impetuous was dangerous. Like the time he was fifteen, when he had pushed that little girl off her bicycle. She was riding near him and he was on his bike and he . . . just had to . . . ride up next to her and push her down. Watch her fall and hit the pavement and cry out and oh, it was special, oh, it was fun to see that. But right away it got bad, the other kids from the neighborhood surrounding him and some of them wanting to hurt him for what he had done. And then the grown-ups showed up, and he had to produce some tears and swear to God that it had been an accident. He even had to tell the little slut he was sorry.

The grown-ups believed him. Yes, it was an accident. They had to believe him, and they wanted to believe him because who could believe that a teenage boy could be so callous, so cruel? So vicious. Who wanted to believe that?

He learned from that, though. Learned that he had to hide things. Learned not to show himself in daylight and open spaces.

You're not a child anymore, Raymond. Not a child, and who will believe that you accidentally pushed Helen Krans off the top of a building? Who will they seek out for questioning if she disappears?

He touched the hairpin in his pocket.

He touched it and turned it over and he felt better. And for the remainder of his drive home, he kept his speed within the lawful limits.

And when he got home, he took a long, hot shower and he felt even better. He felt calm. He began to put on his pajamas and dressing gown over it, but then changed his mind and put on a pair of jeans and a sweater and boots.

Maybe he would go out, he thought. Maybe he would pay a visit to Helen at her home. She wasn't going to leave town anytime soon. After all, he had told that fool Tassett that he would not switch shifts. Maybe she would be home, and if he rang her doorbell, she would probably let him in.

Maybe he didn't have to let her go.

It could still be done. Yes, of course it could. It just couldn't be done on impulse. It had to be thought out, planned like the rest. He had her hairpin. He had something of hers, and now it was something of his.

He thought about his Mercedes.

He could not drive it to her apartment. It might be seen. He would have to drive out to his private garage and switch vehicles and drive the Ford to her home.

He smiled at that.

Planning was the key. He was no rank amateur. He was a thinker. A problem solver. A cup of tea, he thought. A cup of tea and a couple of biscuits and his mind would be fresh.

He was in the kitchen preparing it when the doorbell rang.

He stopped.

Now that was strange. No one had ever rung the bell at his home.

He looked at his watch. Almost ten o'clock.

The doorbell rang again.

Damn. Whoever they were, they weren't going away.

He turned on the porch light before he opened the door. He

looked through the small window and saw a man in a tan raincoat standing on the step. He was holding a brown file under his arm.

Raymond opened the door. "Yes?"

"Dr. Sheffield?"

"Yes."

The man showed his identification and said, "My name is Lieutenant George Hastings. I'm a detective with the St. Louis Police Department."

"What can I do for you?"

"I'm investigating a homicide. A young lady named Reesa Woods. Dr. Zoller informed me that you were with him and her."

"When?"

"A couple of weeks before her murder."

"I don't remember that," Raymond said.

"Her professional name was Ashley. She was at a wine-and-cheese party at the Adam's Mark Hotel with you and Dr. Zoller. That's all I wanted to ask you about. Just routine. May I come in? It won't take long."

"It's rather late, Lieutenant."

"I know. I'm very sorry to come at this hour. But I needed to get this out of the way. I'll make it short and then get out of your hair."

"Okay." Raymond sighed and he let the detective in.

●

The house had likely been built in the sixties and had been fashionable in the seventies. Large, quasi A-frame living room with a stone fireplace and worn carpet. It was dated and drafty. Hastings suspected that Sheffield had not paid much for it. Or that he rented it.

He walked behind the doctor, his hands by his sides. He stepped away from him when they reached the living room.

Dr. Sheffield gestured to the couch, and Hastings took a seat. As he did this, Hastings kept a constant watch on him. His coat was still on, but it was open and his .38 snub was within quick reach.

Dr. Sheffield said, "Did I understand you to say that you spoke with Dr. Zoller?"

"Yes, sir. He was a colleague of yours?"

"Yes. He resigned. Now he works in private practice."

"How long did you work together?"

"Not long. A few months."

"I see. Would you say that he's a capable man?"

"I believe so. We're not close friends."

"Just a professional relationship then?"

"Yes. He was, is, a good physician."

This from a relatively young doctor, Hastings thought. He said, "In your opinion?"

"Yes, in my opinion."

Hastings said, "Dr. Zoller informed me that you and he attended a wine-and-cheese party given by a pharmaceutical company approximately two weeks ago. There was a woman there called Ashley that Dr. Zoller ... met. Do you remember meeting her?"

"I told you before, no."

"You may not have remembered the name. But she was a young, attractive lady with brown hair. A little on the petite side."

Raymond Sheffield shook his head. "I'm sorry. I don't remember."

"Well, Dr. Zoller said you spoke with her."

"I can't speak for what Dr. Zoller saw. Or what you claim he saw," Sheffield said. "It was a party. I talked to a lot of people."

"So it's possible you met this Ashley?"

"Yes, I suppose it's possible."

"What did you talk to her about?"

"I didn't say that I talked with her. It's possible I did, though. If I did, I'm sure it was just small talk. 'Where are you from? Do you go to school?' That sort of thing."

"So she was young enough that you thought she might have been a student?"

The young doctor looked at the detective for a few seconds. "Yes, I suppose so."

Hastings said, "You understand that she was killed?"

"I understand it now. Is it why you came to question me?"

"You didn't read about it in the newspaper?"

"No. I don't read the newspapers much."

"Work a lot, do you?"

"Yes. I work a lot."

"Are you an intern at St. Mary's?"

"No. I'm a full-time staff physician."

"Did you go to school around here?"

"No. I went to Dartmouth medical school."

"Oh. Well. So you're new to the area?"

"Yes."

Hastings was quiet for a moment. Then he said, "How do you like it out here?"

"It's okay. The pace is a little slower."

"Not for me," Hastings said. "I moved here from a small town in Nebraska. But St. Louis is a nice place to live. A good place to raise your children. Do you have children?"

"No."

"Are you married?"

"No. I'm divorced."

"Oh." Hastings flipped through some pages in his notebook. He said, "This situation is a bit delicate."

"Why is that?"

"Well, to be frank, the nature of this investigation requires that I ask you questions about Dr. Zoller. And I think you may be uncomfortable with that."

"Is Dr. Zoller a suspect?"

"No, sir. I did not say he was a suspect. Please don't misunderstand me." Hastings bristled, as if he had inadvertently revealed something. He said, "But he was with Reesa—Ashley—he was with her as a customer. And I have to...check that out. Do you understand that?"

"Yes."

"You are aware that she was a prostitute?"

"No. I didn't know."

"You met her and you didn't know?"

"Lieutenant—"

"Oh, that's right. You're not sure if you met her."

"Correct."

"Do you remember meeting any prostitutes?"

"... That night?"

"Yes."

"No. I don't remember meeting any prostitutes."

"It's okay if you did. There's no crime in talking to one." Hastings smiled. "No crime in being with one, really."

Raymond did not smile back.

Hastings said, "At least, it shouldn't be. They're in business just like anyone else. Right?"

"I suppose."

Hastings removed a photograph from the file. He stood up and walked over to the doctor. "Do you recognize her?"

"No. I presume it's the woman you've been asking me about."

"Yes."

"The one Dr. Zoller was with."

"Yes."

Hastings stepped back to the couch. He put the photograph back in the file. Then he removed another one. This time, he held it up from the couch. "How about her?"

Raymond Sheffield studied it. Then he said, "No."

"Her name is Adele Sayers. Do you recognize that name?"

"No."

"She was killed too. We believe by the same person that killed Reesa Woods. There's a third victim. Her name was Marla Hilsheimer. Do you recognize that name?"

"No."

"Did Dr. Zoller ever tell you about another girl who called herself Estelle?"

"No. He did not discuss his private life with me."

"Did Dr. Zoller ever talk about a woman who sold real estate? A tall woman with red hair?"

"No. I told you—"

"I know what you told me, but I don't think you're being truthful."

"If that's what you think, then we have—"

"Just a minute," Hastings said. "Let me tell you what I think: I think you're a young physician who probably has a very good future ahead of him. And you believe that Dr. Zoller could not under any circumstances be capable of . . . well, you know. And you want to protect him. I understand that. But this is a homicide investigation. And whether it makes us uncomfortable or not, we have to cooperate."

"I have been cooperating, Lieutenant."

"I hope so, but I have not told you that Dr. Zoller is a suspect in the murders of these three ladies. Can we agree that I have not told you that?"

"Yes, we can agree that you have not said that."

"And what I discuss with you is not something you should discuss with Dr. Zoller. Do you understand that?"

"Yes, I understand it. You don't want me to interfere with your investigation."

"That's correct, thank you. Now, it's my understanding that you didn't know about these other two victims either. Correct?"

"That's correct. I didn't. I told you, I work long hours."

"Okay. But surely you must have heard of this Springheel Jim character?"

"...Who?"

"Springheel Jim."

"Who's that?"

"Oh, some loser wrote a letter to the paper claiming responsibility for the murders. He called himself Springheel Jim. It was obviously a fraud, but it got a lot of people upset. Myself included."

For a moment, Raymond Sheffield did not say anything. Now he was studying the detective. Then he said, "Why would that upset you?"

"Because it's a distraction. Some punk wrote the letter to get a kick. We tried to get the press not to run it, but we don't have any control over them."

"That's unfortunate."

"What's unfortunate?"

"Excuse me?"

"You said that was unfortunate. What's unfortunate?"

"It's unfortunate that you can't control the press."

"Oh, yeah. Well, we never can win with them. If we don't catch the guy, we're screw-ups. If we do, we get heat for not doing it sooner. Then they get into 'what sort of man would do this' and all this armchair psychoanalysis. They expect us to *know*. They want us to know. But we don't have any answers. You know what I mean?"

"Not especially. I'm not a policeman."

"Oh. Well, of course not. But I thought being a doctor, you might have some insight into the human condition."

"Insight into the human condition," Raymond repeated, as if the detective had said something that was out of his league. He smiled. "No. Not particularly."

Hastings said, "I suppose the media just wants a good story. The usual homicide's pretty boring. Most of our work is just cleanup, really. I handled a case last month, two kids on a bus, one stabs the other to death. You know what it was about? A jacket. One kid wanted this other kid's jacket, and the other kid wouldn't give it to him. So he killed him. Stabbed him to death and took his jacket. If it's not that, it's a fight over what channel to watch on television or the wrong sort of look given on a street corner. Nine times out of ten these people know each other. Something stupid and pointless and meaningless. Not much mystery involved. We're just cleaning up the mess. I guess you clean up messes too."

"Excuse me?"

"At the hospital. I guess you clean up messes too."

"I wouldn't call it that. I'm a surgeon."

"Oh, well, you know what I mean. I wasn't trying to belittle what you do."

"You haven't."

"Does it wear you down?"

"Does what wear me down?"

"What you see. The grief, the sadness. You know, the pointlessness of it all."

"No. I guess I don't see it as pointless. Lieutenant, I don't mean to be rude, but it is late."

"Of course. Sorry. I guess I'm tired. Rambling." Hastings stood up. "Well, I won't bother you any further." He made eye contact with Sheffield, giving him his official, serious look. "You understand what I meant earlier?"

"What's that, Lieutenant?"

"That it would not be appropriate to discuss this interview with Dr. Zoller?"

"Yes, Lieutenant. You've made that clear."

At the door, Hastings turned to him and said, "Oh, one more thing. There was another young lady at the Adam's Mark. An Asian woman named Rita. Do you remember her?"

"An Asian woman."

"Yes. Rita Liu." Hastings spelled out the last name.

"Another prostitute?"

"Yes."

"No. I don't recall anything like that."

"... Oh. Well, okay."

"Is something the matter, Lieutenant?"

"Well, it's just that she said that you were speaking to her. But maybe that was a misunderstanding. Between us, I think she may be a bit unstable. You know how they can be."

"Yes."

"In any event, I wouldn't worry about it. Thank you again for your cooperation."

Raymond Sheffield nodded and closed the door behind Hastings.

FORTY-TWO

It took Raymond almost an hour to switch cars.

He had to drive the Mercedes out to his property where he kept the black Ford. His secret car to help maintain his other identity. He felt better when he was in the Ford. He felt hidden, submersed. He kept the car at the speed limit and was aware of other vehicles in traffic. He drove toward the city disguised. We're all strangers to each other, he thought. Bodies in motion, each of us unaware of the other. Or, the Other. He was an unknown specter. Unknown and unknowable.

Better yet, he felt in control again. Better than he had felt in a while. He had let the woman at the hospital rattle him. He had let her silly personal defects get in the way of his thinking. His projects. But then the policeman had come to his house and made him feel better. The policeman had cheered him up. The policeman had come and seen . . . nothing.

God, he had been right. It was genuinely not in them to understand. *We're not saying Dr. Zoller is a suspect, mind you . . .* Zoller? *Zoller?* As if that little toad of a man could pull it off. Zoller. It was hysterical. There's your distraction, Lieutenant Hastings. Let Dr. Zoller explain to his wife and second-rate children and second-rate clinic partners that he'd been schtupping a whore. Oh, the scandal. Oh, the glory . . . Let Dr. Zoller explain where he had been after they found Rita Liu's body. Maybe it would be in the river. Maybe it would be in the woods.

Yes, it would work out for the best. There would be a certain symmetry to it.

He remembered seeing the little groundling at the hotel. Zoller hadn't paid her much heed. He obviously preferred the dressed-up little white-trash experience that Ashley could provide him. The great, esteemed Zoller had been a little loose with his tongue that night, telling Raymond that he used to prefer the black girls—sugar, he called them—but there was no beating a good white-trash fuck.

Fuck, Zoller had said. Using the *f*-word, the vulgar little man. Oh, Ted. Ted, Ted, Ted. Like to fuck the little white-trash whores, do we? Like the dirty little hayseeds? What a filthy little man. And now he was being investigated by the police. Oh such joys, such joys.

When Raymond had reached Rita Liu on the telephone, he'd had to give her a false name and promise her fifteen hundred dollars to get her to meet him at the hotel. But it hadn't been easy getting her to that point. At first, she'd wanted to know if they had met before. Raymond had said no, they hadn't, and then she'd wanted to know how he had gotten her home number. He had reminded her that she was in the phone book, and then she'd wanted to know, okay, how had he known her real name? She'd said that he was supposed to contact her through the agency.

Raymond had said that a physician friend of his had recommended her but that he was not comfortable revealing the doctor's name because the man had a wife and family. And by that time, he was sure that she knew he was talking about Zoller. And Raymond had persisted, pleading gently and kindly, and eventually she'd agreed to meet him at twelve thirty, but said that he'd have to be generous with his donation. She hadn't bothered to use the word *gentleman.* She had seemed in a bad mood when he called and not much better even after he'd talked her into it. Irritable and tired. But the money had brought her around. It was always money with these types.

Now he took the Kingshighway exit off the interstate. The light was yellow as he approached. Raymond stepped on the accelerator and made the left turn as the light turned red. He heard no horns in protest.

•

In Rita Liu's apartment at Lindell Towers, a handheld radio squawked.

Hastings answered it.

"George," Klosterman said, "we lost him."

"Where?"

"He got off I-64 at Kingshighway and drove through a red light. We were a few car lengths back from him and we got caught at the light. Murph was driving ahead of him—we were doing a front and back—but Murph drove past the exit. We didn't expect him to get off."

"Kingshighway—why didn't he keep going downtown?"

"I don't know. He's still in the Ford."

"Goddammit."

"I'm sorry, George. What do you want us to do?"

"Go to the hotel. We'll see you there." Hastings put the hand-held down.

Rita Liu looked at him. She was still in her black cocktail dress. An overcoat on top. She was ready to go the hotel with Hastings. They had been preparing to leave.

She said, "What happened?"

"They lost him."

"At the hotel? He's supposed to go to the hotel."

"I know."

"You know? You guys lost him. What about your plan?"

"Just cool it, will you?" Hastings said. "Come on, let's go."

He walked her out of the apartment. They took the elevator. When the door opened in the lobby, Hastings looked out before letting Rita come out. No one there but the desk clerk. They walked out the front door.

Hastings had parked the Jaguar a block down from the apartment building. It was in a diagonal space in a row of cars separated from Lindell Boulevard by a small grass sitting area. He looked into the backseat of the Jaguar to make sure no one was there, and then he opened the passenger door for the girl. Put her in the car and came back around the back and that was when he saw a black car make a sudden hairpin turn, its headlights catch-

ing him in their wide glare. The engine roaring as the car accelerated toward him.

Hastings ran forward, trying to draw the driver away from the
Jaguar and the girl inside. The car changed direction with him,
pointing at him as it hurtled forward. Hastings ran and jumped
on top of the trunk of a Toyota and was about to jump off when
the black Ford smashed into the next car and pushed it into the
Toyota, and Hastings felt himself flying through the air and then
heard more than felt the impact as he hit the next vehicle and
slumped to the ground, unconscious.

FORTY-THREE

Rita got out of the Jaguar and ran out to the street. She couldn't see George. She saw a black car piled into two other cars. Then Raymond Sheffield stepped out of it.

It was him. God, it was him. The man from the Adam's Mark Hotel and the hospital parking lot. A lunatic. He looked in between the wrecked vehicles, checking on George before he turned and looked at her.

"Come here," he said.

Rita turned and ran.

"I said come here!"

Rita ran and she heard him come after her. Heard hard footsteps rapping on the street. She tried to run faster, but she was in high-heeled shoes and it was a balancing act. She poured it on to see if it would make it easier, and it did for a little while, but it still wasn't fast enough. This time she turned around to see the fucker coming after her. He was older and she was in shape, at least three times a week at the gym. She would've been faster than he, too, but not in fucking high heels. She gauged the distance and slowed and lifted a leg, and pulled off one shoe as he drew closer, and then she hopped and dropped the other shoe and he was even closer then, but not on top of her. She ran hard, picking up the pace, regaining bit by bit the distance she'd had on him before, but her feet were coming down hard on the concrete. and then she was approaching another street, where there were only a couple of cars approaching. She slowed and waved her arms, but it did no good, one car driving past her and then the other, and now he was gaining on her.

He wasn't yelling at her anymore, not demanding that she stop, and somehow that made it worse, chasing her the way an animal would, the way a tiger or a panther would, with quiet, cold purpose. Chase her and catch her and pull her down and kill her. And she kept on running and she saw a bus up ahead and it gave her hope, the bus stopped, but then the bus disengaged its brakes and she heard that and the bus started moving ahead and then it was gone and she cried out, anguished, and she was at the enclosed bus stop, a bench with a plastic rain cover on it. No one was sitting there, no one. She looked through the clear Plexiglas and saw him coming, saw that he could see through the glass and see her and what was she doing standing there? What was she doing there waiting to die? And it was an effort for her to stand there as he continued running to the bus stand, coming to the far side of it and running an arc around it, and when he committed himself to the arc, she ran around the other way, back to the apartment building, thinking that if she could just get to the front door, smash her fists on the front door and the desk clerk would see her before the killer could fall on her, but now the distance between them was closer and she was running out of energy and her feet were hurting and she was coming back to the wrecked cars. She looked for George but couldn't see him. Where was he? Was he alive? Had he been crushed between the cars? And who could say why she ran to him instead of the apartment building, she was tired, God so tired and she went to the place between the cars and there he was, on the ground, a stripe of blood running down his temple.

She crouched next to him, tried to lift his head and shoulders. "George, George..."

He would not wake up.

•

He had worried when he saw the bus. He had worried that she would be able to run in front of it, get the driver's attention. If that happened, the bus driver might stop, and then it would all be over. Unless the driver accidentally ran her over, and that wouldn't be too bad as long as it killed her, as long as it crushed the little whore. But then he realized that his worries were in vain because the bus pulled away before she even got close. And it was good because she had invested her energy in the bus, gambled on it, and it hadn't paid off, the bus driving away and leaving her alone.

But then she ran again, the stupid little tramp, but he felt even stronger as he went after her this time. She was faltering now as she ran back up Lindell, and now the fool was going back to the cop, as if he would be able to do anything for her.

Did she think she could hide with him, crouched between the two cars?

Raymond thought about what line he would use when he caught her. Give her a little something to think about in her final moments. Something like, "Time's up."

He got to the corridor between the cars. Saw the girl crouched next to the dead cop.

Raymond smiled, as the girl looked up at him.

"Hey," Raymond said and stopped.

The girl had a gun pointed up at him.

Raymond said, "What are you—"

And the girl shot him.

The first bullet struck him in the stomach and he grunted. The girl pulled the trigger again and put one in his chest. Then twice more as he went to the ground.

Rita saw the figure about seven feet away from her. A crumple of a man and the crumple made a stir and Rita fired the last bullet into his head and that was that.

FORTY-FOUR

For most of the night, the area was filled with police vehicles and ambulances. Local media was there as well, their lighting already set up for the earnest correspondents. Already they were reporting that the police had apprehended Springheel Jim, even though the department spokesman was telling them not to jump to conclusions.

Detectives Howard Rhodes and Tim Murphy kept reporters away from Rita Liu. She had given Hastings's gun to Sergeant Klosterman. She asked Klosterman if she could wait in her apartment and Klosterman told her that she could.

Hastings was on his back on a stretcher in an ambulance. Two paramedics working over him and Klosterman was sitting nearby. It was Klosterman who told Hastings what had happened when Hastings regained consciousness.

Hastings said, "He's dead?"

"Yeah. She used your gun."

Hastings felt like a glass bottle had exploded in his head. He had to struggle to concentrate. He said, "But—how could he have walked into that? I mean, he must have known I'd have a weapon on me."

"I guess he didn't think of it. Or, more likely, he didn't think she'd be capable of it. Or maybe he thought she wouldn't reach it in time."

"She used all five?"

"Yeah. The last one in the head."

"Always good to be sure," Hastings said. "Where is she now?"

"In her apartment. I told her you were going to be okay." Klosterman smiled. "She calls you George. 'How's George? Is George going to be okay? What about George?' Did you two become friends?"

"Shut up … God, I remember hearing something, shots, I guess, but beyond that … nothing. I guess I fucked up."

"No, you didn't. We did. We shouldn't have lost him at the light. I'm sorry, George."

"Forget it."

"Listen, the band's all here. Wulf, Captain Combrink. The chief and deputy chief, all of the big brass."

"So they think we got the right guy?"

"Well, don't you?"

"I have no doubt. But I want them to know it too."

"Well, don't worry. Escobar called from County PD. They searched Sheffield's house and found Marla Hilsheimer's bracelet and Adele Sayers's earring. They were in his desk drawer. I guess he never thought he'd be caught. I'm sure there'll be additional confirmation."

"Good."

"Also, we found a leather strap in his car. It might have been part of a whip. Or a dog leash. Planning to use it on her, I guess."

Hastings said, "He didn't know her."

FORTY-FIVE

They kept Hastings at the hospital overnight for observation. He awoke at ten A.M. and was out the door by ten thirty. He met his ex-wife and daughter for lunch at Hershel's and told them that he was okay but didn't want to talk about the case or anything they had seen on the news. The lunch was quiet and surprisingly free of drama.

When they finished, Amy came over to his side of the booth and took his arm when he stepped out. She must've noticed the stiffness in his walk when he got to the restaurant. He steadied himself on her shoulder and she looked up at him and said, "He was a bad man, wasn't he?"

Hastings didn't like it when she read about murders in the newspapers. But she had a curious nature and she was too old for him to stop her.

"Yeah, honey," he said. "He was a very bad man."

•

After lunch, Klosterman drove him to his car, which was still parked by the Lindell Towers. The wrecked vehicles had been removed. There was no damage to the Jaguar.

Klosterman said, "George, don't come to the station today. Go home. Take a couple days rest."

Hastings said, "You asking me or telling me?"

"Telling you. Anne wants you and Amy to come over Sunday for dinner. Can you make it?"

"I think so. I'll call you."

He watched Klosterman drive away.

He looked around the area before he got in his car, trying to picture what had happened there only thirteen or so hours before. Dark, now light. Then he stopped, deciding it was better to put it behind him.

The Jag started on the first turn of the key.

•

That night, Carol brought him dinner. Over Chinese takeout, he told her most of it, or as much as he felt he should. At times she covered her mouth, but she didn't cry.

She said, "The papers say he was a doctor. He worked at an ER."

"That's right."

"These serial killers, aren't they usually sort of . . ."

"Losers? Yeah, typically. As typical as any serial killer can be. I don't know. He was educated. I think he might have even been a good doctor. But he was no genius."

"Because he fell for your trap?"

"My trap pretty much blew up in my face," Hastings said. "No, it's not so much that. He went for the bait, but he could have passed it by, and maybe we would have never been able to catch him. He came after Rita when he knew she would have access to a gun. My gun. If he didn't know, he should have known. I don't think that's the act of an evil genius."

"He wanted to kill her," Carol said. "Isn't that the mark of most lunatics? They want to kill even when it doesn't make sense to kill?"

Hastings said, "He wasn't a lunatic. He was a man who enjoyed doing wicked things. And he hated women."

Carol smiled, giving in. She didn't want to have that argument again, or at least not until he was up for it. She said, "The conversation you had with him, the one-on-one, did it—did it creep you out?"

"I guess so. I was scared of him. But I'm scared of any murderer. But no, it wasn't like I could look in his eyes and see evil. He wasn't that obvious. He was pretty arrogant, very full of himself. But you could say that of most doctors."

"Or homicide detectives."

"Or lawyers." Hastings smiled. "What he seemed like was a jerk. I couldn't read serial killer in him. It'd be nice to have that ability."

"I don't think so."

Carol McGuire regarded Hastings. She was a perceptive, sensitive woman and she knew there were times when he wanted to be alone. She said, "I can stay over tonight, if you want me to. If you'd like to be alone, that's okay too."

After a moment, he said, "I think I'd like to be alone tonight. Get to bed early. Can we meet for coffee tomorrow morning?"

"Sure."

FORTY-SIX

Rita answered the door in a pair of sweats and a white V-neck undershirt. She wore no makeup. Her hair was down and damp from a recent shower.

Hastings thought of the first time he'd met her. Her hair pulled back in a ponytail. He had thought she looked plain then, like a college student. He didn't see her that way anymore.

Rita said, "Hey."

"Hi."

"Come in. Please." He followed her into the apartment and she said, "Would you like something to drink? I don't have any tea."

"No. Nothing, thank you."

She went around the corner.

Hastings looked at the daybed. Saw clothes folded and luggage packed. He looked around the apartment. "Are you moving?"

He heard her voice from the kitchen. "Yeah, I think so."

He walked to the kitchen doorway and looked in. She was standing in front of the sink, washing glasses.

Rita said, "Maybe you've heard. I've become famous."

Hastings had seen it in the morning paper at the coffee shop and read it after Carol had left. On the cover of the *St. Louis Herald*: CALL GIRL KILLS SPRINGHEEL JIM. Her photo in a black dress and overcoat, near the front of Lindell Towers.

Hastings said, "I saw it in the paper. And on the news. I'm sorry."

She shrugged and kept her focus on the kitchen sink. "What are you sorry for? I'm the most popular girl at school."

"That's why you're leaving?"

She turned and gave him a look. "What do you think?"

"I think you've got nothing to be ashamed of."

"I see. Is that what you came here to tell me?"

"I came here to thank you. For helping us and for, well, for saving my life. And to tell you I'm sorry."

"You already said you were sorry." She turned off the taps. "It's like you told me the other night—you use what you can."

"Yeah, I said that. And the truth is, I'd probably do it again. Well, I mean, I'd probably try to do it better."

She smiled at him. "Yeah, I would hope so."

For a few moments neither of them said anything.

Then she relaxed and said, "Oh, what the hell. I wanted to get out of St. Louis anyway. It's an okay town, but it's not for me."

"Where will you go?"

"Chicago. I've got friends there and I can finish school there too. Start over." She looked around the place. "You know, I'll miss this apartment, though."

"It's a nice apartment."

She walked out of the kitchen and into the living area, her shoulder brushing his as she went by. She took a seat on the daybed.

Hastings turned and leaned against the doorway.

She said, "I guess you'd tell me that it was worth exposing me to stop him from killing other women."

"I didn't want to expose you."

"I know you didn't. But at least you got rid of him."

"*I* didn't."

"Right," she said. "Well, I'll accept the gratitude for helping you catch him. But I didn't save your life. I saved my own."

"Okay," Hastings said. "Well, thanks just the same." He started moving to the door.

"Hey, are you leaving?"

"Yeah, I've got . . . stuff." He turned to look at her. "I wish you the best, Rita."

She smiled at him from her place on the couch, her legs tucked up underneath her. A smile he'd never seen from her before, a friendly warmth in her eyes. "Are you sure you don't want to stay awhile?"

Oh God, Hastings thought. For she had never looked more desirable to him than she did now. Her face and figure, real. The woman, real. Real to him now.

"Ahhh, I gotta go." He opened the door. He turned to look at Rita Liu one more time before he went out.

"You know, George," she said, the smile still in her voice. "You're not so cool."